HURON SUNRISE

Landon Beach

Landon Beach
Visit my website at landonbeachbooks.com

Printed in the United States of America

First Printing: January 2024
Landon Beach Books

ISBN-13 978-1-959783-01-5

For Gram, from whose house I witnessed many Huron sunrises.

HURON
SUNRISE

from *Magnum P.I.*, Season 3, Episode 1

Magnum: "Ivan?"

Ivan: "Yes?"

Magnum: "Did you see the sunrise this morning?"

Ivan: "Yes. Why?"

PROLOGUE

Kalamazoo, Michigan – June 1984

D ressed in a pair of Sesame Street pajamas and standing on her tiptoes, the two-year-old toddler, Rachel Roberts, pulled on her bedroom door handle with her tiny, pudgy fingers. Behind her, sunlight spilled into the darkened room from around the edges of her pull-down window shade, making the shade appear as if it were an all-white picture that had been hung on the wall with a thin, golden frame on three sides.

She had awakened to loud noises—*bangs* and *slams*—and shouting and was curious to find out what was happening outside the sanctuary of the pastel-colored walls of her room.

The handle was heavy, and she dug her top front teeth into her bottom lip as she continued to pull. She had only been able to open her door on her own for the past few weeks; each time, she had struggled to tug the lever far enough to feel the massive rectangular object inch away from the door frame, always exposing a sliver of space that let in a puff of air like a tomb that had been cracked

1

open after many years. The opening was a gateway to other spaces of the house where she did not spend a lot of time—those spaces were her parents' domain.

As the brass fixture lowered, Rachel's heels sank into her bedroom's cushy, sky-blue carpeting. She was about to crack the door open when she heard footsteps thunder down the hallway away from her room. She froze. There was the sound of a door slamming shut, followed by muffled shouting, perhaps from the kitchen or the living room. *Is that mommy? Or daddy?*

Or mommy and daddy?

She opened the door a few inches and peered out. The hallway was dark, and she could hear the sound of the box fan at the end of the passageway, which her father placed in the open window during the early morning hours and in the evening to cool the house. He had told her that the daily June temperature was in the 90s and that it was something called "dry heat," which she didn't understand. She just knew it was hot inside of the house and outside of it every day. And sometimes, when they were near the place her father called "downtown," the smell was bad; he had said words like "cemetery," "Riverview Drive," and "treatment plant," but she did not know what they meant.

Rachel nudged the door open and poked her head out, looking both ways as if making sure the train tracks were clear before crossing them. The brown-carpeted passageway was empty, and the door to her parents' room was closed, as was the door to the bathroom. She felt the cool air from the fan and saw its white cord, like a twisted lightning bolt against the navy-colored walls, dangling down and plugged into the wall socket below the window.

Footsteps to her left. She swiveled her head in time to see her mother enter the portion of the living room visible from where Rachel stood. She had on shorts, a t-shirt, and the sports shoes that she wore when she would push Rachel in the stroller.

Maybe we're going for a walk.

She had not seen much of her mother in the morning hours lately and was unsure where she had been sleeping as Rachel had entered her parents' bedroom in the middle of the night after bad dreams and found only her father asleep in the large bed. Once, she had found no one in the bed or bedroom and had become even more scared, running down the hallway in terror before finding her father sitting at the kitchen table in his robe, drinking apple juice. But when she had hugged him, his breath had not smelled like apple juice.

Rachel's father entered her field of vision. He was in his slippers and bathrobe, and his hair was messy. Her mother turned around, and the two stood, facing each other in front of the grass-green-colored davenport.

* * *

"But I bought tickets for us to see *Temple of Doom* this Friday night with everyone. We'll get dinner and then go watch the movie with all of our friends. It'll be like old times, I promise." Clark Roberts knew it was a desperate and ultimately futile final attempt to save the marriage—a last-ditch effort to highlight a special memory between them, leveraging nostalgia to awaken their once strong bond and reload their relationship. He had known when he purchased the tickets that Tina would not be going with him, but he had bought them anyway, remembering when they had gone to see *Raiders* three years earlier with their close group of friends and how they had come home afterward, still energized from the incredible cinematic experience, and made love like they never had before. A month later, Tina found out she was pregnant, and they celebrated their good fortune. Life had seemed easy, with natural progressions to inevitable happiness.

"They all know I've been seeing him," Tina said.

"I—I don't care. They're forgiving. They know we've had a rough patch. I'll—I'll do anything."

"Clark," she said, pausing, "I'm leaving."

3

His chest felt hot, and he dropped to both knees with tears in his eyes. "Please, don't go. I'm begging you. We can get this turned around; I *know* we can. And so do you."

She frowned. "We never had anything to turn around."

"How can you say that?" he yelled. "We've got Rachel!"

"*You've* got Rachel. Like you said, I'm a horrible mother."

"You know I didn't—"

"You'll find a better mother for her."

"She's two years old!"

"You'll hear from my lawyer. I want nothing to do with either of you. Start over, Clark. It will be better for both of you."

She turned to walk away, and he grabbed her wrist. "My God, you can't just *leave* her!"

"Let. Go. Of. My. Arm."

He released his grip, tears flowing down his cheeks; Tina began walking away.

Then, he heard, "Mommy? Daddy?"

Clark looked down the hallway and saw Rachel standing in the middle of the carpet. He turned to Tina. "Look at her!"

Tina did not look. Tina did not stop. She opened the door, said, "It's better this way," and left.

The house's frame seemed to shake, and the walls rattled with the closing of the door. One of Clark's bowling trophies—a miniature glass bowling ball mounted on a wooden stand—fell from a wall shelf, and the glass ball hit a corner of one of the davenport's end tables and shattered. Clark ignored it and turned to hug Rachel, who was crying and running toward him.

As they embraced, she shouted, "Mommy!"

4

PART I

Sundial

Landon Beach

I

South of Hampstead, Michigan – Monday, June 30, 2025

"I've been watching you do it for years, darling," Topaz Kennedy said to Rachel Roberts over the phone, "Knew all along what you were doing, of course, but I never stepped in as long as what you wrote met the needs of the titillating tale you were telling."

"Was it obvious?"

"Of course not, love. I only picked up on it because I know *you.*"

Rachel listened to her long-time agent while reclining in a wicker chair in the corner of the newly constructed deck extending out from her second-story writing room. She gazed out at the dark water of Lake Huron beyond the white strip of beach that lined her and Stan Atwater's property. She had always wondered if Topaz had noticed that Adrienne Astra was an avatar of Rachel Roberts. Her agent's words had confirmed that the answer to that question was *yes.*

When Rachel created the character of Adrienne Astra, she did what most amateur writers do: She made the character's background mirror her own. And so, after her first draft of *Morning Glory Mayhem!*, book one in the series, she had revised her background notes and changed Adrienne's roots just enough to give Rachel the necessary artistic distance to let the character exist and grow on her own. Then, in draft number three, she decided that the less the reader knew about Adrienne's background, the better. And so, she removed almost all of the backstory from the novel and decided to keep Adrienne's origins shrouded in mystery for most of the series. It had worked better than she or Topaz could have imagined. Most fan letters after each novel centered on one topic: Who in the hell *is* Adrienne Astra?

Rachel's notes left no doubt. Margaret Carol Crandall, who would later be given the name of Adrienne Astra when she officially joined the covert company Worth-Gideon, Inc., which would later become Worth, Tipler, and Associates, had been raised by her father after her mother and baby brother had both died during childbirth when Margaret was three; Rachel Roberts had been raised by her father after her mother had left them when Rachel was two. Looking back, killing off Margaret's mother had been the lie Rachel had told herself while growing up: *My mother died when I was two.* Later, she realized that the deeper reason for her decision to have Margaret's mother die was that Rachel wished that her mother was dead and never felt the pull to try and find her . . . and confront her.

Her entire creation of Adrienne Astra was based on her own life story. Rachel had been raised by a loving and heartbroken father. In her early twenties, she had been given the opportunity of a lifetime to become a published author and compete against the best writers in the world. And soon after, she had risen to the top of the profession, becoming the best . . . all while doing it under another name, Riley Cannon, with her real identity being kept secret. The outline of Adrienne's life was based on Rachel's lived experiences. After graduating college, Margaret Crandall had been given the rare prospect of competing for a spot with

8

a secret organization to become an elite assassin. She had passed the trials and been welcomed into an off-the-books company that functioned like a secret society (much like the fabled smoke and mirrors of the publishing industry). Once accepted into the company, Margaret had been given the name Adrienne Astra, and her prior identity had been "erased." Now a member of the organization, Adrienne had used her skill set to accumulate unthinkable levels of wealth.

And, now, both author and character were completing their journeys. Rachel Roberts, aka Riley Cannon, was 43; Margaret Crandall, aka Adrienne Astra, was 45. Rachel was completing her six-book series, which had taken her just over twenty years to do; Adrienne was homing in on the elusive mega-villain named "Control"—a mission that had taken *her* over twenty years to complete—and the final showdown in the climax of book six loomed large.

The final book in the 'Round the Clock Series was titled *Sunrise Kama Sutra*, which Rachel thought was an ironic name for a novel that marked an ending or separation because rituals of intimacy suggested repeated joinings or beginnings to new pathways of connection or even methods of renewal to sustain pairings, allowing the union to enjoy an extended, healthy, and happy existence.

I'm saying goodbye to Adrienne forever, Rachel thought, *which is to say I'm saying goodbye to myself.*

This thought, coupled with the scene she had written and sent to Topaz earlier in the week, had prompted Rachel to call her agent tonight.

"So, admitting to you that I have known that Adrienne has been you in disguise all along, mighty Cannon, the question is … why the jingle tonight? I mean, I was happy to answer your question. I admit, it threw me for a loop when you started right in with the business about your connection to Adrienne, but then I wasn't surprised because you're very close to wrapping up this book. You are obviously putting the advance reader copy of *The Blue Hour Sanction* to good use with the scene you wrote this week. It's perfect. Hightower loves it.

Freeman's performance was sublime. You have, what, around thirty-thousand words left? You're right on schedule. Then we can discuss you taking a break and jumping in with both feet again. I mean, we can't go a decade without a book like before now, can we? But I think a year or two off would do you some good."

"Topaz, this book is it for me."

"Now, don't you start in with all that talk again, thespian! I thought we had worked through that."

"This is my last book. Writing that scene this week—"

"Is precisely why you cannot quit! You've never been better. Industry needs hits more than ever. Did you hear what I told you about what Hightower said? And he never says that about a first draft!"

Rachel sighed. She knew it would be difficult for her agent to accept that their time was coming to an end after more than twenty years together. But, lately, Topaz had been more irritable than usual. Rachel had probed in roundabout ways, but her famous agent had refused to divulge what was bothering her.

The scene that she had written this week had made Rachel cry. And that had not happened since the first book.

The Blue Hour Sanction, Adrienne Astra's origin story, was on schedule to be published in December, six months before *Sunrise Kama Sutra* hit the bookshelves, e-readers, and audiobook library of readers and listeners on Tuesday, June 30th— right before the July 4th weekend. After five novels, Rachel had thought that publishing Adriene's origin story right before the series finale would be a great way to provide some backstory in an entertaining manner to give the final novel the attention it deserved while still holding back a few secrets. It was also a practical decision. There was too much ground to cover in book six, and adding an origin-story thread would have made the book too long and thrown off the pacing. *"Better to let it rip in a stand-alone-ish action novel, darling! It's bloody brilliant. Glad I came up with it."*

Which she hadn't, but Rachel had let it go as usual.

Then, Rachel had put her agent in a tough position. The night before she was to begin writing the origin story, she had taken off with Stan Atwater to elope. After they had been married in Vegas, she had called Topaz with the news that they were jetting off to Honolulu for a month, which Stan had incredibly cleared with Hampstead Police Chief Corey Ritter. *"But, you can't do this, Cannon! That novel has to be finished so that it comes out exactly six months before book six! Oh, congratulations on getting married, by the way, but still . . . well . . . Cannon, you can't go to Hawaii!"*

But she had, and now she realized that the intense feelings she was experiencing today had started when she had sat down and faced the computer, mere feet from where she was now, and decided that someone else would have to write the origin story with her notes. Thankfully, when Topaz accepted that Rachel was not returning from Hawaii for a month, she caved and said, *"Fine. I've got an old friend who can help us out."*

On her second night in Waikiki, on a moonlit beach with her new husband, Rachel had told Stan who she was. In the days that followed, she had opened up about the uncertain feeling she had inside herself, which she couldn't quite explain.

When they returned to Michigan, she had started working on the final novel. And, to her surprise, the relief from not having to incorporate Adrienne's backstory into the book had made the writing flow like it hadn't since the third book in the series, *Enemies in the Evening.* And yet, there was still a nagging notion, an uncomfortable awareness that there was more to finishing this novel than she could comprehend. As the plot progressed and Adrienne began making moves to counter the supervillain Control's evil deeds, setting up the inevitable clash later on, a new wave of clarity washed over Rachel. *There is something I need to do. What is it?*

The answer had come to her a few days later.

I don't have to pack an entire origin story into the final novel, but I could enrich it with a callback.

The scene was a reunion between Adrienne Astra and one of the competitors she had faced on an island in Lake Superior, attempting to make the final cut and join Worth-Gideon, Inc. Because book six was about resolutions, Rachel thought that it would be interesting to have Adrienne, who had only been known as "Core" to her two other competitors, meet up with the other candidate, "Grid," who had only survived that horrible night because Core had saved her life. The other candidate, "Indigo," had been torn to shreds by a pack of wolves.

Adrienne had never known what had happened to Grid because she had never seen her again after the island. Adrienne had progressed to the next training phase, and Grid had disappeared. Rachel thought it would be the perfect opportunity to bring Adrienne face to face with someone from her past, where her life as an assassin had started, right before propelling her into Act III, where her journey would end.

From her notes, Rachel knew that Grid's real name was Debbie Nunes and that she was a heptathlete from Georgia. If she had finished first in the island course and successfully made her first kill, then her Worth-Gideon name would have been Una Tabor. However, after suffering horrific injuries on the island course, her time at the company had come to an end. She had recovered after multiple life-saving surgeries and then many rounds of plastic surgery, all paid for by the company, and then been given a new identity . . . a new life.

Her name was now Daphne Brighton, and Rachel had her become a collegiate assistant track and field coach. Daphne had a husband named Rod Brighton, and they had two children—a girl named Debbie and a boy named Chris.

At the end of Part II of *Sunrise Kama Sutra*, Rachel had Adrienne start to pull the strings tight around Control's network, and it was here where Rachel found the perfect moment to provide her main character with an opportunity for introspection.

The scene ended up being one of Rachel's favorites of all time.

Adrienne watches day number one of the NCAA Track & Field Championship Meet on TV. About to get up and pour herself another cup of morning coffee, Adrienne stops when she sees the camera zoom in on a heptathlete and her coach standing on the infield, seemingly discussing strategy. Adrienne thinks that there is something familiar about the coach—her build and the way she moves. Then, the coach turns, and Adrienne sees her profile and is transported two decades back in time to the night of the island course . . . the frigid water; the caribou's insides, warming her arms and hands; the screams; the snarling wolves; and the sight of Grid fighting for her life. Adrienne also notices that the coach, even in ninety-degree weather, is wearing a long-sleeved shirt and pants. Hiding the injuries, she thinks.

Adrienne immediately grabs her laptop and looks up the coach online: Daphne Brighton. She can tell that Grid has had some facial plastic surgery and that her eyes are a different color—colored contacts, no doubt—but the shape and intensity of the eyes have not changed. After performing a successful one-hour surveillance detection run and feeling confident that no one from Control's organization is following her, she gets on a plane and travels to the location of the meet. After arriving, Adrienne finds out what hotel Coach Daphne Brighton is staying in and her room number. Adrienne checks into the hotel.

13

Later that evening, she waits in the lobby and watches as the heptathlete enters through the parting glass doors of the hotel. She is soon followed by her coach, and Adrienne's pulse quickens as her in-person assessment of Daphne Brighton confirms to her that she is Grid. Her height and build are exactly as Adrienne remembers. After the coach passes by, Adrienne gives her a grin and nod of approval. Grid has stayed in immaculate shape; there is no limping or favoring of either arm. *It must have been one hell of a rehab from those injuries,* Adrienne thinks.

The coach steps into an elevator with her heptathlete, and the doors close.

At this point, Rachel had hemmed and hawed over how Adrienne could get the coach back down to the lobby. There were dozens of discarded attempts, most of them involving Adrienne making a phone call to Daphne's room — Adrienne saying, *"This is Core. You were once Grid. Meet me in the lobby in five minutes,"* and, *"You were on an island in December of 2001. Be at the lobby bar in ten minutes, and come all by yourself,"* etc. Finally, Rachel decided that simple deception would work the best. Adrienne had the front desk call the coach and say that an Olympic scout wondered if she could speak to her for a few minutes regarding her heptathlete. It was an invitation that no coach could turn down.

Then, Rachel had written the scene and did something she had never done before. She had Topaz send the scene to her narrator, Suzanne Elise Freeman, asking her to perform it and email the recording back to Topaz. When Rachel received the forwarded email with the audio file, she had poured a glass of Riesling, closed herself off in her second-story writing room, and pushed play . . .

* * *

14

Adrienne watched from her booth in the hotel bar as Daphne exited the elevator. Her one-time competitor looked right and left as if scanning for threats and approached the front desk.

The clerk pointed toward Adrienne's table in the darkened bar, and Adrienne observed Daphne nod and then step off toward her.

How long will it take her to remember me? Adrienne thought. *Will she remember me? I'm wearing glasses and have my hair styled in a pixie cut. I've put on and maintained ten pounds of muscle over the past twenty years, but I look basically the same as I did on the island . . . just a few more wrinkles here and there.* As she viewed Daphne take confident, powerful strides toward the booth, a vision appeared in her mind. Snow falling as she sprinted along the fence line of Grid's paddock . . . hearing Grid's shrieks first, and then seeing her on the other side of the fence, yards away from the gate, fighting for her life against two enormous and hungry wolves . . . watching herself climb over the fence and join the fight to help her fellow candidate, knowing it might cost them both . . . gritting her teeth and thrusting her knife into one of the wolves . . . carrying Grid to safety . . . the sound of a motor getting louder and then the headlights of an all-terrain vehicle approaching . . . waking up alone in a hospital room, wondering what happened to Grid . . .

A few yards from the booth, Daphne smiled at Adrienne and extended her hand.

Adrienne rose and shook her hand.

"Daphne Brighton," her old cohort member said.

Her grip was firm but not overpowering. However, Adrienne knew that behind the coach's pleasant greeting was an aggressive animal that might have won the spot with the company that night. *Perhaps, if she had only made a spear like Adrienne had . . .*

"Heather Jennings, USA Track and Field. Pleasure to meet you, coach."

Adrienne sat down, and the booth's red leather cushions made a cracking sound as Daphne slid in across from her. The flickering candle on the table bathed the women's faces in an amber glow.

Before they could speak, a waitress stopped at the table and placed a bottle of Molson Golden in front of each woman, then moved to another table and started taking orders.

"I hope you don't mind me ordering a beer for us," Adrienne said. "I'm an old Minnesota girl, and there's nothing like a Golden after a hot day outside."

It was a lie, of course, but she did it to study her subject. When Daphne was "Grid," she had slipped at one point when they had been given a bucket full of bottles of American light beer and said to their head trainer, "Flo, what is this piss? You don't have any Molson Golden around, do you? It's the only beer I drink." Adrienne had thought she was cocky, but Flo had quickly humbled her by taking a bottle out of the bucket and breaking it over Grid's head. Because of the incident, Adrienne had never forgotten the words Molson Golden.

She watched as Daphne studied the bottle in front of her. The drops of condensation ran down the side of the emerald bottle, and the coach just stared at the red maple leaf on the golden label. A few more seconds passed before Daphne reached out her huge right hand and grasped the bottle. Her eyes rose and met Adrienne's. "I haven't had one of these since . . . well, it's been a long time."

"I'd be happy to order a different brand for you." She grinned and then laughed. "Got no problem slamming two of these down."

Daphne gave a polite grin. "I'm fine," she said and took a sip.

So did Adrienne.

"Solid girl you've got—she could win it all tomorrow."

Daphne seemed not to hear her as she swallowed and closed her eyes briefly before opening them and setting the bottle down. "Thanks. Heather has had a good senior season, but no one has reached out to me. I didn't think she was on

16

anyone's radar. When did you become interested in her? I haven't seen you at any of the meets this year." She took another sip. "How did you hear about her?"

Okay. She's in the booth, and it's quiet here. No one followed you to the airport; no one was on the plane with you; no one followed you from the airport to the stadium; and no one followed you to the hotel. It's time. If somehow you're wrong, she won't recognize anything on the paper. Then, you can make up some story, finish the beer, and disappear. If you are right, you'll know by her reaction.

Adrienne pulled a folded piece of paper from her pocket and handed it to Daphne. "Here's how."

On the piece of paper, she had written:

Kerrie Raven

Flo Fleming

Albert Munny

Core

Indigo

Grid

Daphne took a pair of glasses from her purse and put them on. Carefully, she unfolded the paper.

Adrienne observed.

The opening of the eyes followed by a swallow . . . the start of a gasp, cut short by the complete cessation of breathing for a few seconds . . . the right hand turning into a fist; the fingers of the left hand tapping on the table and then rubbing her right arm . . . the glazed stare at the paper . . .

It is her. Adrienne slid her a second piece of folded paper. Written on it were the words:

I am Core.

Daphne met eyes with her for a beat and then glanced down at the second piece of paper. Her left hand shook as she raised it off the table and opened the paper. A second after looking at what was written down, her eyes shot up to Adrienne's and then narrowed as she tilted her head.

Adrienne removed her glasses, and the two women sat motionless, looking over each other.

"I won't bother looking around. Is there anyone else here?" Daphne finally asked.

"No. We're alone."

Daphne exhaled and picked up her beer bottle, pointing to the label. "You remembered, didn't you?"

Adrienne gave her a nod, and then Daphne brought the bottle to her lips and took a long pull.

"May I see one of your arms?"

Daphne set the bottle down, paused, and then slid back the right sleeve of her moisture-wicking shirt until Adrienne could see the top of her forearm—Daphne's palm was flat against the table. Everything looked as it should, but then Daphne rotated her hand until her knuckles touched the table, and Adrienne saw the array of thin scars. At first, they looked like someone had haphazardly stabbed her skin with a knife, but Adrienne knew what she was looking for, and soon two bite patterns emerged.

"They did a nice job," Adrienne said. "I still remember what it looked like that night."

"Four surgeries on this arm, six on the other, and eight on my legs over the years," she said, covering her arm back up with her shirt sleeve. Daphne shook her head. "I've got a million questions for you, but I assume this will be a short meeting."

"Not too short," Adrienne replied, taking a swig of beer.

"What are you doing here?"

"I wasn't looking for you. I just happened to be watching the track and field finals this morning . . . and saw you. It's strange because I have never watched them before. But, for some reason, this year, I wanted to." She paused. "I had to see if it was you. What we went through was so long ago, but I have always wondered what happened to you after that night. All they told me was that you were no longer with the company and that I would never see you again."

"What gave me away?" Daphne leaned toward her and lowered her voice to a whisper. "As you can see, I've had some work done on my face. I'm shocked you could tell it was me from watching TV."

"I figured you would look a little different, but your build and the way you moved made me wonder. We were so close, competing with and studying each other, over those six months, that I suppose your mannerisms were burned into my memory."

"You aren't still with the company, are you?"

Adrienne waited a few moments to respond. "No, those days are over."

"So, *are you* Heather Jennings from USA Track and Field?"

Adrienne smiled. "Heather Jennings? Yes. USA Track and Field? No. Sorry about that. I needed a way to get you to come down and meet me."

Daphne nodded. "Not a bad move. So, are you saying you saw me on the TV this morning and flew here right away to meet me?"

"I am."

Daphne laughed. "That's crazy."

"I know. How long have you been coaching?"

"About fifteen years. I've had six girls make it to this meet in that time span, and every time they did, I wondered if Kerrie Raven would appear out of the shadows and speak to them. I had my guard up, though, and was determined to prevent them from being recruited." She took a breath, looked up at the ceiling, held it for a few seconds, and then exhaled. "It never happened, though. I had my guard up for all the heptathletes and never saw one approached by anyone." She leaned forward. "It took me a few years to . . . recover . . . from that ordeal."

Adrienne realized there was so much she wanted to tell Daphne, starting with the fact that the island trials had stopped after their group had gone through. However, she knew she could tell her nothing and had to keep her guard up even though seeing the woman across from her brought back memories she had long ago suppressed. She was in her mid-forties now and about to complete a mission that had taken over twenty years to complete—the systematic destruction of Control and her global criminal empire.

Daphne glanced down at the first piece of paper and tapped her finger on Kerrie Raven's name. "So, how is *that* old bitch?"

"I wouldn't know. It's been years since I've seen her."

"I hated her."

"Me too."

Daphne leaned back against the booth's back cushions. "How about Flo?"

"She left the company about a year after we went through the island course."

"Makes sense. How long did you stay in?"

Adrienne remained silent.

Daphne gave her a knowing look. "I shouldn't have asked."

"You're fine," Adrienne said, giving her a warm pat on the arm.

"I got curious once and saw that Worth-Gideon had changed its name to Worth, Tipler, & Associates. Gideon retire? Was there a falling out?"

Adrienne paused. *If you only knew.* "I do have to get going soon. Can't stay in one place for very long. One of the costs of the work I did." She thought of Tipler, one of the company's employees who had been sent to clean up in Switzerland after Flo and Munny had been killed. Then, a few years later, Tipler died on a mission to Guam, tracking a lead that he thought could ultimately reveal Control's identity. Then, after Jock Gideon left the company, Byron Worth made a surprising move and used "Tipler" in the company's new name. Hence, Adrienne had always found it awkward to answer "Who is Tipler?" when a new employee asked.

Daphne leaned forward and lowered her voice to a whisper again. "I know. You can't answer. There were a handful of times over the past two decades when I wondered what kind of *employee* I would have made . . . and what kind of person I would have become. I thought about it during the first snow for a few years." She finished her beer. "You look good."

"You would have been fine," Adrienne said. "Other than the surgeries, has life treated you okay?"

"Better than okay. After being lost for those first few years, I found love and then discovered what real love was when I had my two kids . . . and that reality drowns out any curiosities I had about what might have been if our roles had been reversed that night. I cannot imagine my life without my husband and two kids." Her eyes became glassy. "Thank you for saving my life."

She hadn't expected this.

What did I expect?

A memory crossed her mind: Grid leaping at her, attempting to kill her while they were still on the boat—the dark outline of the island in the distance beyond the ink-black water. "I'm glad I did," Adrienne said. She wondered what it would be like to have a family or a job that ran on a schedule. "Tell me about your family," Adrienne said, motioning to the waitress for the check.

"My husband's name is Rod. He's an elementary school music teacher. My boy, Chris, is fifteen, and my daughter, Debbie, is nine. They're both into sports and band—a perfect mix of me and Rod—so we've got a busy schedule. What about you?"

Adrienne pursed her lips and then finished her beer. She said, "Still single."

And as the words left her mouth, Adrienne Astra felt an emptiness she had never known. The last time she had seen her mentor, Flo, alive, Flo had told her to have something to come home to after each mission or risk losing her soul. It was at this moment that she realized her mentor had been right.

What parts of life have I missed? Have I wasted my life?

The answers would not come to her now. It would take time.

She was engaged to Byron Worth. After saving him from the clutches of his one-time friend and co-owner of the company, Jock Gideon, they had decided to commit to each other finally. The wedding would be after they took down Control. Then, they would retire and sail around the world together.

"Sounds lonely," Daphne said.

"It can be."

"Did you ever go back and visit the town you grew up in or the university you attended?"

"No." She was telling the truth. The moment she had made her first kill and become Adrienne Astra, she realized that she had not only killed a drug kingpin but also killed her former self, Margaret Carol Crandall, forever. In her mind, there was no Shelter Harbor, Michigan; there was no University of Michigan. However, now that she had been asked about revisiting her prior life, she suddenly felt the pull to return. Sitting in a first-class seat at 35,000 feet earlier today, she had thought that meeting with Daphne would be enough to make peace with the past. Now, she realized that it would not. Adrienne wanted—*needed*—to see her hometown.

She also needed to visit Ann Arbor and walk through campus . . . and see the U-M Track and Field Stadium, which she had heard replaced the historic Ferry Field, where she had competed.

"Did you go back?" Adrienne asked.

"Seven years ago, I finally got the courage to do it."

"How was it? Did anyone recognize you?"

"Not a soul. And it was cathartic. Raven, Flo—they made us give up our past. Raven threatened me in the hospital room where I was recovering from my injuries on the island, saying that if I ever went back home or to the college I attended or told anyone from my former life that I was still alive, I would be killed. Well, when I turned forty, I decided it was time to go back. I admit that I visited my hometown in the summer when I could wear sunglasses, and I pretty much stayed in my car. But it felt good to see everything again. So much had changed; so much had stayed the same. My house seemed smaller. The trees in the backyard were enormous.

"When I traveled to my college campus, it was easy to blend in. Everyone just walks along the sidewalks, looking at their phones. No one said a word to me all day. The only place I had to be careful was around the track because my coach was still there—thankfully, our paths had not crossed at any meets. I saw her working with the sprinters on the far side of the field. I wanted to hop the fence, run over, and give her a gigantic hug. We had been close. That was the difficult part of returning, but it was all worth it. I needed to cry those tears in the car on the way to the airport that day. My coach retired after that season." She reached out and held Adrienne's hand for a moment. "Go back if you can."

Her mouth became dry, and she felt tears building behind her eyes. A twenty-plus-year emotional veneer was crumbling . . .

Mercifully, the waitress arrived with the check, and Daphne offered to pay, but Adrienne had already taken cash out and handed the bills to the girl. "Keep the change," she said. The waitress thanked her and moved on to another table.

"Tell me one thing, though," Daphne said. "Was it worth it, working for the company? Did you do the world some good while you were employed there?"

There was silence for a few moments.

What do I tell her? Adrienne thought. *Yes? I think?*

"Wait a minute," Daphne said. "You mull it over while I visit the restroom, and then tell me when I get back. Deal?"

23

"Deal."

Daphne slid out of the booth but paused, standing over Adrienne. "I'm glad you made it. And I'm glad you risked coming to see me."

Before Adrienne could answer, Daphne headed away toward the bar restrooms.

Adrienne waited until her old rival disappeared through the doorway, and then she took the two pieces of paper, stuffed them in her pocket, and exited the bar.

As she drove away in her car, she looked through her rearview mirror at the hotel.

Goodbye, Grid. Thank you.

* * *

After hearing the performance, Rachel realized that, like her character, it was time for her to "go home" and face something she had been avoiding her entire life: her mother. She knew she could not write the conclusion to Adrienne's story without attempting some closure in her own life. If she was standing in a valley, then Part III of *Sunrise Kama Sutra* was somewhere over the mountain range in the distance. Adrienne could not face Control in the final showdown until Rachel had faced her mother.

Her last thought before calling Topaz tonight had been, *How much has the memory of my mother been* controlling *me for the past forty years?*

"I've been running from my past for too long now, Topaz. It's time to face it, and doing that will give me the answers I need to finish Adrienne's journey in a satisfying manner." She paused, hearing the wind chimes on the first-floor porch below. "I cannot write another word until I have answers—whether I like the answers or not."

"But, do you have the *questions*, darling?"

24

"I think so."

"Well, let's talk more about this. I must say I'm relieved, child; I thought you were hanging up the paper and pen for good."

"I am. Topaz, I meant what I said. The sun eventually sets on everyone's career."

There was a pause, and then Rachel heard loud crashing sounds on the phone.

"Topaz? Topaz, are you okay?"

2

The sounds grew louder—crashing, smashing, and then the piercing sound of glass shattering. "Topaz!" Rachel yelled.

There was silence again, and then an out-of-breath Topaz Kennedy came back on the line. "Not your career, Madame President. *Not. Yours.* You've got the wrong word, Cannon. The *right* word to describe the state of your career is in the title of your new novel. It's sun*rise,* not sun*set,* for you, ma'am. In fact, after we release this book, we'll just be getting started. Our next stop will be the prequels. Going to hit it. Hard. Remember, Hightower and I still have our printed-out copies of *Ice Station* locked away in our homes. Do you realize what a hit that Adrienne Astra prequel story will be in a few years? And Freeman doesn't even know about it! What a *gift* you will bequeath her with, wise woman!"

"Are you okay?"

"Heavens, yes, it was the TV. I've turned it down. Now, where were we? Ah, yes, talking about the prequels. It's a brilliant idea, isn't it?"

"*The Blue Hour Sanction* did everything we wanted it to do. I have nothing else to say about Adrienne's origins, Topaz."

"Hmph," Topaz grunted.

"It's time to say goodbye to Adrienne."

"Nonsense! Forget what I said about the prequels. Adrienne has *at least* five good years left in her tank. I mean, look at me, child, I'm *mumble, mumble* years old, and *I* could be carrying out her missions. Oh yes, I've given it some thought, and I think you should use me as the bar for Adrienne to try and reach. She'll never make it, but she'll give it a go, won't she? Now, enough of this retirement rubbish. You're forty-three . . . the absolute height of your powers, Cannon! *3 A.M.* fucking *Phone Call* is still holding at number one on the *Times* list after a year! Can you imagine what book *six* will do? And book seven, and book eight, and book—"

"Topaz, book six is it."

There was a long pause before her legendary agent spoke again. Rachel could hear the ice clink in Topaz's ritualistic evening glass of scotch. "I'm going to douse you in empirical evidence, okay? All your major competitors have tried to take you down this past year, all represented by my nemesis, the prissy, backstabbing, loathsome agent, Aya Gunner. Remember, darling? Yes, of course you do. In August, it was Ivan Bacca's book, which never made it higher than #5 on the list; in October, it was Jackie Donahue, well, the ghostwriter for her anyway—got stuck at #2; in March it was Judge Macy Ashberry—ha!—barely made the list at #15; and then in May, it was our most delicious victory—we pummeled Saw Walden and his newest Shane Steel novel, which, as we all knew, was just a political treatise masquerading as a military-thriller. Blasted them all, darling! Did you ever notice, Cannon, that I never have my other clients release a book during the same year as you do?"

Rachel did know. Topaz had told her about the complaints from the other authors, but ultimately, the agent whom all other agents were measured against had prevailed. And Topaz's stable of authors was impressive. There was Rachel's thriller-writer partner-in-crime, M. Scott Sala, the romance novelist queen of the charts, Aphrodite Belle, the literary snob, Jaffa St. Thiery, and the mystery writer phenomenon, Dallas Darcy. Topaz merely referred to them as her children.

Other industry insiders called them "The Big Five." Aya Gunner called her four power clients "The Fantastic Four."

"It's so goddamned stupid to name them after a comic book superhero team," Topaz had remarked.

"I *have* noticed that they don't release books in the same year as I do," Rachel said. "They're all releasing books this year, right?"

"Naturally, my dear. Want to get their books out—" She paused. "What's the blasted phrase Aya Gunner uses these days on social media when one of her authors launches a book?" Rachel heard the ice clink in Topaz's glass again, followed by Topaz smacking her lips. "Ah, I remember. Time to release such-and-such stupid title *into the wild*. Ugh. Anyway, yes, we want to get their books out and give them a chance before your novel is released *into the wild* next summer."

"Who's going first?"

"Sala is releasing his Nehemiah Stone prequel, *Secret Voyage*, next month. See, angel? Prequels are *hot*. I just listened to Shawn Frost's recording last week. Got a copy from David Killian. Now, *there's* an agent who could claim to call his clients the Fantastic Four—Shawn Frost, Corie Woods, Courtney Tyson, and Seraphina Devereaux. He's been trying to represent Freeman for years, but our star lady narrator continues maintaining her independence—like a gun for hire, Cannon!" Rachel heard Topaz take another sip. "Ah, now, where was I?"

"The order of publication for this year."

"Right! Oh, one more thing. Did you know that Shawn Frost was starring in that new movie, *The Baroness of Monterrey*, with none other than Jessamine Jean Baptiste? And that there's been rumblings of drama?"

"I knew the film was being made but had forgotten they were starring. Don't even know who's directing it. I stay off the internet, remember?"

"Of course, I remember, and I've never understood why. Me? I've got to be in the loop. Well, you see, Miss Off-The-Grid, they got Henri Pascal to come out of retirement to direct it. Bonkers, lass. Bonkers! You do know who Jessamine Jean Baptiste is, right?"

"Who doesn't? She's an incredible actress; I saw her in *The Kaleidoscope* last year."

"Oh, how I loved that one. Reminds you of Grace Kelly, doesn't she?"

"Agreed. And as talented as either Hepburn."

"Exactly, Miss Kael! Now, *The Kaleidoscope* was gorgeous—good gosh, the chemistry between her and Mr. Murphy . . . sizzling—but her best work was in *Tahiti*. Don't give a hoot about the Oscar and Golden Globe she won for it. I'm a sucker for a story about an embattled woman who finds peace . . . and gets her *revenge*."

"The newspapers can't get enough of her, but I haven't read about any drama regarding the picture."

"Why still bother with those inky sheaves?"

"I—"

"Never mind. Well, the reason it hasn't made the papers yet is that there are just *rumors* of drama at this point. I knew them well before *Deadline* and *The Hollywood Reporter* put out their *breaking news*—I've got insiders everywhere, Cannonical."

"Is the picture in trouble?"

"Heavens no. One way or another, Henri always comes through. However, the juicy details are that Sir Gentry Hill—for my money, the greatest character actor to ever live, and I don't care if he's seventy-one—has been complaining that Ms. Jean Baptiste has been difficult to work with. I love it. There's blood in the water. Imagine that. Our glamor girl is not perfect. Hmph! Ah, the first chink in the armor is always the most intriguing; the fairytale unravels—Rapunzel's hair gets cut, and she falls from the tower and breaks her neck. Ha! Apparently, Jessamine has a 2-story motorhome worth 3.2 million dollars—even more luxurious than Will Smith's. I guess she's been hiding out in it, refusing to work because of the 'conditions.' Sir Gentry is furious. And, here's the best part: Somehow, Mister Shawn Frost is caught up in the middle of it!"

Why did I ask? She's stalling and doesn't want to talk about the ending of my career. I haven't even told her yet what I need to do to finish the book. Rachel cleared her throat. "Topaz, this will be my last book."

"I'll get to that, but first, I'm finishing my list."

"Topaz—"

"Hush. Now, where was I? Yes, two months after Sala's Nehemiah Stone origin story, Aphrodite Belle's *Heart Mirror* will be released, and it's a tear-jerker, Cannon. Cried for hours. Then, we have pompous Mister Vocabulary, the master of syntax, Jaffa St. Bastard and his trim, seventy-three-thousand-word exploration of a painter named Dorian who falls in love with an A.I. version of his deceased wife, Pelagia, and is unable to paint because he cannot break away from his den where a projector displays a 3D version of dead wifey. For over two hundred pages, Dorian sits in the dark and converses with her as she walks along the seashore, swims in the deep blue Mediterranean, or sits on the couch beside him. The algorithm that Dorian's friend has created puts her in a different outfit each day. There's even a chapter where Dorian attempts to make love to Pelagia. I tried to talk Jaffa out of it, but he and his goddamned editor ganged up on me and somehow got the publisher to agree to leave the chapter untouched. Dorian gets his thingy caught between the bloody couch cushions! And we call this *art?* Nonsense. Have I mentioned Jaffa St. Bernard's editor before? *Julian* Benedict. Now, there's a monster, dear; he'd even slice up your oracle, J. Rudolph Hightower, and that's saying something. Remind me later; I have news about him. Well, the slim exploration of machine and man is titled *The Den Widow Sea.* Preposterous! God-damnit, I don't want to arrange any promotions for that bloody book!" Topaz sighed, and Rachel heard ice cubes slosh and then clink against her agent's glass. "Anyway, a month after that, I find my comfortable footing once more as dear Dallas Darcy publishes book thirty-seven in his Gary

Burt Detective Series. And number three seven—dear God, almost two books a year for twenty years—is one of his best titles yet: *Gary Can't*. Not even a Halloween mask could hide my enthusiasm for that one. Darcy has Gary facing his demons head-on, and it's time. This will allow him to stretch the series past forty books, which has always been our goal since I signed him a year after you. Been a Gary Burt fan since day one. Conversation closed."

"Topaz, we need to talk about—"

"Damn it, Cannon, they're all threatening to leave me!"

Before Rachel could answer, Topaz hung up the phone.

3

Rachel tried to call her agent back, but the call went straight to voicemail.

. . . they're all threatening to leave me!

The words ran through her mind as she opened the deck door and entered her writing room. Her enormous cat, Hemy, emerged from underneath the desk and rubbed his furry girth against her right calf muscle as she paused to pick up her Moleskine notebook from the desktop.

"Change is hard, Hemy," she said.

The cat followed her toward the door to the hallway.

She opened it, turned off the light, and they both left the room.

When Rachel reached the downstairs living room, her husband, Stan Atwater, was lying on the couch, watching the Detroit Pistons game on the TV.

"How did it go?" he asked, muting the TV.

"Not well," she said, sitting down in the recliner. "I didn't even get to tell her what I am going to try and do."

Stan sat up. "Really? I thought that was the whole point of calling her?"

"It was. Things went off the rails when I reminded her that I'm retiring after this book."

He rubbed his chin. "She's going to fight you every step of the way. You're her biggest client."

Ugh, thought Rachel. *Her other clients.* "She told me that the other authors that she represents are threatening to leave her."

"What did you say to that?"

"I didn't get a chance. She hung up right after she said that. I tried to call back, and she wouldn't answer."

"Why would her other clients threaten to leave?"

She knew the answer. Jealously. All four of them knew who Topaz's number one client was and that it wasn't changing. Riley Cannon's books sold the most copies and made the most money; that was all that mattered. When she had disappeared for over a decade, the other writers had thrived, enjoying the spotlight; when Riley Cannon had made her comeback with *Dark After Midnight,* all four had faded once again. They were not happy. With Riley Cannon out of the way, Topaz knew that her rival agent, Aya Gunner, would make a play to steal her clients. After all, Topaz had only acquired them *after* she had become famous because Riley Cannon's books had become a phenomenon, and there had been rumors for years that the sales had little to do with Topaz Kennedy and more to do with the fact that the books sold themselves. They were addictive, successful movie adaptations had been made, and the mystery and accompanying theories of who Riley Cannon was would not die. Competitors claimed that the publishing house and Topaz had spun the success of the books to make it look like *they* had been the reason that Riley Cannon and her series had become a twenty-year sensation. Rival agents and publishers had called it publishing voodoo when trying to lure Topaz's clients away. But it hadn't worked.

Until, perhaps, now. Topaz had been complaining to her about thirty-nine-year-old megalomaniac Aya Gunner for months. *'The bitch had an intermediary tell Dallas Darcy that Aya could be doing so much more for his career.' I'll gut her, Cannon, and take her clients!"*

She's always been a bit over the top.

However, Rachel knew that the moment she announced her retirement, Topaz would be vulnerable. The clandestine campaign would cease, and Gunner would come out of the shadows and make a play for Topaz's clients.

Rachel told Stan all of this and then added, "This is why she doesn't want me to announce that I am retiring. With me as a client, she can still claim to represent the number one bestselling author in the world, which gives her leverage with her other four clients. No one can create as much visibility for an author as Topaz can, and that will keep even envious authors tethered to her."

"You know I'm fine if you change your mind," Stan said.

She laughed. "Gold digger."

"You know that's not what I mean."

"I know." She stood up and walked toward the couch.

Stan Atwater was anything but a person who married for money. She had waited to tell him who she was until after their engagement. *If I don't, then I'll never know if he proposed to me because of the money.* When she did tell him—and how much she was worth—she was relieved when he said, *"You're not going to make me quit my job, are you?"*

They had been married for almost a year now—he had not changed, and the secret of who she was had remained between them and Topaz. He had neither upgraded his wardrobe nor started to collect toys such as boats, planes, cars, etc. He enjoyed her for who she was, and she trusted him and admired his dedication to his job and community. She could not deny that her anonymity helped to keep them grounded, for he was not suddenly thrust into attending cocktail parties with wealthy people whom he did not know nor forced to take lavish vacations to places he did not want to see nor pressured to spend money on things he did not need in an attempt to bring him up to speed with the other members who resided in his new tax bracket. The second-floor deck was constructed so that they could sit with each other and enjoy a morning cup of coffee, watching the sunrise before he headed to work, or a bottle of wine on a weekend night. He was an early riser, and she liked that about him. He was also a deep sleeper who did not move around once he went to sleep. Sometimes, she would lie awake and study his frozen form. Everything else at her house had remained the same except for the addition of his clothes in the master closet and his tools in the garage. He loved Hemy, and the cat had approved of him from day one.

What she had not told Topaz was that the primary reason she was retiring was that she and Stan wanted to start a family.

"No, I'm more certain than ever that this will be my last book," she said, snuggling up next to him.

"Will you try and call her back tonight?"

"No, I'll give it a few days. But I'm not waiting to get started on what I need to do. At least she knows I have to take care of something before writing Part III of the book. As I told you before, her main priority is getting the novel to the finish line. So, whatever I need to do to make that happen, she will support me."

Stan kissed the top of her head. "You okay?"

"She has practically been my mother for the past twenty years, and now I'm somewhat leaving her. We'll talk every once in a while about foreign rights, royalties, or film adaptations, but that will be about it."

Rachel felt him wrap his arms around her. He squeezed and said, "What do you need from me?"

He was so in tune with her wants and needs that Rachel had grown to feel safe and supported in his presence. He would offer advice if asked, but he always asked her what she needed first and resisted the urge to do something when her answer was, *"Nothing."* He was also the most generous lover she had ever known, which had made her feel free and at ease when their bodies joined. She felt the urge to make love to him but knew that she needed to wrap up her business first. "You're already doing it, holding me and listening to me." She looked at her watch and then kissed his muscular forearm.

"Are you still going to call Obadiah tonight?"

"Yes." She tapped his arm, and he released her. Facing him, she motioned with her eyes toward the bedroom. "After that . . ."

He nodded and lay back down on the couch.

After a few seconds had passed, she could hear the sounds of the basketball game again and blew him a kiss as she left the living room.

Five minutes later, she was sitting in bed, dialing Obadiah Ben-David's number. He answered, and after a few minutes of small talk, he said, "It's good to hear from you, but somehow, I don't think you rang me to catch up. Thing is, I was going to call you in the morning."

"Really? Why?"

"You go first," Ben-David said.

She grinned. They had grown even closer in the past year and a half, although it had been a few weeks since they had last talked. "I have a proposition for you."

"I'm listening."

She had wondered how to ask him. Her partner was blunt and did not like extended preambles to answers. She decided to be direct but general at first. "I would like to hire you to help me find someone."

"Who?"

"I'll get to that."

There was silence on the other end for a few seconds, and then Ben-David said, "Before I answer your question, there is something you need to know."

Oh my gosh, he finally proposed! Ben-David had been dating Tilly Michaels, the owner of the local bookstore, The Hampstead Pages, for a year and a half. He had discussed possibly asking her to marry him with Rachel a month ago, and Rachel had told him to do it.

When did he ask her? It had to be within the past twenty-four hours because he would have called me with the news if it had happened any earlier.

"I think I know what you're about to say," she said.

36

There was a pause. "I don't think so, my friend."

Oh, it's the other thing! He's finally figured out that I am Riley Cannon. But how?

Just as her mind registered that his voice suddenly sounded tired, he said, "Rachel, I have cancer."

Santa Andreas Island, five nautical miles west of San Miguel Island, Channel Islands, Santa Barbara County, California – Monday, June 30, 2025

*E**mpires built on hate and division do not last,* thought Andre Kurt Andreas, Chief Executive Officer of A. Andreas Enterprises, as he exited the five-hundred-square-foot, glass-enclosed shower off his master bedroom.

Unless you are in the arms dealing business.

He gave a sly grin and peered back at the two voluptuous and gigantic—six-foot-three and six-foot-four—twenty-five-year-old women, one Caucasian, one African-American, who stood on the turquoise tiling underneath separate silver shower heads, washing their hair. The sex between the three of them had been ideal, a well-rehearsed transition of positions that had led to exciting rhythms and slippery sensations underneath the torrents of hot water. When they had entered his shower paradise, complete with teak benches, four shower heads, and automatic-dispensing cylindrical canisters of soap, shampoo, conditioner, and lotion, the five-foot-seven-inch Kurt had been in the middle of the 3-person conga line, which, according to their heights, looked like an "M" moving toward the high-above (in his case) jets of liquid relief.

He closed the door and reached for his white terrycloth robe hanging on a silver hook mounted on the navy-colored wall of the bathroom. On the robe's breast pocket were the initials "A.K." sewn in with crimson-colored yarn, which not only stood for his first and middle name but, by providence, he claimed to clients, also stood for his favorite weapon to sell worldwide: the AK-47 assault rifle.

He picked up his after-shower brush from a shelf next to the hook where his robe had hung and pulled the wire bristles straight back through his thick black hair, dyed once a week to hide his seventy-two years of age. His skin was tanned to a smooth and even bronze color from his daily visit to his vertical tanning hexagon, equipped with fans that blew cool air straight down at him while he stood inside the hex for five minutes every morning before his sixty-minute swim in the saltwater lap pool located in the gymnasium building next to his twenty-thousand-square-foot island mansion.

As Kurt slipped on his navy-colored flip-flops that had been specially made to support his high arches—they were officially called "orthopedic recovery shoes," which he thought was ridiculous—he heard a faint knock coming from his bedroom. He heard giggling in the shower and was tempted to hang his robe back up and ignore the knocking, but it got louder, so he left the giggling coming from the wet, curvy bodies and entered the bedroom.

He padded across the lush, sky-blue carpet and opened the door.

Standing before him was his head of security, Ivan Volkov, whose head almost touched the top of the doorway. His black and gray goatee was like steel wool, and Kurt had never gotten used to the fact that Ivan's mammoth shoulders and arms looked out of place compared to the giant's narrow waist. However, this afternoon, Ivan's nervous eyes captured Kurt's attention. They looked uneasy and were not the usual cold, black, seemingly lifeless circles in the center of the white globes of his eyeballs. The eyes remained the same whether Ivan was greeting a world leader who had come to Kurt's island or if Ivan was using an axe to cut off a traitor's legs just above the knee. Kurt had never seen the eyes as jumpy as they were today.

"What is it, Ivan?" he said.

Ivan answered in his deep baritone voice, just a hint of his Eastern Ukraine accent still noticeable. "Trouble."

Immediately, Kurt's mind went to his guest list.

First, there were the two honeys back in the shower. *It couldn't be about them.* They'd been vetted a year ago and enjoyed their weekly trip out to the island to spend a few days with him, sunbathe on the beach or by the pool, get paid, and then return to the house he had bought for them in northern California, just outside of Modesto. A hired overseer kept an eye on them when they were on the mainland, and there had been no trouble since they had started the relationship with him nine months ago. They were leaving in the morning on Wednesday, July 2nd to celebrate the 4th of July at home. He had toyed with the idea of inviting them to stay for an entire week, but his mistress would be back on Thursday, July 3rd, and even though she knew about the two pillars, it was best not to push it. *No, whatever Ivan has for me, it cannot be about them.*

Next were Academy-Award-winning actor Zachariah Lafontaine and his mega-agent Jolly Otto, who had both arrived in the late morning and *were* staying for the week to enjoy a low-key celebration of the 4th . . . and, to escape a public relations nightmare. Lafontaine—tall, slim, with a deep tan and a mop of brown hair—was in his early forties but had a full-time staff devoted to making him look like he was thirty. Cheating the aging process was one thing they had in common. The other item was their shared narrative of being globalist climate change activists and disruptors. The enormous power that Lafontaine had accumulated through his acting and his production company, Hotspur & Hal are Hamlet Productions ("Triple H" Productions for short), had given him the coveted megaphone to spread his agenda, which just happened to align with Kurt's. Then, yesterday, it had all been turned upside down. Lafontaine owned a yacht, a private jet, a helicopter, and an armored limousine, and Kurt had warned him about flaunting his use of them. *"If you have to take a jet across the world to a climate summit where you're going to give a speech and then vacation for two weeks, people will look the other way because, right now, a jet is the only practical way to get there. Hence, always align your vacations with climate conferences that are close by. Get there, stay there, and enjoy. Location shooting for a film you're in? You're still fine there, too, because that's your job. Perhaps if the location is close and accessible by water, like that thriller you filmed last year up in Alaska, you can sail there. Don't use your power yacht. How many times do I have to tell you to get a sailboat? Anyway, do not use your other toys often, or, at the minimum, try to do it unnoticed. If you don't announce your schedule to the world on social media, you have some flexibility and might sneak in a trip or two. You've got a friendly media, so they'll look the other way too— especially if you invite a few moguls as a VIP guest to one of your premieres or vacation with them every once in a while. That's what I do. That way, if I'm photographed on their fossil-fuel-guzzling mega-yacht, I can always claim that I was merely a guest, and though I am leading the charge to find clean, environmentally friendly energy alternatives, I do realize the reality of the current situation that we are all in. And I would never be disrespectful to my host and friend."*

His speech had reached Lafontaine's agent, Jolly Otto, and Jolly, a short, muscular man with a shaved head and a reputation for incinerating any of Lafontaine's Hollywood enemies, had instituted protocols to adhere to Kurt's philosophy. But . . . that stubborn actor didn't always listen to Kurt or Jolly, and that subversive spirit of defiance—one set of rules for me, one set for everyone else—had finally backfired. Yesterday, at a Senate hearing on climate change, after Lafontaine's fiery remarks castigating big oil companies and anyone who drove or rode in an SUV (which was 99% of Congress), a Senator from Hawaii, who was an independent but caucused with the Democrats, had shocked the chamber and lowered the boom on live television. Kurt could still see and hear her delivering her statement, which had been replayed on every nightly news show last evening: *"Zach, I'm a big fan of yours, have been for years, but I have to admit, I'm not as big a fan as Trice Givins. Does that name mean anything to you? No, I didn't think it would. How about Bryan Seltzer? Ah, yes, I see the recognition in your eyes. He was your personal assistant for the past three years, correct? And, as of six months ago, he is no longer an employee of yours, correct? Well, Bryan's friend, Trice Givins, was such a big fan that he wanted to know what a year in the life of a star was like—what a star did, who a star saw, and where a star went. Things like that. Well, for the good of the chamber, we'll skip what Trice learned about the first two inquiries and only focus on the last one: where you went. What you are about to see on the screen are the actual miles you traveled last year using fossil-fueled transportation, the details, and logs and receipts provided by Bryan Seltzer. With the gift of modern video surveillance, your every trip has been checked and verified by an independent, third-party review, and Mr. Seltzer's information is one hundred percent accurate . . . As you can see on the screen, in the year before Mr. Seltzer's termination, you traveled 113,000 miles. Now, there's an asterisk next to that number, and I want to explain why. According to the records provided by Mr. Seltzer and verified by the review members, 38,000 of those miles were either for your job or because you were attending a climate change conference, so we won't count those against you—although, for a three-day conference, you stayed an average of two weeks at that location and traveled . . . well, let's forget that for now. You're a busy guy—private jet, one-hundred-foot power yacht, luxury helicopter, limousine, two SUVs, two sports cars, two motorcycles, and one hybrid that you bought three years ago that has four hundred and twenty-seven miles on it. Sorry, I'm getting off track. If we grant you the miles for work and activist conferences, that leaves you with 75,000 miles traveled for vacations that year. The estimated amount of fuel it took to travel that distance, according to the different modes of travel that you used, is a little over 78,000 gallons. Let me repeat those numbers. 75,000 miles. 78,000 gallons. For vacation.*

"Now, personally, I believe that climate change is a major concern, and we need to hear from people who are making a difference and doing their part to help, but you know who I don't think we should all hear from again? You. But if you do speak in public in the future, chastising your fellow human beings, most of whom are not as privileged as you are, for not comprehending the grave danger the earth is in due to our negligence, then my recommendation is for whoever is giving you air time, they place both of those numbers on the screen below you as you talk."

Just after boarding his private jet (damnit!) to leave Washington D.C., Lafontaine had called Kurt and asked for a quiet place to hide out for a week until the hearing left the headlines. Kurt had granted the favor but made the actor put his agent on the phone at that point. Lafontaine's doctor had given him something to sleep, and he had retired to his jet's private bedroom. When the door had shut, Jolly Otto had said, *"I warned him, Kurty, and he didn't listen. This was a well-timed hit job. That gorgeous female senator from Hawaii, Tera Nailima, who called him out, yeah, well, she got word that one night when Zach had too much to drink at a party, he slipped and said that one night with him in bed, and she wouldn't be a lesbian anymore. I know, I know, he's out of control, but we've got the big picture starting in a month with you know who directing, and I don't want anything to fuck it up . . . Yes, I'll make sure that no one knows he's left his residence. Let the media think he's holed up in there thinking about how he can atone for his sins. We'll use the hangar trick."* When Jolly mentioned that, Kurt knew they'd make it to the island unnoticed. The legendary agent had told him so a few hours ago.

When Lafontaine's plane had entered the private hangar, Lafontaine and Jolly Otto had hidden in the hangar's panic room until the limousine that supposedly had them both in it had left for Lafontaine's mansion. When the limousine arrived at the outer gates to the estate, there were news vans, reporters, and protestors all over the place. But, Lafontaine's security personnel had made it possible for the vehicle to pass through the gates and travel down the winding drive until the driver had safely parked it inside the garage. The crowd outside the gate had remained, thinking that the embarrassed actor was now inside his castle but would hear their discontent when he grabbed a breath of fresh air later. Meanwhile, using a van from the cleaning company that maintained the hangar, a driver smuggled Lafontaine and Jolly to a private drive that led to a remote pier, where they were picked up by a cabin cruiser that took them out to one of Kurt's yachts that was anchored offshore. Then, a few hours before dawn, a helicopter landed on the yacht and picked them up. After a few stops to refuel on Kurt's other yachts spread along the coast, they arrived at Santa Andreas Island in the morning. As planned, no one knew they were there.

At least, that was what Kurt thought. Perhaps Ivan was about to tell him that word had somehow leaked and that they were about to have a magnifying glass put on the island by the outside world. Kurt would not be pleased with this.

He completed his checklist of guests. *Shit. Of all the weeks.* The Governor of California, Sal Reiner, had arrived last night just before dinner, and his mistress, Chrissy Marin, had shown up around 9 p.m. Kurt had seen them at lunch today, but other than that, the two had remained in their room. They would leave tomorrow evening—forty-eight hours was usually the cap on the time the governor could slip away on a "working vacation" and have his chief of staff and the lieutenant governor cover for him. This particular getaway was easy to explain: The governor had some last-minute business to attend to before taking some time off to enjoy the 4th of July holiday with his family. They'd watch fireworks in Sacramento and then stay the weekend with a studio head and his wife and kids at the studio head's beach house in Malibu. Why had Reiner not been caught other times? He was a workaholic who wasn't overly greedy; he only visited Kurt's island once a quarter to spend time with Christy. Reiner worked and traveled so much that his wife and three children didn't give the forty-eight-hour absence a second thought when it occurred once every three months—usually, he was away for longer. Santa Andreas Island was also the perfect location for these discrete getaways: If there was a real personal or professional emergency, he was a little over an hour's flight away from Sacramento.

However, Reiner's visitations were never completely work-free. Kurt's wife, Kitty, would entertain Chrissy for a few hours tomorrow morning while Kurt and Sal had their quarterly meeting regarding Kurt's secondary business. In the past, touching base for these precious hours had kept Kurt's arms-dealing machine running smoothly. Now, he wondered if Ivan's urgency had anything to do with tomorrow's summit.

"You need to come down to the conference room," Ivan said.

"The conference room?"

"Immediately, sir."

Three minutes later, Kurt entered the spacious conference room in his mansion's business wing, wearing khaki shorts, a short-sleeved linen shirt, and his special flip-flops.

The room was empty as Ivan sat across from him and pushed a button on the conference room table. "Bring in the package."

Kurt met Ivan's eyes—they were anxious. He wanted more information on the walk to the room, but for the first time ever, Ivan had said, *"There is something you need to see,"* and Kurt had not pressed.

A door on the far end of the conference room opened, and a man wearing the standard security uniform of black boots, jeans, and a black polo shirt with "A. Andreas Enterprises" stenciled in cobalt blue thread on the left breast entered, carrying a hefty, square package, perhaps three feet by three feet by three feet. As the man set the box on the table between Kurt and Ivan, Kurt noticed that the man had on a utility belt that held a knife, a flashlight, handcuffs, extra clips of ammunition, and a holster that held a Beretta M9 handgun. He was one of Ivan's crew; the only difference was that Ivan's shirt was red.

"Thanks, Jake," Ivan said. "Wait outside."

Jake left the room, and Ivan opened the top of the box. Reaching in, he began to lift something.

Kurt said, "Okay, what the hell is—"

He stopped when he saw the eyes.

Ivan set the glass container on the table and pushed the cardboard box to the side.

Inside the glass container was the floating head of his top informant, who had been embedded in his main competitor's arms-dealing company.

His fists closed, and tears flooded his eyes. "How did they find out?"

Ivan rubbed his goatee. "I don't know, but that's not the most important question, boss." He leaned forward. "The *real* question is . . . What do they plan to do next?"

5

Hampstead, Michigan – Tuesday, July 1, 2025

Rachel Roberts sat across from Obadiah Ben-David in a corner booth inside Darwinger's Gas Station. She had taken a run with her husband at 5:00 a.m., and they had eaten bagels and drunk coffee on their back porch before he had headed off to work. The run and chat had cleared her mind, but seeing her good friend seated before her now made her stomach feel queasy, and she felt that her eyes could start tearing up at any moment.

Nothing was allowed to happen to Ben-David, one of her favorite people in the world.

Their phone conversation last night had ended with Ben-David saying, *"It's prostate cancer, and I'm okay for now,"* but she had wanted to know more. What was the treatment plan? Was he feeling ill? How long had he known? But she had not asked those questions knowing Ben-David's stubbornness. When he had said, *"I'll let you know everything tomorrow at Darwinger's,"* Rachel knew she would have to wait.

It was 9 a.m., and they had just sat down. The summer heat was still a few hours off. However, the station's two large metal fans—"The Darwinger Sentinels," as the locals called them—were already blasting air around the inside of the fabled Hampstead landmark, filling the space with the familiar *hum* that customers had come to expect. Rachel knew that the owner, Lloyd Darwinger the Third, also known as "Baby Lloyd," still refused to install air conditioning in the ancient building, his claim being that sweat was nature's perfume. He had explained to her once that if customers left the booths after having their morning coffee and needed a shower, then he had done his duty: The world would be a little cleaner; each visitor's water bill would be a little higher; and his friends who worked at Hampstead Utilities would be a little happier.

Speaking of the gas station patriarch, Baby Lloyd was at his usual post by the coffee island, monitoring the eight coffee pots and the assortment of coffee accessories. Today, he was wearing a tattered Detroit Tigers baseball cap—the home cap with the white Old English "D" on the front. Rachel had noticed that Baby Lloyd's choice of headwear during baseball season was determined by how well the Tigers were playing. When the wins started stacking up, he wore the hat every day; when a losing streak commenced, the cap would disappear, replaced by his trusty cowboy hat. However, the belt around his waist with a holster that held a six-shooter on each hip never changed.

Did he wear a Detroit Lions hat during the NFL season?

Absolutely not.

Did he *ever* wear a Detroit Lions hat?

No.

Ben-David took a drink of his black coffee and then set the ceramic mug on the table, his huge right hand wrapped all the way around the orange-colored mug with green letters spelling *Darwinger's*. The mugs were a new addition to the gas station's lore. Baby Lloyd's wife, Agatha, had presented them to customers who had been awarded entrance into the Darwinger's Hall of Fame. The selection criteria were not disclosed, but Ben-David had been included in the inaugural class of five members. The other four were Lucille Hawthorne; Lloyd Darwinger, Jr.; the late Tyee Beecher; and, against all odds, Police Chief Corey Ritter. Rachel had overheard some patrons whispering in a nearby booth that the only reason Ritter had been selected was one, he ate the most donuts in the gas station, and two, his political spin of the pivotal role he had played in bringing Kate Warner Foster to justice the previous fall.

In any event, in addition to having their mugs displayed in a glass case next to the coffee island when they weren't drinking from them, all five hall-of-fame members had an 8 ½" x 11" portrait of them hung on the wall above two of the four original booths. A rule had been established stating that, if possible, if a hall of fame member entered the gas station for coffee and donuts, they would be given priority seating at a booth of their choice. Ben-David told Rachel that he had protested the rule in a private conversation with Agatha Darwinger and would not ask a customer to give up his or her seat in one of the booths just because he had entered the gas station for a quick cup of coffee. Agatha had huffed and walked away.

Okay, stop scrolling through Darwinger's history. Your friend has cancer, and you need to get your questions in.

They had hugged in the parking lot, but she still felt the need for physical contact. She reached her hand out and gave his arm a loving pat. She was worried about him, and he was one person that she never worried about. "Has the doctor discussed a treatment plan with you?"

"Sure has," Ben-David said. "Nothing."

"What do you mean *nothing?*"

He shrugged. "Nothing. Doc says that I might never need treatment and called our plan something like *watchful waiting* or *active surveillance.* I laughed when he told me because I've been watchful, waiting, and performing active surveillance in one way or another as a P.I. for the past forty years."

"So, no radiation? No surgery?"

"Nope."

"Are you okay with that?" She took a sip from her paper cup of coffee. "Because I'm not. You . . . you don't even look concerned."

He gave a slight grin. "Pretty good at hiding my emotions, remember?" And now it was he who gave her forearm a loving squeeze. "Truth is, Rachel, I'm scared," he whispered, then paused, looking over at one of the large fans for a moment before saying, "As soon as Doc said the 'c-word,' I had a panic attack. Didn't pass out, but they had to lay me back on the bed and put an ice pack on my forehead and one on my neck." Ben-David rolled his eyes. "I guess because my wife died of cancer, I never got over my fear. Doc even had a psychologist in the room when he delivered the news. Guess it's standard practice now." His hand shook as he lifted his mug and took a careful sip of coffee. "Anyway, I've seen what cancer can do to a healthy person and how fast it can do it."

"Then, why isn't the doctor being more aggressive with the treatment?"

Baby Lloyd had been inching closer to their booth for the last minute, and Rachel met eyes with him. He straightened up and retreated to the coffee island.

"I had the same question," Ben-David said. "What he told me was that since the cancer was small and located just in the prostate and not expected to grow very fast because of something called a Gleason score—and I've already forgotten what in the hell that means—he didn't recommend anything beyond keeping an eye on it. So, for now, blood test every six months and," he said, frowning and pointing at his rear, "an exam back there once a year."

"Did you have any symptoms?"

"No. They caught it during my screening. I complained when I had my first one at fifty-five, but I ain't complainin' no more."

Rachel thought about Ben-David's girlfriend, Tilly Michaels. When Rachel and Ben-David had returned to Huron Heights for dinner in January of 2024, about a month after her secret trip to Key West to confront Ryan, Ben-David had told her over his second beer that he had given their talk before she had left a lot of thought and that he had decided that he wanted to spend his golden years with someone. When she had asked him who that someone might be, he had said, "Would you believe me if I said Tilly Michaels?" Rachel had approved, Ben-David had asked Tilly out the following weekend, and they had been together ever since. Tilly adored Ben-David and lived with him in his A-frame house on the beach.

Rachel also knew that Tilly was a veteran activist from the '60s who wore her emotions on her sleeve and brought great drama, warmth, and excitement to the old professional investigator's somewhat blasé way of life. Minus the warmth, which Topaz Kennedy rarely showed, Rachel thought that her agent and Tilly could be long-lost sisters. However, because of Tilly's warmth, Rachel knew she would be frightened to lose Ben-David. "How is Tilly doing?" Rachel asked. "What does she think about all of this?"

"Like me, she was scared shitless at first, but she's better now. We've got all of my upcoming medical appointments on the calendar out at the house, so I plan to go on with life. Well, all except for the school bus driving. Tilly made me resign. I'm going to miss picking up and dropping off the kiddos."

Rachel knew that he had gotten a bit stir-crazy in retirement and had been driving a school bus for the past half year.

"Know what I won't miss?" He scoffed. "Substitute teaching. The *hell* with that. Lasted one day this past fall. Only reason I even gave bus driving a shot was because they needed me to take Dawn Jackson's route in the spring because of her cancer treatment, and, well, I couldn't say no. I thought it would be as bad as subbing, but I enjoyed it." He paused. "Maybe once I get clear of my cancer,

I'll go back. Then again, Tilly thinks it was too much. Maybe she's right. I'm not as young as I used to be. Don't tell anyone I said that."

"I won't." She took a sip of coffee. "You look great, though. What's Tilly had you doing for the past month?"

He patted his flat stomach. "That's the kicker. I might be in the best shape of my life—even better than the past few years—I've been biking and swimming every day, and I join Tilly and Ben on their marathon weekend walks now." He tapped his lip with his right index finger. "Maybe if my next check-up goes well, I'll see if she'll let me drive the bus."

"She might. I think she's just being cautious."

"Yeah. I also want to return to umpiring for the Hampstead Softball League."

She nodded, took another sip, and then set her mug down. "How long have you known about the cancer?"

"Got the results last week and then met with doc to go over the plan of attack. Was going to tell you all about it this week." He went to say something but hesitated, and the noise blaring from the two huge fans filled her ears once more as if a muted person was suddenly unmuted. Ben-David ran his left hand through his enormous gray beard. "If the news had been bad, I would have told you sooner."

She did know. He was neither a chauvinist nor an alpha male, whatever that meant. And he did not operate under the guise of being a shining knight to rescue his female partner in distress. However, that did not mean that when he needed to act upon his primitive survival instincts, he denied them. *Quite the opposite,* Rachel thought. He could be the Lion in Winter if you crossed him. He was blunt and even direct to the point of telling someone like her that she should *not* tell Stan about her trip down to Key West because it could only complicate things. She wasn't cheating on Stan; she was getting a decade-long question answered that would enable her to move forward without any lingering *"What if...?"* wonderings.

He had been right. She got her answer from Ryan; it was not the one she had expected, but now she was able to live her life without looking back . . .

Except for one thing.

Her mother—which is what she was also here to discuss. After Ben-David told Rachel on the phone that he had cancer, they had not talked any more about her request.

However, therein lay another rub in Rachel's supposedly open-and-honest relationship with the six-foot-eight-inch, two-hundred-and-thirty-pound man seated across from her. Yes, she needed his help in locating her mother. Rachel desired to see her and confront her. Seeing Ryan and discovering the truth about an event she had witnessed that had forced her to run away and disappear from his life led to healing and insight into herself. Could she have pressed on in life with that significant event dealt with and locked away forever? When she had returned to Hampstead for Christmas, she had believed so. Then, she started in on the final book in the saga and soon realized that she was closing a chapter with the one being Adrienne Astra, who had helped Rachel cope with the recurring nightmare of being two and watching her mother vanish from her life. Those nightmares had come and gone over the years and had mostly disappeared until she had started the final book.

Adrienne had also somehow stayed in Rachel's mind after the death of Rachel's father and had carried her through the past few years, like when she had no ideas for *Dark After Midnight* and when she was uncertain about her past and future. Now, with wealth beyond anything she could have imagined as a young girl, she knew that her life ahead, one that could possibly include motherhood— she and Stan had breached the subject, and Rachel was open to the idea—would always partially lay in the shadow of pain and abandonment unless she found her mother and let her know that she existed; she mattered; she was somebody; and she was somebody to someone.

These things she could tell Ben-David.

What she could not tell him was the *practical* reason why she needed to find her mother: Rachel wanted to put her mind at ease to finally finish her twenty-year adventure writing the character of Adrienne Astra. For two decades, the secret of who mega-author Riley Cannon was had been kept secret. Only Topaz and Stan knew who she was. Now that Rachel was about to finish her career, she was considering letting Ben-David know who she was. She had teased it when *Dark After Midnight* had come out, and she had mailed him a copy and watched while hidden in the nearby woods while he walked to his mailbox and opened the package. They had even discussed the matter, and she had answered his questions truthfully. She just hadn't told him the *entire* truth yet.

Perhaps she never would. However, a few thoughts had occurred to her since speaking with Topaz the night before. *After I confront my mother, will I feel like I no longer need to hide behind the name of Riley Cannon? Have I been hiding behind that name? Was choosing a pen name really about privacy, or have I been protecting myself in interviews from having to face questions about my personal life, which would expose my core wound, if people knew who Riley Cannon was? Or, since this is my final novel, is it better to forever keep who Riley Cannon is a mystery? I can have a quiet, peaceful life with Stan, and the media will never get to invade my privacy. But I can trust Obadiah with my secret, right?*

She was certain that she could, and she thought that the opportunity to tell him would be at some point on their journey to track down her mother—just not right now.

Can I trust my secret with Christine Harper? She works in the book industry, for crying out loud! But she likes to talk . . .

Maybe I can't.

"I know you would have told me," she said and then realized that she was leaning forward, the seat of her pants almost off the worn booth cushion. She leaned back and relaxed. "I'm relieved that the doctors caught it early enough. Although, I have to say I'm not a big fan of *watchful waiting* and *performing active surveillance.*"

Ben-David laughed and motioned Baby Lloyd over.

The gas station owner strutted over, holding a full coffee pot, and refilled Ben-David's mug and Rachel's paper cup. "That's fresh blackjack right there," Baby Lloyd said. "You both need any sinkers to go with it?"

Rachel bit her tongue, trying not to laugh. Agatha had complained to Rachel that six months ago, Baby Lloyd had visited Lumberman's Monument in Oscoda and descended the one hundred and fifty vertical feet by taking the two hundred and eighty steps built into the sloping hill that led down to the riverbank of the Au Sable River. At the bottom was a floating museum with displays of lumberjack life on the river over 150 years ago. One of the exhibitions had a list of lumberjack slang:

Blackjack = coffee.

Sinkers = donuts.

Ever since he had visited Lumberman's, Baby Lloyd had refused to refer to coffee and donuts by any names other than blackjack and sinkers.

"He's so childish, " Agatha had said.

Ben-David patted his stomach. "No sinkers for me today, sir."

Baby Lloyd gave a glowing nod, no doubt enjoying that Ben-David had answered him with the same slang, and then turned to Rachel. "Ma'am?" he asked.

"No donuts for me," she answered.

From across the room, she could hear Agatha start laughing.

Baby Lloyd gave Rachel a frown and then rolled his eyes at his wife.

Ben-David patted his shoulder, and the gas station owner returned to the coffee island and started two fresh pots as four regulars had just entered the gas station and slid into a booth.

"You should humor him and speak his lumberjack slang," Ben-David said.

"I'm afraid I'm with Agatha on this one."

Ben-David grinned. "I figured."

Now, that doesn't mean a character in Sunrise Kama Sutra *won't use those terms,* she thought.

They both took sips of their fresh coffees, and Rachel enjoyed the background noises—the fans, the light chatter, an occasional ring of the old-fashioned cash register that Agatha refused to part with, and the chime of the door when it opened.

"So, now that we've clarified my health situation, tell me about your missing person."

She did not hesitate. "Obadiah, I need you to help me find my mother."

"Your mother?" Obadiah Ben-David said.

Rachel Roberts pursed her lips, lowered her voice, and then replied, "Stan and I want to start a family." She let the statement hang in the air for a few seconds; Ben-David's face was stone, not in a disinterested or detached way—which is what most people thought when he looked at them in that manner—but, rather, a calming front of concentration. "The subject came up a few months ago, and after giving it some thought, I have decided that I want to be a mother." She paused and rubbed the tip of her index finger around the rim of her coffee cup. "And the more I thought about becoming a mother, the more I realized that for me to do that, I need to deal with what happened to my family." She made eye contact with her friend. "My mother left my father and me when I was two. I haven't seen her since."

Ben-David ran his right hand over the top of his bald head and held onto his neck for a few seconds before lowering his arm to the table—he tapped the side of his coffee mug with his long, thick fingers. "As my girlfriend would say, 'That's a lot to unpack.'"

She gave a quick grin. "It is."

"Same nagging feeling, like the one you had about Key West?"

"Magnified."

He gave her a knowing nod. "I imagine so."

"Will you help me?"

He did not hesitate. "Yep."

She sighed, feeling a surge of relief run through her body. Knowing that Ben-David would not only help her find her mother but also be by her side, as her friend, gave her a sense of peace and a boost of confidence. This was the second time she had been vulnerable with him, and, once again, he proved to be a steadying force. She had no backup plan and was worried that she would be unable to keep it together today if he had said no. Of course, she would have understood. He didn't owe her anything.

Ben-David had finally convinced her last year to come over to his house to watch *Rocky III* with him and Amos Meyer one Saturday night. She had been skeptical—it was the third film in a series about boxing—but decided to give it a chance.

It ended up being one of her favorite films, too.

There were many lessons that she took away from the movie, and she felt that after watching it, she knew more about both Ben-David and Amos. Still, the exchange between Rocky and his brother-in-law, Paulie, in the beginning, had defined an essential aspect of friendship that she had always been unable to put into simple yet effective terms.

Paulie had said, *"You're wrong; friends owe!"*

And Rocky had replied, *"Friends* don't owe. *They do because they wanna do."*

An exchange inspired by that scene had already shown up in the early chapters of *Sunrise Kama Sutra*—Adrienne Astra explaining the concept of commitment and charity versus the bank account version of companionship. You deposit money into my account, and I suddenly feel the need to deposit money into your account, which conditions us to only do something for the other person because we expect to be repaid. Not good. Unsustainable.

"Is there anything you need to know?" Rachel asked.

"About personal matters between you and your mom? No."

"What about between me and my father or my mother and father's relationship?"

"Maybe. You know that I'll listen."

"Have you ever worked a missing person case?"

"Two, but they were pretty simple. One summer, an eight-year-old boy ran away from home—his parents lived out past Huron Heights—and I found him hiding underneath his grandma's back deck a few miles away the day after his folks hired me. The second case was a teenage girl, fifteen or sixteen, who found out she was pregnant and took off with the eighteen-year-old dipshit who knocked her up. He didn't have his own car and stole his parents' van. Didn't have a job either, so he stole fifty bucks out of his mom's purse. The morning after her mom hired me, I found them having breakfast at a Bob Evans a hundred or so miles away." Ben-David took a long pull on his coffee. "I'm guessing you've already scoured the internet for your mom and came up with nothing."

She had searched for hours—social media, LinkedIn, obituaries, marriage announcements, divorce records, real estate holdings, arrest records, birth announcements, car registrations, Google, Yahoo!, Whitepages, YouTube—everything she could think of.

There had been one result: The divorce between Tina Haines Roberts and Clark Jeffrey Roberts had been finalized on January 27, 1985, which Rachel already knew. When cleaning out his house after her father had died, she had taken possession of his one-drawer, tan file cabinet. In the cabinet was his small collection of personal papers, and in a manila envelope labeled "DIVORCE," she had read the final paperwork. Before searching the internet for her mother, she had re-read every one of her father's files. It proved to be no help locating her, but it refreshed her memory of everything her father had told her about her mom, which amounted to a paragraph.

Her mother, Tina Karen Haines, was born on April 8th, 1955, to George and Doris Haines of East Lansing, Michigan. She had one older sibling, Mary Ann, who had moved out to Arizona before Rachel was born; Rachel had learned that she had passed away two years ago at the age of seventy-two. She had never been married and had no children. Tina's father, George, had died in 1981, and Doris had passed away in 1987. In 1980, at age twenty-five, Tina dropped out of college for a second time and moved to Kalamazoo, Michigan. After her first day working as a waitress at Denny's, she dropped by the Meijer grocery store and met Clark Roberts, who was also twenty-five and a grocery clerk at Meijer's. The two began dating the following week, and a month later, Tina attended the opening night show of *Dial 'M' For Murder* at The Civic Theatre, Kalamazoo's Community Theatre since 1929. Clark was playing Max Halliday, the American crime writer having an affair with Margot Wendice, who has been in a bad marriage for years with her husband, retired professional tennis player Tony Wendice. Six months later, Clark and Tina marry, and Rachel is born a year and a half later. Then, in June of 1984, when Rachel was two, her mother left her father for another man. From the time Rachel was old enough to ask her father until his death by heart attack in 2008 when he was fifty-three, he would never tell her the man's name.

She told Ben-David all of this and watched as her friend cocked his head to one side and played with his enormous beard.

After another sip of coffee, he said, "Not much to go on. One thing has got me a bit mystified, though."

"What is it?"

"That your dad didn't have any of the divorce settlement paperwork in his file. It will be easy for me to look up who the lawyers were, but I'm wondering why he didn't keep his copy of the paperwork. He didn't have it in another file, did he?"

"No. I didn't see it anywhere." *How could I have been so blind? Of course! The lawyers would be a natural place to start.* She started to frown but realized she shouldn't be too hard on herself. She was revisiting a place in her heart and mind that she had locked away for decades, and there would be blind spots and surprises—she would miss the obvious as she had done so many times when writing one of her novels. She would think she had an airtight plot only to have J. Rudolph Hightower poke a hole in it a mile wide. *"How did I not think of that?"* she would yell in her writing room when reading his comments.

Relax. Don't beat yourself up because you didn't think about the lawyers. This is why you have Ben-David, a trusted friend who won't judge you and will see things you cannot. You're also distracted because Topaz is freaking out about her future. She'll be fine, but you won't unless you continue down the path you've started here.

"It is a bit strange, now that I think about it," she said. "Why wouldn't he have kept them?"

Ben-David shrugged. "Don't know."

She was sure he had some theories but would wait until he was ready to share them.

"And nothing came up when you searched all of the variations of your mother's name?"

She nodded in the affirmative. "Tina Haines, nothing. Tina Karen Haines, nothing. Tina Karen Roberts, nothing. Tina Roberts, nothing. Tina Haines Roberts? Just the one hit about the divorce being finalized." She gave him a defeated grin and exhaled. "Still want the case?"

"Even more," he said and finished his coffee. "Sounds like she changed her name."

She drained the last of her coffee and then crushed the paper cup with her right hand. "Any ideas about where we should start?"

She watched as his eyes lowered to the destroyed cup. "A few." After a beat, his eyes rose and met hers. "You're not okay, are you?"

Rachel released her grip on the cup, and it fell on its side. "No, I'm not. But I think I will be once this investigation is over."

"You think about Key West anymore?"

"No. I'm free of it, and that's what I want out of this."

Ben-David took out his cell phone and waved it in front of her. "It's good and bad that technology didn't help us find her yet: good, because it means that I'm going to have to use the old ways, which you know I prefer; bad, because it would have gotten you in front of her sooner . . . if she's still alive."

As usual, her partner had wasted no time illuminating one of the distinct possibilities. Tomorrow would be July 1, 2025. *If she's alive, she's seventy years old.* However, reaching that age is guaranteed to no one. Ever since she had felt the pull to find her mother, she had wondered: *What if she's dead?*

There were, of course, other questions as well: *What if I don't find her? What if she died shortly after leaving my father? What if she's on her deathbed right now? Did she stay with the man whom she had run off with? Where did they go? Did they split up? Did they stay in Michigan? Does she have any other children? Did she go back to school? What kind of career did she have? Is she retired?*

There were many more questions that Rachel had, but Ben-David had touched on the most immediate. If she found out that her mother was dead, then the search would be more of a reconstruction of her mother's life, but Rachel would not get to meet her. If she found out that her mother was alive, then it would still be an exercise in reconstructing her mother's life after leaving Rachel and Clark in 1984, but the stakes would be higher as Rachel might be afforded the opportunity to stand in front of her.

She thought that if that moment came, she would be glad that Ben-David was by her side. Would she then ask Ben-David to give them a few minutes in private? She didn't know.

"The old ways will have to do," she replied. "And I'm glad I've got a master of them in my corner."

"Coming from a computer coder, that's high praise." He put his phone away. "I'm retired but not in a museum yet."

She felt both satisfaction and consternation at the mention of her being a computer coder: satisfaction, because Ben-David had not figured out who she really was yet; consternation, because she dreaded the moment he might find out and wondered what it would do to their relationship. Would he understand why she had kept it from him? Would he see that she had tried to lead him to the answer by putting the novel *Dark After Midnight* in his mailbox two summers ago?

"Speaking of your job," Ben-David said, "when do you plan on taking time off so we can work on this?"

"I spoke with my boss yesterday, and she's fine with me cashing in some vacation hours right now. It worked out well with the 4th of July hitting this week." She paused, reflecting for a moment about her continued commitment to telling the truth . . . just not the *entire* truth. In a way, Topaz was her boss, and Rachel had spoken with her yesterday to tell the mega agent that she was suspending her writing until she found out what had become of her mother.

She joined both of her hands by interweaving her fingers as if she were about to pray. "So, the question is, sir, when can you start?" *And will Tilly be okay with this?*

The corners of his mouth began to roll up into a grin. "I spoke with Tilly last night after our phone call. She might be able to talk me out of driving a school bus while I get a handle on my health, but she's not talking me out of investigating something for a friend." He tapped the table once as if putting an exclamation point on the end of his sentence. "I've got the green light to start today." He paused. "But we won't."

"We won't?"

"We need today to pack."

"Pack for where?"

"Pack a week's worth of clothes and make sure you'll be covered if we have to go somewhere cold. Bring your passport, too." He slid his coffee mug to the side. "We're leaving for East Lansing tomorrow morning. That's where we'll start. Then, we'll head over to Kalamazoo. I'll look up who your parents hired as lawyers. If they're still in business, we might pay them a visit. They'll have records. After that . . . who knows? I don't think we need to go to Arizona to ask around about your dead aunt, but you never know. Chances are we'll be back home tomorrow night, but I think we need to be prepared to follow leads as they develop. Sometimes, locating a person is a matter of timing. Our main challenge is that your parents divorced and left Kalamazoo in their late twenties, so anyone around their age who worked with them would probably be retired by now. My bet is that the lawyers who handled the case were probably in their thirties or forties back then, so now they'd be, at best, retired, and at worst, dead."

She welcomed his decisiveness and was fine letting him take the lead. Perhaps later, she would take the baton and direct their plan, but right now, she was vulnerable and needed to lean on his assertiveness. "I know we're up against it, but you can count on me," she said.

"I know I can. Also, if we have to stay in a hotel, I prefer one with a pool. Swimming had been easier on my joints—especially these past few years. That okay with you?"

She nodded. "I'll pack my suit."

"Thanks. Let's enjoy tonight with our families—I need to take Ben for an extra-long walk after supper . . . old boy has put on a few pounds because I've been giving him extra treats to stay off Tilly's side of the bed. Say hi to Hemy and Stan for me."

"I will. Give Ben a hug."

"Done." They rose. "I'll pick you up at 6 a.m."

"I'll be ready," she said, and at the time, she believed it.

If Rachel had known what they were about to discover when they found her mother, Tina Karen Haines, then she never would have gone looking in the first place.

7

Kalamazoo, Michigan – Wednesday, July 2, 2025

It was nearly 5 p.m. when Rachel Roberts watched Obadiah Ben-David flip the blinker lever up in his black Chevrolet Express van. They were past Riverview, where the sewage plant smelled like rotten ass, and were traveling north on Gull Road. Up ahead, on the left, she could see a Starbucks that, according to her research, had been put in just a few years ago; apparently, author Ryan Steck, whom she had never met, now went there every morning. The vehicle stopped at the red light, and Rachel could see out her passenger's side window the parking lot and structure of arguably Michigan's most famous grocery store chain, Meijer, in the distance. It had been remodeled and added on to twice since her father had worked there, the most recent renovation being in 2022. Also, there was a fun fact about the store chain's name: Michiganders pronounced it "Meijers." *I'll pick it up at Meijers. Stop by Meijers on the way home, okay? Meijers will have it.*

"I can't believe my dad used to work in *that* store," Rachel said. "When we moved to Midland in 1985, there wasn't a Meijer store there yet; it came in 1992. But one in Saginaw opened in 1980, so Dad drove there and back almost every day for seven years. I know what you're thinking: Why didn't we move to Saginaw in the first place? Well, Dad loved acting, and Midland had the beautiful Center for the Arts with two theaters, which he fell in love with, so we moved to Midland instead of Saginaw."

I've been in the Saginaw one before," said Ben-David. "Made many trips to Fashion Square Mall with my friends over the years. In the '70s and '80s, it was *the* place to shop. Never really had anything in my size, but it was fun to walk around. You've noticed there isn't a mall in Hampstead, which is fine by me. Malls mean more people, and more people packed together inevitably leads to more crime." He looked at her. "Not much good has occurred in a mall parking lot after 9 p.m."

The traffic light switched to green, and he turned down the road that emptied into the Meijer parking lot. "Anyway, we'd always hit Meijer last before returning to Hampstead. Best grocery store in the world if you ask me. Always wished Hampstead had gotten one."

"Let's hope it brings us better luck than earlier."

"Well, we can't do any worse," Ben-David said.

The day's first stop in East Lansing had given them no more information. Before departing Hampstead, Ben-David had researched and found that there had been three different homeowners since Doris Haines had died in 1987. The first owners, Bob and Patty Reed, had lived in the house from 1987 to 1991. After another half-hour search, Ben-David had found them. They were living in Jacksonville, Florida, and he had given them a call. Bob Reed had answered and said that, unfortunately, they had never met the previous owner, Mrs. Haines; the real estate agents had handled everything. In the four years that they had lived in the house, they had spoken to their neighbors on only a few occasions, mainly because they lived half a mile away on either side of them. Since then, the area had grown up, and there was now a scattering of houses along the road. Ben-David did not bother checking out the other owners who had lived in the house after the Reeds.

That left the neighbors. One of the original two had sold their home in 1993, and the other family had sold in 1997. Then, in 2014, a man had purchased the first house, had it demolished, and built a new mansion in its place.

Rachel and Ben-David had interviewed both neighbors and gotten nowhere. No one remembered the previous residents, let alone anything about the neighbor in between them, Doris Haines, who had passed away years before they had even purchased their homes. They had driven past Rachel's grandparents' house; strangely, she had felt no emotion. The small house was painted tan with brown shingles and brown shutters, and it was around fifty yards back from the road. Ben-David had pulled into the gravel driveway, and she had just stared at the home. The porch's railing had a few broken spindles, and weeds had overtaken the landscaping beds. The lawn had not been mowed in some time. After a minute, she had said, *"That's enough,"* and they had left.

The Haines were not a church-going family, so there were no leads to pursue there, and Doris Haines had been a stay-at-home mom. Hence, only two threads remained. George's workplace and Tina's high school.

From reading George Haines's obituary, Ben-David had learned that George had worked at Murray's Hardware, retiring in 1978, three years before his death. When Ben-David and Rachel had entered Murray's, the fourth-generation owner, Mike Murray, had told them that he had been in middle school around that time and used to come to the store after school every day to help his dad and grandfather. He remembered old George Haines but knew nothing about his daughter. His father might have, but he had died five years ago.

So, they had gone to East Lansing High School to see if anyone there remembered Tina Haines or her sister, for that matter. What they had found out was that one of Tina's classmates, Joyce Pugh, from the class of 1973, had come back in 1977 and taught high school science for 40 years, retiring in 2017. The principal still had Joyce's number and had given it to Ben-David and Rachel. When they reached Joyce, she said that her high school graduating class was over three hundred students, and she did not know or remember Tina Haines or her older sister.

"I should have started looking earlier," Rachel said as Ben-David pulled the van onto I-69 South after they had eaten a late lunch. *"I could have at least interviewed my aunt."*

"You weren't ready," he had replied. *"There's nothing you can do about your aunt, so don't second guess yourself. I didn't think we'd find much in East Lansing, but we had to try. This wasn't a wasted trip. Seeing where your mom grew up and went to school and where her dad worked gave me a sense of them, and, as you know, that always comes first for me. Let's focus on Kalamazoo."*

They had traveled the hour and a half mostly in silence.

Ben-David pulled the van into a parking spot near the Meijer entrance. "After the restroom, we'll hit the Customer Service desk and arrange a meeting with the store manager."

Her breathing picked up as she looked at the large, red letters spelling Meijer that loomed over the entrance. "I—I . . ."

"You need a minute?"

She looked at him and grabbed his forearm, closing her eyes. "My father took so much pride in working at Meijer's. Everyone knew him at the Saginaw and Midland stores. He worked hard—never stopped, really. Whenever he took me there, or I visited when I was old enough to drive, he was always walking somewhere with a customer, pointing and smiling at an aisle. And the customers couldn't help but smile and nod back."

"My kind of person," Ben-David said. He pointed at the entrance. "You want me to go in alone?"

She opened her eyes and wiped them, then gave his arm a pat. "Thank you, but, no, I'll be fine. I look at this store and see a young version of my dad, full of life, happy where he's at, building a future with my mom, and then *wham!* She just leaves us. I don't understand it."

Ben-David gave her hand a squeeze. "Not everyone can do what you're doing. Most are too vulnerable. This will probably be a quick stop, and then we'll head over to Wentworth and Higgins."

On the way to East Lansing—the closer they had gotten, the more green and white they had seen—Ben-David had told her about the divorce lawyers. Her father had hired a lawyer named Mickey Dunn from a small practice that had closed its doors in 2005 when Attorney at Law M. Carmichael "Mickey" Dunn retired. Searching his name in the obituaries, Ben-David had learned that Mickey had kicked the bucket five miles off the coast of Miami in 2016 at the age of 81 when his sixty-foot yacht had sunk under mysterious conditions. Two survivors who had clung to a life ring were picked up the next day by a deep-sea fisherman who was running a charter party out to a favorite spot. The survivors were both prostitutes who immediately went to the authorities and told them their tale. Apparently, Mickey had terminal cancer and set sail for one last week with ten prostitutes and half a million dollars worth of cocaine for his send-off. Rachel's eyes had opened wide when she read the *Miami Herald* article that Ben-David had texted her. One of the prostitutes, Stallion, was quoted saying, "We were down below with Mickey, and everybody was laughing and snorting and having a good time, and then it's like we were all wet and the boat is sinking, and Sweetness and I made it topside and then like the whole boat starts like tipping and we grab a life ring and jump off. Then, there was like this explosion or something, and the boat went like straight down. We saw nobody after that. Sweet Daddy Mickey and eight of my sisters are like gone." Because the title of her last book was *Sunrise Kama Sutra*, Rachel wondered, after reading the story, if she could pad the shorter Part Two of her novel with a scenario like this. She had filed it away and then listened as Ben-David told her about the law firm her mother had hired.

"It doesn't make a lot of sense to me. Your mom hired the most prestigious law firm in Kalamazoo, Wentworth and Higgins, to represent her. Where did she get that kind of money? Well, William Wentworth and Johnny Higgins were in their mid-fifties when they handled your mother's divorce in 1985, so, as you have probably guessed, they have both passed away. Wentworth in 2012 and Higgins in 2017. However, the business has been passed on to their sons, Gabriel Wentworth and Joey Higgins, and an entire battalion of family members works at the firm. Gabriel and Joey are in their early sixties, and from the website, it looks like their respective daughters, Roberta Wentworth and Anna Higgins, are about to take the company's reins. Bottom line: We should be able to talk to someone who could look up the case and speak with us."

She stared at the floor mat and nodded a few times as if each up and down recharged a courage meter inside her. She felt the stakes of anticipation getting higher. Now, she would be setting foot inside a store where her father had worked, and then she would visit the law offices of the two dead attorneys who had represented her mother. The questions kept running through her mind: *Why and how did she hire such expensive attorneys? Why didn't her father save any of the paperwork from the divorce? How did William Wentworth and Johnny Higgins get her mother out of paying child support? In fact, how did they settle the case in a way that absolved her mother from having any obligation to her?*

This was the mid-1980s, for heaven's sake!

Whereas she was confident that Ben-David's mind was scrolling through possible answers to these questions, Rachel's mind had *no* answers.

All she was able to concentrate on consciously was what *did* make sense. And what made sense was that her father had hired an attorney, Mickey Dunn, who was within her father's financial means at the time. And knowing her father's attention to detail in all matters, there was no way he could have misplaced any of the divorce paperwork. Until now, she had never thought to go through his files looking for it, but when he had died, and she had closed out his financial accounts, curiosity had got the better of her at the time, and she had gone back to the years when she was a minor and studied his statements to see if there had been deposits from her mother. When she found out that there hadn't been, it only added to her pain, and she had closed herself off from any thoughts of her mother. Looking back, perhaps it was the discovery that her mother hadn't given her a dime and not her father's death that had pushed Rachel to contact Topaz and tell her that she was going to take a break from her 'Round the Clock Series . . . a break that ended up being over ten years.

She stared at the Meijer's storefront again. Ben-David was right. This would be a quick stop, and then they'd be on their way to Wentworth and Higgins. And yet, like Adrienne Astra seeing "Grid" coaching track on TV, Rachel felt a hint of excitement knowing that when she exited the van, she would enter the store where her father had worked within twenty seconds.

She exhaled and turned her head toward Ben-David. "You know how many hours of my life have been spent inside a Meijer store?"

He neither said anything nor answered with body language for a few seconds. Suddenly, he snapped his fingers. "Is that why you still go to Midland once a month?"

She gave him a mischievous grin. "To be honest, I alternate between Midland and Saginaw. Don't worry; I still shop at our local grocery store, but I am so loyal to Meijer that I have to go there and give them my business once a month. I use that trip to stock up on stuff like paper towels and such. Plus, I still know the manager in Midland—worked with my dad for years."

"I respect loyalty."

"I know you do." She unbuckled her safety belt. "Let's go."

8

Rachel Roberts and Obadiah Ben-David exited the van, and five minutes later, they were standing at the Customer Service desk, waiting for the store manager to join them. The worker manning the desk, a squat, blonde-haired woman in her thirties named Gail, had called the manager, Shae Barnes, thirty seconds ago. Rachel watched as Gail made small talk with a customer purchasing a lottery ticket. Then, movement caught her eye, and she saw an office door swing open by the drinking fountain. A tall, African-American woman emerged and approached the desk. Her hair was pulled back into a ponytail, and she wore black pants and a cobalt blue blouse with a white Meijer's I.D. badge clipped to her left collar.

After taking a dozen steps, she stopped a few feet away from Rachel, extended her hand, and said, "Hi."

Rachel read the nametag: Shae B., Manager. "Hi, Ms. Barnes—"

The manager smiled and cut her off, saying, "Please, call me Shae."

Okay, I like her already. She remembered that her dad's badge had "Clark R." stenciled in black letters.

Rachel introduced Obadiah and gave Shae a brief history of her father's employment at Meijer.

"I love this," Shae said. "I started as a grocer here fifteen years ago in college and worked my way up. Meijer is family, and we appreciate that your father found a home here for his career." She paused. "Now, you said that you are professional investigators. What can we help you with?"

"You can verify that Clark Roberts worked for Meijer if you want to," Ben-David said.

"I appreciate that," Shae said. "I'll be right back."

She went inside her office and returned five minutes later, grinning. "My gosh, your dad put in over thirty years with us!"

"Like I said, he loved his job," Rachel said.

"Hope he's enjoying retirement."

Rachel frowned. "He passed away in 2008." She could see an oh-shit-why-did-I-say-that look on Shae's face and gave her arm a squeeze. "Oh, don't worry. I'm fine. It was years ago, and he was enjoying retirement. However, he still missed his job."

Shae relaxed. "I'm still sorry to hear that he passed."

"Thanks," said Rachel. She motioned the manager and Ben-David over to an empty spot in the store next to one of the blood pressure machines she had never seen anyone use before. They stopped, and she continued, "We're investigating a missing person from over forty years ago, and there is a chance that someone who knew my father while he worked here might be able to help us out."

Ben-David jumped in. "Know it's a long shot, Shae, but do you have any generation workers here?"

"You mean like people whose parents worked at this store?"

"Parents, aunts, uncles, maybe even grandparents, yes."

"I can do better than that," Shae said. "Follow me."

A minute later, they had stopped at the end of one of the sports equipment aisles. Halfway down the aisle, standing ramrod straight and checking prices on a row of baseball mitts, was a tall, thin, African-American man with a full head of closely cropped gray hair.

"Hi, Harold," Shae said to the man.

With a smooth twist of his head, Harold made eye contact and, grinning, said, "Well, Ms. Shae, how are you today?" He looked at Rachel and Ben-David. "Ma'am. Sir."

Shae waved them to follow her, and they soon stood in front of Harold.

"What can I do for you all?" Harold said.

Shae put a hand on one of Harold's shoulders. "Here is one of our legends, Rachel and Obadiah. You've been here since when, Harold?"

"Nineteen eighty-four." He gave them a wink. "The last time the Tigers won the World Series. Easy to remember."

Rachel felt butterflies in her stomach and locked eyes with Ben-David for a beat. *He could have known my father.*

Shae lifted her hand from his shoulder and gave it a playful tap. "What's your number?"

Harold's grin widened. "Eleven."

Shae turned toward Rachel and Obadiah. "In forty-one years, he's only missed eleven days." She motioned with her hand around the store. "I've got workers right now that have missed more than that in the past *year.*"

"I don't miss work," Harold stated.

Rachel wanted to hug the man. Ben-David gave a few nods of respect.

Shae then explained the situation to Harold but did not say Clark Roberts's name as a courtesy to Ben-David, who had asked her while they were walking across the store, not to mention Rachel's father. The old Meijer warrior nodded throughout Shae's entire presentation.

"Missing person, huh?" he said. "I'll sure help if I can."

"Thank you, Harold," Shae said, turning to Ben-David and Rachel. "I'll be back up front. Please stop by to say goodbye before you head out."

75

Rachel and Ben-David said "Thanks" at the same time, and the four of them enjoyed a quick laugh.

Shae turned and walked away, her heels clicking on the polished floor. When she was out of sight, Rachel said, "Harold, do you remember a worker named Clark Roberts who worked here until 1985?"

At first, Harold's expression remained stoic. Then, a few seconds later, as if the baseball gloves to his left had flown off the shelf and rearranged themselves as a ghost floating in front of him, his eyes widened, and his mouth started to open. "Clark Roberts," he said to Rachel and then peered at the ceiling. "Now, ma'am, that's a name I've not heard in a long time." He rubbed his chin. "A long time."

Then, as if the gloves rearranged themselves again into the shape of an arrow pointing at Rachel, he looked into her eyes, studying them. "Oh, yes. I can see it. I can see it now. You're his daughter, aren't you?"

"I am," Rachel said.

Tears started to form in the older man's eyes. "I haven't seen you since I helped your father load up the last of your old house into the U-Haul on the day you left Kalamazoo." He paused, looking back and forth between Rachel and Ben-David. "My God, what's happened? Who's missing?"

9

From the shade provided by the large canopy of a Meijer-branded umbrella, Rachel Roberts watched as Harold and a younger male Meijer employee approached the concrete picnic table where she and Obadiah Ben-David were seated. The table was one of four and located in the lush plot of freshly cut grass across from the loading dock in the back of the store.

Harold and the younger employee arrived. Rachel could smell fresh sandwiches and realized she was hungrier than she thought, even though she and Ben-David had eaten lunch only a few hours ago. Maybe it was the stress, but she was usually not a stress eater. For a brief moment, she thought about Mark Jensen and wondered how he was doing. She had received a card from him six months ago at Christmas. He had written that cabin life in Colorado was the best. He was still single but enjoying the peace and quiet of the woods. Brother Curt loved his own cabin and was seeing someone that he had met at a bar in the town near where they lived. They didn't game together as much as they used to, but they were still close. Mark had ended the card with an invitation for Rachel and Stan to visit. *When this final book is done, we will,* she had thought.

Harold took the chocolate chip cookies, submarine sandwiches, chips, and three large bottles of Coca-Cola off the tray the younger employee, who wore a badge with "Bryce K." on it, was holding. When the tray was empty, Bryce pulled a stack of napkins out of his apron and set them on the table.

"Thank you, brother," Harold said, sitting across from Rachel and Ben-David. "Now, get back to it."

Bryce bowed and then retreated from the table. After turning around, he started jogging back toward the building.

"It pays to have friends in the deli. Learned that a long time ago." There was silence for a beat, and then Harold smiled and said, "I'm just kidding." He motioned to the food and drinks. "This here is all compliments of Shae." Then, he looked toward Bryce; the young man was almost to the loading dock door. "He's a good kid. One of the few who work with me and listen to my advice . . . could be a manager someday if he sticks with it." He turned back toward them. "Appreciate you both coming out here. Thought it would give us some needed privacy. Shae let me punch out for half an hour, so I'm off the clock." He looked down at the food. "Okay, let's eat and talk."

They dug in, and as she took the first taste of her ice-cold Coke, Rachel thought about her early writing and how she had copied other writers, who, when they had characters meet in the afternoon or evening or even when the characters had lunch, they would always be drinking coffee. Some people she knew had an afternoon cup, but most people, twenty years ago, stopped the caffeine IV after their morning coffee so that they could go to bed at night. Then, with the explosion of Starbucks and Dunkin' Donuts, routines changed, and it was now common for people to order coffee at any time of the day or night.

She felt the cool condensation on the Coke bottle's surface and thought, *If I were writing this scene in 2005, my characters would have been having coffee with their submarine sandwiches, chips, and chocolate chip cookies. Gross. Adrienne Astra will have something other than coffee with her lunches and dinners in* Sunrise Kama Sutra.

Rachel watched Harold wash down a bite of his submarine sandwich with Coke. He wiped his mouth with a napkin and said, "I never would have thought that you hadn't seen your mother in all these years, Rachel. The divorce about killed your dad, but I always thought that Tina would come back around once her fling was over with Mister Bigshot."

"I know nothing about what happened."

Ben-David finished a swig of Coke and said, "Mister Bigshot might be the only lead that helps us find Tina. I want to know everything about him."

Harold frowned. "I might disappoint you because I don't know anything beyond what Clark told me during the divorce." He popped a Ruffles chip into his mouth and chewed before taking another chug of Coke. "Here is what I do know. Mister Bigshot's name was Guy Cole—I'll never forget that name—and he was a lawyer who was in town working for Gibson Guitar Corporation."

Rachel exchanged a knowing glance with Ben-David. *Well, that probably tells us how my mother could have afforded Wentworth & Higgins,* she thought.

Harold did not see their exchange as he was grinning and looking up at the umbrella's canvas. "God, how I love their guitars," he said. "I've still got my Les Paul Custom at home and play it almost every night." His eyes lowered slowly. "Well, the company was founded right here in Kalamazoo by Orville Gibson in 1902 and named Gibson Mandolin-Guitar Manufacturing Company Limited. Fast forward to 1976, and production started to shift from the flagship Kalamazoo factory to the new factory in Nashville, Tennessee. Fast forward another eight years, and in 1984, the Kalamazoo plant closed for good, and Nashville became the new headquarters. It still tears me apart because I had friends who worked in the Kalamazoo plant. Ever hear the saying that 'everything created in Michigan eventually *leaves* Michigan?'"

Rachel shook her head *no*; Ben-David nodded *yes*.

"Well, Gibson Guitars should have never left Michigan. Heck, since that company departed, all Kalamazoo is known for these days is being the birthplace of Derek Jeter . . . went to Kalamazoo Central." He rubbed his chin. "Don't know if you're much into books, but one of my favorite authors, Daniel Silva, was born just outside of Kalamazoo."

Rachel did know that about Silva. In fact, she looked forward to his new book each summer.

Harold skipped the rest of his sandwich and chips and took a huge bite of his cookie. "Anyway, your dad told me that Guy Cole was a lawyer from a big firm in Palm Springs, and that firm did a variety of work in the entertainment business but specialized in the music industry, including manufacturing companies. So, Gibson hired the firm—I can't remember the name—and they sent Guy Cole to Kalamazoo to help during the final months of the transfer. He was staying at the historic Henderson Castle, and I guess, from what your father told me, one morning, he stopped in at Denny's for breakfast, saw your mother working there, swept her off her feet with his charm and wealth, and that was it." He paused. "As a side note, in 1986, the company almost went out of business but got rescued by three guys who bought it and turned it around. Did any of the blame for the near-collapse land on Guy Cole's shoulders or his firm's? Hell no."

Ben-David finished writing in his pocket notebook and set it on the table. He ran a hand through his beard, wound the end around his fingers, then pulled his hand out of the gray field and tapped the top of the concrete table. "So, a smooth-talking lawyer on assignment from his firm in Palm Springs stays in Kalamazoo for a few months in 1984, meets Rachel's mom, they have an affair, and then she divorces Clark Roberts, leaving him with two-year-old Rachel. She leaves with Guy, presumably back to his place in Palm Springs, and is never heard from again. Clark takes sole custody of Rachel, sells his house, and transfers from the Kalamazoo Meijer to the Saginaw Meijer but settles in Midland so that when he's not working at Meijer, he can continue to participate in his passion, community theater."

"And now you know more than I do." He chuckled to himself. "I'm glad he stayed with acting, though. He was somethin', I tell you." Harold shifted his gaze from Ben-David to Rachel. "Do you act? Please tell me that you do—it had to run in the family."

"No, I never took it up."

He raised his eyebrows. "Work at Meijer?"

"No, again," she said.

He gave her a playful pout. "Damn. The arts run in your family, ma'am."

Don't I know it, Rachel thought.

"She's a computer coder," said Ben-David.

"Oh, no. Those machines are pure evil."

They all enjoyed a quick laugh, and then Rachel said, "Harold, you told us inside that you helped my dad load up the U-Haul the day we left Kalamazoo."

"Yes, ma'am."

"Were you a close friend of my father's?"

"I wouldn't say close friend. He was a few years older than me and in a different place in life. He was married and had a child, and I was still single and dating." He pulled his wallet from his back pocket and took out a picture. He showed it to them.

It was a professional photo of a young Harold with his arms wrapped around a beautiful African-American woman. They had on matching red turtlenecks.

"Me and Chloe. Married thirty-eight years this past March."

Rachel gave a polite smile and watched as he put the photo back inside his wallet. "But you were friends with Dad, right?"

"For certain," Harold said. "He was my mentor at Meijer, and there was nobody better. I was blessed to have him show me the ropes."

"Dad was a pretty private person. How did you know about my mother and Guy?"

"I just think he needed someone to talk to when it was going on. I saw a change in him at work and asked him about it one day. As I recall, about a week later, we were on break, and he opened up to me about it. Then, when the divorce was final, he asked if I would help him pack up the house. Chloe and I were dating by then, so she watched you while your dad and I loaded up the truck."

Ben-David said, "Did he ever talk to you about the divorce settlement?"

Harold took another bite of his cookie and followed it with a sip of Coke. "What do you mean?"

"Neither Tina nor her parents ever saw Rachel again. And Tina never paid a penny in child support."

"Doesn't surprise me."

"Why do you say that?" Rachel asked.

"Well, first, I didn't understand why he was leaving Kalamazoo. I understand Midland had a nice performing arts center, but The Civic Theatre here in Kalamazoo was second to none. I told him, 'Hey, man, she's heading to California. You got a raw deal, but there's no reason to up and leave. We got a good thing goin' on here at Meijer. We're bound to move up together.' He told me that he just needed a fresh start. Too many memories here. I respected him for that."

"Did the two of you stay in touch?"

He pursed his lips and shook his head. "No. Chloe and I thought about him a lot over the years, but it was just one of those things. People move away; you fall out of touch. Chloe and I were starting our own family, and—do you have any kids?"

"No," Rachel said.

"Well, when you have kids, it feels like about twenty years go by in the blink of an eye, and you're suddenly in your forties and haven't talked to anyone from your twenties since your children were born." He looked down at the table, and Rachel thought she saw his eyes tear up again. He did not look up but said,

"Meijer sent out a newsletter every month, and every once in a while, they would include an article about someone retiring who had made a huge impact. Well, I read the article about your dad when he retired and considered reaching out, but then thought, 'No, it's been too long.' I regret that decision to this day."

She reached over and squeezed his hand.

A few seconds passed in silence, and she released his hand.

"You have your father's kindness," he said.

"What you said about his decision to leave Kalamazoo aligns with what Dad told me about why he moved us to Midland. But let's get back to your reaction to my main question about why my mother's parents never once visited me and why my mother never paid any child support. You said that it didn't surprise you."

"Yeah, sorry. Got sidetracked by my guilt. It's mostly a wasted emotion, but I'll be damned if it isn't a necessary one sometimes to keep us in line. You watch; I'll probably be extra nice to people the rest of the day because of how badly I feel about not keeping in contact with your dad . . . something that was completely off my mind when I woke up this morning. Ha! Life."

He finished his cookie.

"Or, maybe I was trying to stray so you'd forget what I said."

"Why would you do that?"

"To protect you." He sighed. "I don't want to hurt you. You've been through enough already, living without a mother who left you and grandparents who didn't want to be a part of your life."

"Please, tell me."

He exhaled. "I don't wanna—"

She leaned toward him, a fierce determination in her eyes and her body shaking with . . . what? Anger? Fear? Annoyance? Anxiety? Disgust? She couldn't narrow it down. "*Tell* me," she snapped at him.

10

Rachel Roberts sat forward and rested her elbows on the concrete table; she put her head into her hands and rubbed her eyes. "I'm sorry," she said to Harold. "I didn't mean to get upset."

When she had removed her hands from her face, she saw Harold nodding, seeming to understand how emotional the subject was to Rachel. Even *she* did not know what kind of powerful feelings the search would bring out in her; now that she had uncharacteristically been rude to someone, she wondered what the intensity of her emotions would be as they got closer to finding her mother. And what if they found her? Would she lose control? As her knees bounced up and down beneath the tabletop, she couldn't decide whether there would be tears or clenched fists if she found and faced Tina Haines.

"No offense taken, Rachel," Harold said.

"Thank you for understanding."

He nodded. "I'll tell you what I know. It's not much, but it may answer some questions and generate others."

"We'd be grateful," Ben-David said.

Harold drank from his Coke bottle and then screwed the top back on as if his hand was a wrench and he was counting the number of turns it took to tighten

84

it. When he could no longer move the cap, he set the drink down. "I knew your father well enough to be able to ask him about the divorce before I helped him load up the moving truck. I think I was in the same boat as everyone else who knew him, mostly workers at Meijer and his pals in the community theatre circle. We all wanted to know why he was moving away. It was obvious that your mom was leaving town with the lawyer, Guy Cole, but we didn't understand why your dad wanted to split. When I asked him, he told me why, and he explained what had happened in the divorce."

Harold paused and rubbed the middle finger of his right hand in circles on the table surface.

She glanced at Ben-David, who was ready to write in his notebook.

"The first answer is easy, although it wasn't easy for any of us who knew him to hear. He wanted a fresh start. Too many memories in Kalamazoo. Said all he could think about was the empty, cold side of the bed where your mom used to lie beside him. When he went to the theater, all he could see from the stage was Tina in the audience. He couldn't concentrate anymore. Couldn't eat at Denny's. And at the Meijer store, all he saw down every aisle was Tina, who used to shop there with him when his shift was done.

"And then there was the hospital where you were born and the park they used to take you to. He told me that he had to get out of here. I had never met his parents, so I asked him if he was moving closer to them. Told me that he lost them when he was young."

Rachel said, "Yes. I never knew any of my grandparents."

Harold motioned with his hand as if he was selling the vast expanse of land Rachel could see from her seat. "Did he ever bring you back to Kalamazoo?"

"No," she said. "It was the one place he said was off-limits. He never discouraged me from coming here on my own, but I never did."

"What do you think of it, now that you're here?"

"I like it; it has some similarities with Midland and Saginaw. There is a part of me that wishes I could remember more from when I lived here. What I have are mostly images." She motioned her hand at the surrounding area. "If this place is anything like Midland, then there are places I am sure no one would recognize nowadays. Everything has changed so much."

"Oh, it has. Even this store. Much bigger than it used to be."

There were a few moments of silence. Then, Rachel could hear a lawn mower starting in the distance.

"Lawn care day here at Meijer," Harold said.

Ben-David entered the conversation. "So, he wanted to get away from the bad memories. Understandable." He tapped his notebook with his pencil. "But what about the divorce?"

Harold smiled and pointed at Ben-David. "You've got a good partner, ma'am."

"He doesn't like loose ends," Rachel said.

Harold took a napkin and wiped the condensation off his Coke bottle. Then, he used the wet napkin to wipe his forehead. "Yeah, the divorce . . ." He gave Rachel a frown. "I'm sorry for what I'm about to say."

A thousand thoughts raced through her mind, dominated by a stream of questions: *Did Mom's lawyers have something on Dad? Was it a case of blackmail? Dad never talked much about the divorce, but was it because he was hiding something?*

Am I about to discover something about my father, my hero, my champion, the man who gave everything for me, that I did not want to know? She steeled herself. This was one of the risks of traveling down this road. *You knew what you were getting into.*

"Your mom didn't want you," Harold said. "Before she met Guy Cole, your father had already taken over as your primary caregiver. I think nowadays, she would have been diagnosed with postpartum depression, but this was the early eighties. Your dad told me that she wanted nothing to do with either of you and did not plan on paying child support. I guess when Guy hired Wentworth and

Higgins, they were ready to go after your dad for a bunch of stuff that Guy and your mom had made up; they were going to bloody him up. And I mean the kind of beating where it would be difficult for him to find a job."

"But that would have meant that Tina would have to care for Rachel, which is what she didn't want," said Ben-David.

"You're right, but here's the thing: Clark feared that if it came to that, she and Guy would take Rachel with them to California and then put her up for adoption. Clark had his lawyer look into it." Harold raised his eyebrows. "And his lawyer found that there are ways to do that if you've got the right connections. So, in the end, I think your dad saw that if he took full custody of you, everything else would go away. And that is exactly what happened. When I helped him load up the moving truck, he said it was as if the marriage had never happened and you had been left on his doorstep in a basket carried by a stork. Guy and Tina were gone; Wentworth and Higgins and your dad's lawyer, Mickey Dunn, had settled the divorce and taken their cuts of cash; and your dad had sold his house and transferred from the Kalamazoo Meijer to the Saginaw Meijer."

She didn't want me, Rachel said to herself over and over again.

All the years of wondering were suddenly compressed into Harold's singular statement. If Harold's memory could be trusted, and there was no reason for her to doubt it, she had her answer. After all, he had tried to warn her; he gained nothing by lying. Why hadn't her father just told her the truth? The only reason she could come up with was that it was too painful for him to relive. And in that way, he had protected her from the truth. What good would it have done to know that her mother wanted nothing to do with her? Because of her mother's absence, Rachel already knew that on some level, but it had never been explained to her as directly as Harold just had. She had read about postpartum depression and knew it was a difficult situation for new mothers and families to navigate. What if her mother had gotten help back then? She dismissed the thought. *She had plenty of time to consider what she had done in the years after the divorce.*

In a strange twist of fate, the *woman* in the relationship had abandoned the man and left him to raise their child. Now, she wondered what she would have done if her father had told her the truth while he was still alive. Would she have rushed to find and confront her mother? Maybe. Maybe not. Would she have been able to handle that type of revelation? She didn't think so. When her father was still alive, she had still been running from her past, keeping her mother out of her mind. In fact, from when they left Kalamazoo until the day he died, she had only become more loyal to her father with each passing year. She never even thought of bringing up her mother to him out of fear that it would hurt him in some way.

This is why he didn't keep a record of the divorce, she thought. There was nothing to keep. It was a clean split designed to erase memories and the people involved. *He didn't want me to know.*

She first felt Ben-David's hand on her shoulder, then the tears running down her face. There was only a glassy mirage of Harold in front of her, and she wiped her eyes with a napkin until she could see him. His head was lowered. "It's okay," she said. "I wanted the truth, and it took a lot for you to tell me." She blew her nose. "Thank you, Harold."

"She had such a good thing with you and your dad. I just . . . well, I am grateful to have met you finally after all of these years. Always wondered what happened to you." He leaned his head toward his right shoulder and squinted. "I must say, though, you look familiar to me." He bit his lower lip. "I wonder why that is?"

If I have to guess, it's because someone in your family reads Riley Cannon novels, Rachel thought. "Maybe it's because I resemble my father," she said.

"Yeah, that's probably it. Although, you've got your mom's height."

"Dad was six-foot-one, so I figured she had to be short."

"Short and had a temper."

"Sounds like she was an unhappy person," Ben-David said.

88

"Yeah," Harold said. "Still want to find her, Rachel?"

"I do," she said, surprising herself with how confidently she had stated her intention.

Ben-David gave her a nod of encouragement and a look in his eyes that said, *"I'm with you."*

"Is there anything else you can tell me that might help us locate her?"

Harold thought for a moment and then said, "No. Where Guy went, she went. I'd start there."

She gave his hand a squeeze. "Thanks for today, and thanks to you and your wife for caring for me and Dad when we moved."

His eyes filled. "I should have stayed in touch with him."

"He could have stayed in touch with you too," she said, "so don't give it another thought. You were in each other's life at that time for certain reasons. Today might be one of those." She paused, contemplating whether or not she should bring in a piece of writing to bookend her point.

She went for it.

"Are you familiar with the poem 'Desiderata' by Max Ehrmann?"

He rubbed his chin. "Can't say that I am."

"My father introduced me to the poem when I was young, and I try to live by those words. Here is a section appropriate for today," she said. "Beyond a wholesome discipline, be gentle with yourself. You are a child of the universe no less than the trees and the stars; you have a right to be here. And whether or not it is clear to you, no doubt the universe is unfolding as it should."

As the last words left her mouth and entered the ears of Harold and Ben-David, Rachel once again felt comforted by Ehrmann's composition. She had referred to it often throughout the years and realized today that, perhaps, she was guilty of not always following its precepts.

Now that she was running toward her ultimate fear instead of running away, she felt empowered. Harold had risked hurting her, albeit at her request, but he had not shielded her from what he believed the truth to be. Would she and Ben-David find her mother? She wasn't sure. This afternoon was proof of everything that could happen in one day.

Try *forty-one* years.

"You remind me so much of him. He loved to share quotes from literature too—especially the plays he would study during his breaks at work and late at night after you had gone to bed."

"He never lost his love of theater."

"I'm glad."

They finished their meal, thanked and said goodbye to Shae inside, and then thanked and said goodbye to Harold in the parking lot—she had hugged him, and Ben-David had given him a warm handshake.

And now she watched as the old, reliable Meijer clerk ambled back toward the store entrance. He let a car pass in front of him and then crossed the curbside lane. As the glass doors slid open, Harold paused for a few seconds and then headed inside. He did not look back.

"How are you doing?" Ben-David asked.

"All kinds of emotions going on inside," she replied, watching the glass doors shut behind Harold.

"I didn't know we'd catch a break like this today."

She turned toward him. "Do we need to visit the esteemed law offices of Wentworth and Higgins?"

"No. The hell with those assholes. We've got everything we need. While you were having a private chat with Shae and Harold, I looked up Guy Cole."

"You found him?"

"Sort of. Both good and bad."

"Let's have it." She was determined, all business now.

"Bad—I read his obituary—died three years ago. He is survived by his wife, Lilly, and three children, Max, Jordan, and Stephanie."

"So, either my mother changed her name to Lilly and changed her mind about having kids, or she and Guy did not stay together."

"Correct. He was indeed a lawyer out of Palm Springs. Started at the big firm—Jacobsen, Hudson, and Sherwood—entertainment lawyers, just as Harold said. Guy would have been working there during the Gibson plant move. Then, Guy's obituary said that he started his own firm in 1990. Ready for the name? 'Cole Train.' Double meaning. One, it was an obvious nod to John Coltrane; two, it was most likely a nod to the American musical variety television program *Soul Train*, which Don Cornelius started. When I was growing up in the early seventies, that show used to depress every single kid."

"Why?"

"Because it aired every Saturday at 11 a.m., which always signified the end of Saturday morning cartoons."

"I can't believe we're talking about this right now."

"Hey, you asked," Ben-David said, laughing. "Let it be known, though, that once I got past my cartoon phase, I actually enjoyed the show and watched it pretty regularly."

"So, Guy Cole continued his career as a lawyer in the entertainment business."

"That he did. His firm is still alive and well in Palm Springs."

Rachel met his eyes. "Palm Springs."

"Are we about to be airline passengers?"

Rachel motioned for him to unlock the van. When she heard the click, she opened her door and said, "Yes. Get us to the Kalamazoo airport. I'll get our tickets on the way there." She stood still, feeling the heat from inside the vehicle smother her. "We're going to California. Now I *have to* confront her . . . if she's still there."

She would soon regret what she found.

II

Paradise Cove Bluffs, California – Wednesday, July 2, 2025

Andre Kurt Andreas sat in a black leather chair in his semi-circular office with floor-to-ceiling windows located on the northwestern corner of his beachfront mansion's third—and top—floor. It was a few minutes after nine p.m., and the sun had set an hour earlier, leaving a fading orange glow on the deep blue Pacific's horizon. Two high-speed motorboats crisscrossed paths, patrolling the waters just offshore, and farther out, one of Kurt's smaller yachts, a 200-foot Oceanco, lay at anchor.

Just outside the door to the office was Ivan, armed and wearing a headset to maintain communication with Kurt and Kurt's guest, the home's gate guard, four armed men stationed at strategic points around the property, and the gate guard at the entrance to the private drive leading to the mansions on this stretch of beach in Paradise Clove Bluffs; there were twenty men inside armed for war in case they were needed. Security was tighter than ever, for the woman seated across from Kurt in a matching leather chair was the number one arms dealer in the world . . .

The President of the United States, Susan Kantor.

"So, what you're telling me, Kurt, is that Millard may make a move on you, correct?"

"I think so," Kurt replied.

"How soon?"

"Tough to say. I've been looking into it the past few days, and from my sources in France, nothing unusual is happening. Millard is still in Paris."

She exhaled and crossed her legs.

If only the country could see her now, Kurt thought.

She wore running shoes, baggy gray sweatpants, and a black hoodie. The black Nike baseball cap with the white swoosh on the front was on the coffee table between them, and her messy brown hair was pulled back into a short ponytail. She wore no makeup. And even so, he still considered her looks stunning—high cheekbones, smooth yet tight skin that had not been maintained through surgery or injections, penetrating blue eyes, and perfect teeth achieved through multiple dental surgeries. They had once compared notes about what they did to stay—What was the phrase she had used?—ah, yes, "Forever thirty-five." She was notorious for waking at 4 a.m. for an hour of cross-fit before taking a half-hour swim followed by a massage, shower, and then eating the same breakfast that she had for three decades: oatmeal with fresh blueberries, 2 cups of black coffee, and a liter of ice water. Yes, underneath the sweatsuit disguise was a five-foot-ten-inch President who was more physically fit than ninety percent of the women half her age.

"Any idea how Louis was found out?" she asked.

"None. We inserted him five years ago and never had a problem. His cover was perfect."

She uncrossed her legs. "No doubt they tortured him before killing him."

"His head showed up at *my* island."

She exhaled and leaned back, sinking deep into the oversized leather chair. "We still need to do business with everyone," Kantor said.

Kurt knew what she meant. There were entities in the world that were important for the U.S. Government to do business with, but because of who the entities were, the U.S. Government could not do business with them *directly*. A cutout was needed, and for three decades, that cutout had been him: Andre Kurt Andreas, the Silicon Valley anti-hero who was a member of the famous 1970s and 1980s "Gates Cohort."

When the Soviet Union fell in 1991, Kurt had seen the money to be made in arms dealing before anyone else. In fact, he'd predicted it when the Berlin Wall came down. Warren Buffett may have been called "The Oracle of Omaha," but Andre Kurt Andreas was soon referred to as "The Oracle of Ukraine." Vast stockpiles of larger weapons—tanks, helicopter gunships, planes, missiles, light machine guns, and mortars—and small arms—assault rifles, handguns, grenades, bullets, mines, etc.—were in storage facilities all across Ukraine in preparation for what the Soviet Union thought was the inevitable clash with the West one day.

The irony of the situation in Ukraine during the past handful of years was not lost on Kurt. The U.S.'s spending had caused the Soviet Union to produce more weapons and ammunition than Ukraine could possibly need. When the Cold War ended, and Ukraine broke away, then those stockpiles were the very things that made Kurt Andreas one of the wealthiest men in the world, as he had innovated and worked tirelessly to empty that nation of its stockpiles . . . only to witness thirty years later that very same country get invaded by Russia—perhaps Ukraine could have used some of those arms in its defense—and see his own nation send billions of dollars worth of arms and ammunition to help Ukraine retain its sovereignty. And what was the kicker? Because of his connections, Kurt Andreas was able to dominate the Pentagon's bidding board for contracts to send the arms and ammunition back into Ukraine.

Thirty years ago, he had helped to empty the stockpiles. Now, he was helping to rebuild the stockpiles.

However, this was not the business partnership that Kantor was hinting at. The ones she wanted to preserve were the gray ones—the ones where the lesser of two bad actors on the world stage was supplied in the hopes that it would eliminate the other, who was more of a threat to the U.S. *"You and I hate knowing who the U.S. is in bed with, but we still sleep at night because the alternative is unimaginable,"* she had said to him years ago. They had built their trust on that statement.

And now, because of Louis's execution, those secret business relationships were being threatened. Frenchman Hans Millard had also become wealthy in the 1990s and, apart from Kurt, was the primary arms dealer in Europe. Kurt had spies in every competitor's operation, but he had never been able to crack Millard's until five years ago when Louis had broken in. Now, there would be consequences.

"Agreed," Kurt said. He also knew that if he and his operation were to disappear, Kantor would have no trouble having another one of her cutouts contact Millard and make a deal. Yes, she and Kurt were friends, but she had stayed with Kurt over the years because, in the illegal deals, he moved products efficiently, at a cheaper cost than the competition, and ensured that nothing was traceable back to the U.S. Government.

She raised her eyebrows and opened her palms. "So, what happens next?"

"I had a competitive pricing advantage over him because of Louis. Now, he's going to tighten his circle. He'll start to dominate the area within a month, which weakens our position. If he decides to disrupt my supply chain, then we've got a real problem."

"But that's not what you're most concerned about, is it?"

She had read him. There were always obstacles in the arms dealing business, but rarely any that necessitated him meeting with her in person. Other Presidents he had worked with over the years had formed elaborate cutouts so they could never be linked to him. However, ever since he had been introduced to Susan Kantor in 1992 at the celebratory party when, at the age of thirty, she had won her first Senate term—Kurt had donated millions to her campaign—he had known her to be obsessed over control. Yes, they had indirect routes to get messages to each other, but when the situation called for it—and this one did—she preferred to meet in person. They had been in business together for over thirty years, but in the 1990s, they had started a decade-long affair that had them both questioning whether they wanted to join forces personally. He had considered leaving his wife, Kitty, for her, but he and Kantor ultimately decided it would be bad for both of their career aspirations. She wanted to be President, and he did not want to become the First Gentleman. He wanted to become the wealthiest person in the world, and she did not want that to interfere with her ambition for power. "You can still read me," he said.

She smirked.

"Yes, at the present, I am concerned about losing my life."

She reached across the table and gave his hand a sympathetic squeeze.

He both loved and hated when she did that—loved it because there was nothing like her touch, hated it because it always disarmed him.

"Do you really believe he would do that?" she asked.

He did. "It would be the most effective way to accomplish his goal, but it's also the riskiest."

She took a sip from the bottle of water he had set on the table for her. "You know what I am going to ask you."

Again, he did. "Regardless of how he attempts to disrupt the supply line, you want to know if anyone will be able to discover that the United States was behind the deal?"

She raised her eyebrows and set down the water. "It was risky enough to sneak over here tonight. But I'm six months into my second term and have to know."

96

Kurt drank from his water bottle and took a measure of the world leader before him. He respected her and was always impressed by her audacity and ingenuity when she wanted to meet with him in person. Because he was afraid to answer her question, his mind drifted for a moment to how she had arrived at his house undetected and with only one Secret Service agent.

After contacting her through a series of cutouts—the main one being Governor Reiner—two days ago, he had finally received word this afternoon that she would meet him at his beach house at 9 p.m. Before becoming President, she had been the Senior Senator from California for twenty-eight years and, as the Commander in Chief, visited her home state often during her first term. Hence, a visit, even an impromptu visit, never appeared to be anything out of the ordinary. Because of the urgent need to meet him, she had planned a quick visit to Sacramento to meet with the Governor and kick off a pre-4th-of-July barbeque at the Governor's mansion. After the meal, her Chief of Staff had announced that she would sit down with Governor Reiner to discuss immigration reform, climate change, the state of the entertainment economy, and a host of other issues. Again, it made sense to the press since the Governor was an ally of President Kantor's—also the President's choice to succeed her—and she had not paid a visit to the Golden State during her second term yet.

The barbeque that afternoon had gone well, and Kurt had watched the coverage on T.V. as Susan Kantor wore an apron and scooped baked beans out of an enormous pot and deposited them on guests' plates. Then, she had gone inside to prepare for her meeting with Sal Reiner. Then, her secret service bodyguard, Mark Andrews, who had been her head of security when she was a senator, had swung into action.

She donned the disguise she was in now, and she and Mark were hidden in one of the guest's SUVs and driven by another secret service member to a grocery store parking lot, where they emerged and got into a van driven by a member of Kurt's security team, who did not know whom he was picking up, just that he was to drive them to a small farm in the Sacramento Valley where a helicopter was waiting to transport them to a private hangar at the Sacramento airport, where they would fly out on one of Kurt's private jets.

They landed in Santa Barbara, and a helicopter took them to Kurt's yacht, anchored offshore. Then, one of the speedboats picked them up and drove them to the beach. Kurt had owned the beach house for two decades, and his neighbors knew that many celebrities and other wealthy guests arrived at his estate via the ocean. Normally, he would have watched the President of the United States and her Secret Service bodyguard arrive on his beach with great amusement, but when they had come ashore ten minutes ago, he could see, from the high post of his third-floor office, that she was moving with a sense of purpose. However, he thought Mark Andrews had done an excellent job hiding his identity underneath a floppy sun hat, sunglasses, and white Nike sweatsuit. If the neighbors had noticed, they probably thought he was hosting a pair of athletes.

The return trip would be the reverse of this, with the exception being that in Sacramento, the President and Mark would switch into a pizza delivery car, driven by the same secret service agent who had dropped them off at the grocery store earlier, and arrive at the governor's mansion with pizza for a late-night snack. But, just before the car made it to the front gate, the President and Mark would be let off to be escorted back into the mansion via a secret entrance.

It was a lot of moving parts, but Kurt and the Governor had done this all before when Kurt needed to speak one-on-one with the President. Each time, no one had ever known that she had left the Governor's mansion.

Kurt also knew that Susan Kantor enjoyed the excitement of going undercover and relished her stolen moments as an ordinary citizen who was not being watched or hunted. Even though she was here to speak with him, it wasn't all she was here for. In one of the guest suites down the hall, Mark Andrews was waiting for her with a bucket of champagne on ice. It was a thirty-year affair and none of his business, but he did wonder tonight how she would be able to compartmentalize what they were discussing to enjoy her twenty minutes in the bedroom with Mark.

I couldn't do it, he thought. *After I saw Louis's head in the glass jar, it was like someone had poured ice water on my groin.*

He had sent the two pillars home to Modesto early.

Kurt examined the lid of his water bottle for a few seconds and then screwed it back on. He had guessed her question because it was the question he would be asking if he were in her shoes. *Will anyone be able to discover that the United States was behind the deal?*

"Kurt?" she said.

He knew that the best answer he could give her was *probably not, but maybe.* And that was not the answer she wanted to hear. However, they had always been honest with each other.

He set his water down. "Susan, whenever we arm someone, there is always the risk that those weapons could be used against us later. Now, that's nothing you haven't heard before. We must always be innovating, making something better than what we sell to maintain a tactical advantage. It's a cycle and an expensive one at that." He looked her in the eyes. "And we've both gotten rich because of that never-ending cycle."

She didn't nod in agreement, but she didn't dismiss his statement either. On the legal side, the small arms trade was worth close to $5 billion. On the illegal side, it was worth nearly $2 billion. She knew the rest of the numbers because he had told her. There were well over 600 million small arms and light weapons in circulation around the world—and almost half of them were in the United States. He had heard once that there were more gun stores in the U.S. than McDonald's restaurants.

"On the home front, my operation is sealed tight," Kurt said.

He was using his old playbook, starting with the good news, which always seemed to placate her. He even knew that she knew what he was doing, but he didn't care. Weapons, ammunition, gas masks, body armor, etc., were made in the United States with materials from other countries—similar to how pencils were made—and tremendous amounts of these products were loaded into crates and placed onboard merchant vessels in the port of Los Angeles. Then, these ships would leave port, passing by the Channel Islands, and head north to travel a great circle route west across the Pacific. However, a few times a month, one of the ships, whose captain and crew had been bribed, would meet one of Kurt's yachts in the middle of the night and transfer a few pallets to the specially designed aft deck of the yacht where they would be lowered into a hold. Doctored paperwork would be provided to the merchant, and when the ship reached its destination on the other side of the world, ready to transfer arms legally, no one would notice a pallet or two that had gone missing. The yacht would then return to Santa Andreas Island, where the cargo would be offloaded and stored in a secret underground system of storehouses, ready to be shipped anytime Kurt Andreas brokered an illegal deal with one of the entities that the United States could not officially be tied to but needed to supply for political purposes. The island had the perfect infrastructure to be a headquarters to base his operations: There was the fleet of AK ships that prowled the Pacific, which constantly changed names whenever there was a pickup and docked in a natural harbor that was safe from the elements; a landing strip long enough for a C-130 to land for imports and exports if need be; and his warehouse complex. To the outside eye, it looked like another rich person's island: private jet, private yachts—including the four-hundred-and-fifty-foot flagship, *Blue Kurty,* that had cost $600 million to build—a private golf course, private beaches, private pools, etc.

"Never had a problem that I can recall," Kantor said.

Now, she was using her playbook, which was to be polite and agree with his positive statements.

Both of them knew the "but" was coming.

He leaned back and felt the cool leather against his neck. "And we know that our customers in the Middle East and around the world have always paid and been discrete about their dealings with me."

She gave him a nod.

He also had headquarters strategically placed in central locations close to his customers.

So did Hans Millard.

"But, as much as I've automated things over the years, it's still a game of bribes, blackmail, and beating your competitor's price."

Kantor laughed. "I thought we were talking about your business, not mine."

He gave a short laugh in reply. "I still do all my banking through Switzerland and offshore accounts. I always make sure that I am paid in advance. I have an entire shop that forges and notarizes certificates and documents. I've got shell companies set up that I've used for years . . . got plenty of insurance. And, well, you've seen my pilots and sea captains in action. They're well-paid and don't ask questions. If anyone screws up, then they get a meeting with Ivan." He stopped short of saying that the employee never left that meeting alive. He knew that she was comfortable with the necessity of killing, but she did not want to know the close-up, look-them-in-the-eye details about how someone left the earth. The exception being her political enemies—then, she wanted every detail.

"I agree with everything you've said so far," she added.

"But—"

"Knew it was coming," she said, cutting him off while she leaned forward.

"But, bribes work two ways. And without Louis being our eyes and ears, we will start to lose some bids to Millard. And when you lose bids, sometimes your allies, who have stayed quiet about certain business arrangements, jump ship and start talking. Now, I think we're okay for the time being, maybe forever. However, there is a slim possibility that if Millard takes away enough of our business, he might discover 'the deal' and a few of the customers we were selling to."

He watched as she took in the information. There were a few eye blinks, then a glance at the ceiling followed by a long stare at the darkening Pacific Ocean. "It will be easier for him to disrupt your supply chains overseas; we agree on that point. And, yes, he would probably like you out of the picture. But, if he does decide to try and kill you, then it won't be the only thing he comes to this island to do."

He pursed his lips and swallowed. They had come to the same conclusion.

She turned back toward him and stretched her arms to the ceiling. "He'll either want to take all your stored products on Santa Andreas or destroy them."

He and Ivan had discussed the matter yesterday. If Hans took Kurt's products, he'd be in a superior position with more inventory and less competition. If Hans destroyed Kurt's products, then he would create scarcity and could charge more for his existing inventory. Both Kurt and Hans knew that other suppliers would be unable to wedge in and make lowball offers.

Other than Hans trying to kill him and consume his business, Kurt was scared of something far greater. What if Kantor made a deal with Hans? He had also discussed this with Ivan, and his head of security had encouraged him to meet with the President to try and get a read on which way she might go. So far, she had given him no indication of switching sides. But the stakes were high. If she sided with Kurt, and Kurt lost, then Hans Millard could possibly expose the ties between the U.S. and those they were secretly arming.

"I think we need to watch him," she said. Then, she grinned and said, "I saw the security around your place tonight, so, my friend, I don't think you're in any danger of being killed." Kantor gave him a playful tap on his arm. "You're too God damn important to me."

This put him at ease and stoked his confidence. She was standing by him. And why shouldn't she? He'd never let her down in over thirty years. "I'm flattered, Madam President."

"Oh, get off it. You know how much I love you."

"Hard not to," he said.

She nodded but then became serious. "Let's keep all of our options on the table regarding Millard, understand?"

This meant *We may need to kill him.*

Well, Kurt had ordered that kind of thing before—hated to do it, especially to a worthy competitor that he had played what he called "the great game" against all these years.

But Millard is fifteen years my junior, and if it comes down to him or me, he's going to be the one to disappear.

"Understood," he said.

She sandwiched his right hand between hers and said, "Good."

"Anything else?" he asked.

She stood, grinning. "Lafontaine still hiding out on your island?"

"Now, whatever gave you that idea?" He already knew the answer: Governor Reiner had blabbed.

"He's such a little shit," she said. "But he does have a lot of money." She rubbed Kurt's arm. "Not as much as you . . ."

He felt the start of an erection.

"But every dime of his helped get me re-elected and helps to push my agenda."

"Think it'll blow over?"

She gave his biceps a tight squeeze and then released. "Yes. You'll make sure that he issues a public statement, pledges more money, and starts listening to his asshole of an agent. When he issues the statement and the money is deposited in the proper accounts, I'll call off Senator Nailima." She paused.

103

"When I heard what he said about her, I was the one who told her. I also ensured she was on the hearing committee and gave her my blessing to make him sweat." The President laughed and started to walk away from Kurt toward the door. "It became an inside joke between us." She reached the door and turned around. "We see each other now and then, and I can tell you from first-hand experience that he would never turn her . . . and I wouldn't want him to." She opened the door, and Ivan escorted her down the hallway.

The last sounds Kurt heard were the opening of the guest suite door and then its closing.

* * *

Inside the bedroom, President Susan Kantor saw her lover, Secret Service Agent Mark Andrews, sitting in a lounger wearing only his Jockey shorts and holding a glass of champagne. There was another filled glass on the table in front of her.

She picked it up, and as the first sweet and heavenly drops touched her lips, she thought, *A final toast to you, Kurt.*

She swallowed and set the glass down, assured of her decision to call Hans Millard tomorrow morning. He was not in Paris. He was in a cabin in Banff . . . a mere three-hour plane ride away from Los Angeles.

Andrews rose from the chair, and she began to undress.

PART II

Midnight

12

Palm Springs, California – Thursday, July 3, 2025

I *can see why movie stars built vacation homes here to escape from L.A.*, Rachel Roberts thought as Obadiah Ben-David drove the black Chevrolet Suburban they had rented from Hertz at the Palm Springs International Airport down the palm-tree-lined street of old residences that featured floating planes and large, plate glass windows to provide natural lighting. Whereas L.A. was a packed theater with assigned seats, Palm Springs was an amphitheater with open seating, filled to only twenty-five percent of its capacity. Like the movie stars who had found peace and privacy here away from the limelight, Rachel had opted for a quiet life in her secluded residence south of Hampstead. She had only considered moving to one other place: Key West . . . but her mistake had eliminated that option.

Ben-David had the air conditioning turned to "Max A/C" as the temperatures outside were 106 degrees and would only drop to 79 overnight.

Rachel had discovered that the vehicle's radio had SiriusXM, and she had selected Channel 70: Siriusly Sinatra. They were drinking iced coffee and listening to The Chairman of the Board's live performance of "Don't Worry About Me" in the Copa Room at the Sands Hotel and Casino in 1966 when Sinatra was fifty and, in Rachel's opinion, at the height of his powers. She had explained to Ben-David that the music was conducted and arranged by Quincy Jones, and Count Basie and his orchestra accompanied Sinatra. *"Simply stated, 'Sinatra at the Sands' is the best live album ever recorded,"* she had said to him when the song had come on. Ben-David had replied, *"I've never heard of it."*

Now, as she looked out the window at the cloudless sky, she thought, *I also stand by my decision to use Palm Springs as the location for villain Aristotle Baron's vacation home in* Enemies in the Evening.

Speaking of Frank Sinatra, she had placed Baron's Richard-Neutra-designed "Kaufmann Desert House" between Old Blue Eye's and Dinah Shore's former homes in Rancho Mirage, and she had positioned Baron's mistress's house in Palm Desert between John Ford's and Kurt Russell's former homes. She had taken an aspect of Sinatra's home and one of the singer's routines and changed them to suit her needs for Aristotle Baron. Sinatra's swimming pool was piano-shaped; for Baron, the retired art thief, she designed a pool in the outline of Bob Ross's hair and chin—a gigantic teardrop. Sinatra had famously raised a Jack Daniels flag between the towering twin palms on his property to signal to his neighbors the start of every cocktail hour. Therefore, Rachel had Aristotle Baron raise a 'Friends of Laphroaig' flag in her novel. She usually visited each place she wrote about, but this had been one of the few times she had not. The scenes set in Palm Springs in *Enemies in the Evening* were such a small part of the novel that she had trusted the internet and J. Rudolph Hightower's notes about the area since he had a vacation home there. Now that she was here, she felt relieved that she had gotten the details right.

Ben-David slowed the suburban and then parked on the curb as Rachel's phone announced that they had arrived at their destination.

"Took us long enough to get here," Ben-David said.

On the way to the Kalamazoo | Battle Creek International Airport last night, they discovered that direct flights from Chicago to Palm Springs were only seasonal between October and May. So, the best they could do was drive over to the Detroit Metropolitan Airport, stay the night at the airport's hotel, the Westin, and then catch a flight to Denver the next morning with a connecting flight to Palm Springs in the afternoon. "The important thing is that we're here," Rachel said.

"Looks exactly like the picture."

Rachel agreed. Before them was a Desert-Modern-styled home dominated by glass and floating planes. She had looked up the home on a Palm Springs real estate website and found pictures of the inside; the home had been listed by Guy Cole's widow, Lilly, a year ago and then taken off the market. It was a classic open design of 4,000 square feet with four bedrooms and five bathrooms. A pool and a cabana were in the backyard, surrounded by a beautiful garden.

"Ready for this?" Ben-David asked.

Rachel turned off the radio.

"It's different actually being here," she said, looking out the passenger's side window at the house. "In a minute, I could be standing before my mother. Or, in a minute, I could be standing in front of a complete stranger who knows nothing about my mother. I see this house and know that Guy Cole purchased it in 1987, two years after my mom would have come to Palm Springs with him. From what you learned yesterday, the house he lived in from 1975 to 1987 has been demolished. So, I'm thinking that even if his wife Lilly isn't my mom, there is still a good chance she lived here for a while."

The vehicle was still running, and the cool air from the front vents felt good, but coupled with her nerves, she shivered.

Am I ready for this?

Ben-David took a drink of his iced coffee. "Forty-one years is a long time."

"And then, I look at that house and remember the house in Midland where my father raised me: twelve hundred square feet, two bedrooms, and one bathroom. And—" She paused, rubbing her eyes. "Suddenly, I'm a kid again, and I'm jealous that I didn't get to grow up in a house this nice, and I'm angry that my father never got a taste of living in a beautiful place like this until the end of his life when I bought him a new house."

"You bought your dad a house when you were in your twenties?"

She had made a mistake. The combination of feeling safe with Ben-David and the freedom she knew she had to display her emotions in front of him had led her to reveal something about her past that had surprised him.

Oh, God. I cannot deal with telling him who I really am right now. There must be a way out. Think!

There was. Claiming that she was a computer coder offered her the escape route from the line of questioning that was sure to come if she didn't answer him right now.

"Well, I took care of the downpayment. As a coder and software engineer, I was making triple what he was and wanted to repay him for all he had done for me," she said. It was near the whole truth. "I wanted to buy him something larger, but he refused."

Her partner nodded. "That was kind of you."

Did he buy it? She could not tell, but he did not ask any follow-up questions. She returned her attention to the house. "And I think of my mother possibly raising the three children—Max, Jordan, and Stephanie—and I think of all the family memories in that house. Memories that she could have been making with me and my father."

Her voice trailed off, and she did not speak for another minute—the only sound was that of the air conditioner's fan above the low hum of the SUV's idling engine.

What is the first thing I say to her?

She did not know. However, what she did know from her father was that her mother was taller than she was, around five-six. Accounting for age, perhaps five foot five now. So, if Lilly Cole's height was not in that ballpark, then Rachel would know she wasn't her mother. "We'll know from her height," she said.

"Five-six or five-five, right?"

"Right." She closed her eyes, and all she could think of were the words that Joan Didion had written in her novel *The Year of Magical Thinking*, which was about the grief the author had felt about losing her husband.

You're safe.

I'm here.

Words that Rachel's mother had never said to her.

There was a car parked in the driveway.

Is it hers?

What if one of her children is here? What would I say to him or her?

Ben-David cleared his throat and said, "I can go up and knock on the door, get a gauge of things if you want to stay in here?"

No one would ever be fully ready to do this, she said to herself. *I could have thought about this moment and planned my speech for years, and it wouldn't have helped me right now.* She looked at Ben-David with glassy eyes.

"That's kind of you to offer, old friend, but I need to be with you." She inhaled through her nose and then exhaled through her mouth. "Okay. Let's go."

Less than a minute after ringing the doorbell, Rachel heard the lock turn and saw the handle start to move. For a second, she was transported back to her room when she was two years old and was pulling on the handle to open her door. She could hear mommy and daddy shouting and wanted to know what was going on . . .

The door opened, and a tall, lithe woman with black hair, blue eyes, and wearing a sun dress—who looked to be somewhere in her fifties, definitely not *seventy*—studied them.

"Yes?" the woman said.

She's not my mother, Rachel thought, *but who is she? This cannot be Lilly, can it?*

"Is this the residence of Lilly Cole?" Ben-David asked.

The woman grinned. "Has been for many years. Can I help you?"

"You're Lilly Cole?"

The grin disappeared. "Yes," she said, leaning her head to the right. "Now, what is this?"

Feeling more at ease, Rachel didn't wait. "Ms. Cole, my name is Rachel Roberts. This is going to sound crazy, but a little over forty years ago, my mother, Tina Haines, left me and my father for a lawyer named Guy Cole. That was your husband, correct?"

Lilly stood there, frozen for around ten seconds. She tried to speak, but all that came out was, "I—" and her mouth closed.

Rachel continued. "I am sorry to show up here unannounced, and I realize that your husband passed away three years ago. My father died in 2008, and I never knew where my mother went." Her voice was strong but not threatening, approachable but in no way sad. Despite being uncertain in the SUV minutes ago, she now felt determined and free to get right to the point. Somehow, the fact that her mother had not opened the door had released her of a weight that, at the moment, she did not understand—even more so because she had still yet to find and confront her. "Well, this man beside me is a friend and P.I. from Michigan, where Guy met my mother. He is helping me to track down my mom."

Ben-David showed Lilly his license.

Lilly looked at the license and nodded.

"In the early nineteen eighties, Guy had been sent by the entertainment law firm he was working for at that time, which was here in Palm Springs, to Kalamazoo, Michigan, to be the counsel for a company that was moving to Tennessee. My parents and I were living in Kalamazoo, and that is where Guy met my mom." Rachel paused, seeing Lilly close her eyes. "Look, I'm not here to cause you pain today. I'm married now, and my husband and I want to start a family. However, I realized that to do that, I needed to find my mom before I could move forward. The only piece of information we have to go on is that she moved out here with Guy."

Ben-David put his license away and said, "Miss Cole, did your husband ever mention a former girlfriend named Tina Haines to you?"

Lilly's face remained still for a moment, and then she shook her head back and forth. "No. He never mentioned that name to me." She turned to Rachel. "You said he helped break up your parent's marriage?"

"Yes," she answered.

Her eyes got glassy, and she got out, "I . . . I don't believe it. He never told me anything like that, and we knew *everything* about each other. Are you sure you have the right man?"

"He bought this house in 1987," Ben-David said. "Were you with him then?"

"No. We met in June of 1990, and we were both single—I was twenty-two, had just graduated college, and planned to attend law school. He was over twenty years older than I was, but it was just one of those instances where age didn't matter. Everything was right. I had started a summer internship with his law firm."

"Jacobsen, Hudson, and Sherwood."

"Why, yes. Then, I discovered he was leaving in a few months to start his own firm."

"Cole Train."

"How do you—"

"I'm a Professional Investigator, ma'am—"

"I thought it was Private Investigator."

"Usually is. But in Michigan, we're called Professional Investigators." He rubbed his beard. "I'm good at my job, and that's how I know about your husband's employment record."

There was silence for a few beats, and then Lilly continued. "We started dating, and he asked if I wanted to work for him at his new firm. I said sure." She shrugged. "So, I moved in with him, attended law school, and we got married in 1992."

Rachel took a step closer to her. *Butter her up a bit,* she told herself. "I believe you, and it sounds like what you and your husband had was special."

"It was."

Rachel gave her an affirming nod. Lilly Cole had done nothing to hurt her emotionally; her deceased husband, Guy Cole, had. The fact that he was dead had diluted any negative energy that Rachel might have fallen prey to had he been alive. Hence, she found it easy to talk to Lilly, and in some way, she pitied her. Not that Guy Cole had owed her every detail from his past relationships—most people protected their images by either not mentioning a former relationship or putting their spin on why the union had disintegrated when recounting their former partners to a new lover. However, Rachel was sure it was not easy to hear that your life partner had destroyed another marriage, even though it had happened before you met him. She wondered how she would feel if a stranger showed up on her front doorstep one day and told her that Stan had helped to cause a divorce because he had been a part of an extramarital affair. As the first answers—angry, disappointed, confused, and sad—entered her mind, she refocused on Lilly.

Now, play dumb. "Any kids?"

"Three. I practiced law at the firm for a year, and we decided to start a family. So, I took time off until our youngest was in Kindergarten, and then we worked together until he retired."

Ben-David angled in, and Rachel was grateful. Mentioning kids had somehow touched the nerve she had been trying to avoid. She was thrown off for a moment and didn't like it. "So, he lived here for around three years before you met, right?" asked Ben-David.

"Yes."

He swept his hand in the direction of the neighboring houses. "Any of these folks here when you first moved in?"

Her eyes scanned the neighborhood, and she eventually pointed at a smaller house two lots over that had tan-colored siding with a dark brown roof. "I think only Mrs. Mallory was here when I started living with Guy. Everyone else either moved in after 1990 or moved away." Her eyes started to well up, and she wiped them with her hand before any tears could escape. "You'll have to excuse the emotion; it's just that I haven't thought of the neighborhood in that way in so long." She pulled her cell phone out of her pocket and waved it before them. "Since Guy passed away, I've been spending too much time on this stupid thing." She slid it back inside her pocket, saying, "I do miss some of them who have moved away."

"Do you know if Mrs. Mallory is home today?" Rachel asked.

"Oh, she's always home. Eighty-one years old, and her only child, Tony, who's my age, lives with her and takes care of her."

"Mrs. Mallory got a first name?" said Ben-David.

"Yes, it's Harriet. Why do you want to know that?"

"Just the way I work."

Rachel and Ben-David shared a glance, and then Rachel said, "Thank you for taking the time to speak with us, Lilly."

"Thank you," added Ben-David.

Lilly placed her hand on the door handle and went to say something but then took a slow step back, nodded once, and closed the door.

As they walked down the sidewalk, Ben-David said, "She was telling the truth."

"How do you know?"

"People who are hiding something don't act like that."

"Like what?"

"One, she was in shock, couldn't believe her husband could have done that. Two, she answered our questions and knew she didn't have to." Half a dozen paces later, they were in front of Harriet Mallory's house. Ben-David stopped. "I was surprised by how direct you were with Lilly. You okay?"

"I was surprised myself," Rachel said. "Yeah, I'm fine. Let's see if Harriet remembers my mom."

Ben-David motioned toward the front door. "After you."

13

Rachel Roberts stood facing the barn-red door and waited . . . and waited.

"Ring it again," said Obadiah Ben-David.

She pushed the doorbell and heard it ring inside.

Thirty more seconds passed. Then, she heard the door being unlocked, and seconds later, it was opened.

Immediately, she smelled marijuana as a short, bald man with an enormous belly that stretched his white t-shirt tight stood in front of them. He had black sweatpants on and wore sky-blue-colored Crocs. His eyes were bloodshot, and he squinted at the sun. "Yeah?"

Ben-David took the lead. "Tony Mallory?"

Tony rubbed his right eye. "Yeah?"

"My name is Obadiah Ben-David, and this is Rachel Roberts. I'm a Professional Investigator—"

"Oh, shit, man. I know what it smells like, but you see, she's got—I mean, my mother—she's got a prescription for medical marijuana, and—"

"Tony, I don't care about the weed. It's legal here," said Ben-David, cutting him off. He leaned forward and sniffed. "And, your clothes and body reek of pot, so I don't think that you're eighty-one-year-old mother is the only one who's smoking tree in there."

Tony's eyes shifted back and forth between Rachel and Ben-David. "Uh … Okay." His eyes settled upon Rachel once more. "Who's she?"

"We'll get to that."

"Bruh, I don't recognize her at all. That's all I'm sayin' upfront."

You're sayin' *a lot more than that,* Rachel thought.

Ben-David snapped his fingers. "Tony, we're trying to locate someone who may have lived in this neighborhood many years ago."

Tony blinked his eyes a few times and then looked up at Ben-David. "Right, right."

Rachel pointed at the Cole house. "Do you know Lilly Cole?"

"Aw, no, man, is she the one that's missin'?"

"No," Rachel said. "We just spoke with her a few minutes ago."

Tony ran his hand over his bald head and then started to play with the wispy ponytail coming down from the thin layer of gray hair near the top of his neck. "Good, Good."

"Did you know her late husband, Guy Cole?" asked Ben-David.

"Guy? You bet I did. Like a father to me."

Rachel heard a withered voice from inside say, "Tony, who is it?"

Tony turned and said, "It's nobody, ma. I'll be back in just a sec." He stepped outside and closed the door behind him. "She'll be fine."

"How long did you know Guy?" asked Ben-David.

"Since my junior year in high school. He moved in then. Still remember the night his car pulled up to the driveway. I was in my car with my girlfrie—well, anyway, it was 1987 because I graduated in '88."

Rachel almost laughed at how proud he seemed when he presented the dates.

"'87, huh?" Ben-David said.

"Yes, sir. Seems like yesterday, doesn't it?"

118

Ben-David said, "No." There was silence for a few beats. "Did Guy live alone there?"

Tony laughed. "Oh, ho, ho—no . . . no. Had himself a fine lady. Well, at least until—ah, whatever."

"Until what?" Rachel said.

Tony bit his lower lip.

"Her name Tina?"

His eyes got big. "How in the fuck did you know that?"

She raised her eyebrows.

"Oh, um, sorry for my language. Shit." He slapped his own face. "Aw, man! Sorry."

Ben-David and Rachel met eyes.

She was here, Rachel thought. She gave Tony a quick grin. "So, what happened to Guy and Tina?"

He rubbed both eyes furiously and then flexed both hands twice before feeling his 5 o'clock shadow. "Mom didn't like me going over there, said she didn't trust Guy. You know, greasy lawyer and all that. I don't think she liked him moving into our neighborhood." He paused. "Dad liked him fine, and, like I said, I got tight with him and remained tight." He pointed toward the Cole residence. "And I never had a problem with Lilly. Hit their car once when I was . . . well, they forgave me." He got up on his tiptoes and bounced up and down a few times.

Weed isn't the only thing he's on, Rachel said to herself.

"So, Guy and Tina."

"Yeah, yeah, yeah. Well, they moved into the house, and 'all was well,' you know? There was talk of marriage and all that, and then, one day—" He paused and laughed. "I'm harkening back to my storytelling days. Wrote a screenplay once about a teddy bear that comes alive at night and murders bad-behaving

119

kids—called it 'Deady Bear.' Submitted it to Nicholl way back in the nineties." His eyes drifted to the blazing sky above. "Never made it."

Rachel decided to throw him a bone. *Focusing on writing again* has *to be better than what he's doing now.* "Maybe you should pick up the pen again," she said.

He smoothed his ponytail three times and replied, "That's a fascinating thought."

She touched his sweaty arm. "If you believe in yourself, you should never give up."

He closed his eyes and nodded . . . *like a tortured soul in deep contemplation*, she thought.

Rachel wiped her hand on her shirt. "You said it looked like Guy and Tina were going to get married."

Tony opened his eyes. "Yeah, everyone in the neighborhood thought it was a done deal. I know I did. Then," he said, smacking his palms together, "boom, out of nowhere, she leaves him."

"Leaves him?"

"I'll never forget it. He always left really early for work, like at five a.m. or some nonsense, and so I was a senior in high school and got picked up here by my buddy around eight a.m. As we drove by Guy and Tina's place, Guy's car was gone as usual, but I had my buddy stop the car for a minute. There was a U-Haul in the driveway. At first, I was confused, but then I figured someone, maybe a family member, was dropping something off. My mind was put at ease when Tina came out the front door, saw me in the passenger seat of my buddy's car, and waved at me." He paused, scratching his nuts and snorting before shaking his head as if to get water out of his ears. "Anyway, I waved back, and we sped out of there because, as usual, I was late for school." He laughed and then bounced up and down on his tiptoes again. "I got home that night after football practice and saw that Guy's car was back in the driveway. Didn't think any more about it. Then, like a week later or something, I decided to skip school. So, I'm walking by his house and think, 'Whoa, what's his car doin' there?' because it's nine in the morning. Then, I realized I hadn't seen Tina all week, which was weird because she was always outside—taking a walk, jogging, or visiting with one of the neighbors. I mean, she and my mom weren't close, but they'd say hi now and then on the sidewalk." He laughed to himself while raising his arms and pointing his two index fingers directly at his ears; he started to move his fingers in circles. "Gettin' off track again. Ahem. So, I walked over and knocked on Guy's door. He used to buy pot from me once every couple of months, so we knew each other. Well, he opens the door, and he is rough. I mean, rough— unshaven, half a bottle of Jack in his hand, eyes that—" He laughed. "—kind of look like mine right now." He suddenly straightened up and jerked a thumb back at the door. "Second-hand Mary Jane from mom earlier. No, no, no, she's got a prescription."

"Tony," Ben-David said, looking down and leaning toward him, "What did Guy say?"

"Man, you're powerful," Tony said, inching away. "You, like, scare the shit out of me and stuff."

Ben-David took a step toward him.

"All right, all right, I'll get to the point. Guy invited me in and poured me a glass of Jack. His house was a mess. Garbage everywhere, broken dishes and wine glasses on the floor . . . like he had thrown them against the wall or somethin'." He exhaled. "Anyway, he sat in his easy chair, and I plopped on the couch. After a few sips of old number seven, he told me she left him for another dude. I asked him, 'Who?' He said that he had spent the last three days searching for her because she had only left him a short note, telling him that she was leaving him. He eventually got smart, checked with the U-Haul company, and tracked her down."

She leaves my dad for Guy and then leaves Guy for someone else within three years, Rachel thought. This made her even more angry, and she asked, "Do you know the man's name?" She felt Ben-David's reassuring hand on her shoulder. It felt good, safe. She needed it.

"Sure do," said Tony. "He had such a unique name, didn't think I'd ever forget it. And I didn't. Then, he got famous, and I knew I wouldn't forget it." He paused. "Hey, you know what? You never did tell me who it was that was missing."

Rachel steeled herself and said in a matter-of-fact way, "The missing person is Tina Haines, Tony."

He snapped his fingers. "Got it. Makes sense."

"Why do you say that?" asked Ben-David.

"Because of what I'm about to tell you. After she left Guy for Mister Famous, I never saw any pictures of Tina with him. I mean, I got it: She was moving up by leaving Guy for him, but they must have broken up soon after she left Guy. I don't know where she went. No one does. Interesting that you've come here to look for her because here is where the trail went cold for our neighborhood. Mister 'The Universe Is Mine' has been married for a long time now, so who knows where Tina ended up." He laughed. "As soon as I say his name, you won't believe who she left Guy for." He raised his eyebrows. "Ready?"

They waited.

"Ladies and gentlemen, the man Tina left my neighbor and close friend Guy Cole for was Andre Kurt Andreas."

14

Rachel Roberts felt the relief of the SUV's air conditioning system as cool air blew through the vents and touched the perspiration on her face. Obadiah Ben-David pulled the vehicle into the Starbucks parking lot and left to pick up the drinks that Rachel had ordered through the app on her phone. As she watched him disappear inside, she took out her phone and continued to Google Tina Haines and Andre Kurt Andreas.

It had been fifteen minutes since they had left Tony Mallory, and, surprisingly, in all that time, she had found nothing connecting her mother to the man *People* magazine had deemed "The Outlaw of Silicon Valley" when he had appeared on its cover in 1995. She learned from his Wikipedia page that Andre Kurt Andreas, who now went by just "Kurt," had no children but had married Kethryn Pappas in 1989. Under the "Personal" tab, other marriages or affairs were not mentioned. Kethryn's nickname was Kitty, and she was the CEO of the non-profit humanitarian (food and medicine to third world countries) and philanthropic (books for underprivileged kids) wings of A. Andreas Enterprises, which Kurt had founded in 1982. There was only a scattering of pictures of Kitty on the internet over the years. She seemed to be of medium height, was extremely voluptuous, and had black hair. She was wearing oversized sunglasses in most pictures and only photographed from a distance. From her past twenty years in the wealthy Lakeview subdivision, and from what she had written about in her novels, she knew that people changed names, got plastic surgery, and started life over. Hence, she couldn't rule out the possibility that Kitty Andreas was her mother.

Tony had said that Guy wanted to win Tina back and that he had helped him search for her after she had left Guy for Kurt. However, compared to Andre Kurt Andreas, they were both so far out of their league that neither of them could even gain access to the Country Club he belonged to, let alone get past the manned front gate of his house. Their most elaborate ruse had been when Guy rented a limousine and high-end tuxedos, which he and Tony had dressed up in— Tony, the driver, and Guy, the high-powered Attorney-at-Law. Tony had told the gate guard that lawyer H. John Kirenhouse, Guy's alias, had a meeting with Mr. Andreas. The man called the mansion from his guard house, and Guy had the limo speed off. *"Somehow, man, he was able to let her go. Then, he met Lilly, and life was good. We never talked about Tina again. Uh, why do you want to find her?"* And Ben-David had said, *"She's an old friend of mine."* Tony had nodded approvingly, and Ben-David had asked, *"Any idea of how she and Mr. Andreas had met?"* After Tony had said, *"Naw. That's the thing! Guy never found out how they even met!"* they thanked him and left.

So, Rachel thought while looking out the passenger's side window, *either my mom changed her name to Kethryn Pappas and married Kurt, becoming Kitty Andreas . . . or she and Kurt broke up within a year of meeting each other, and she disappeared without a trace.*

Her phone beeped. It was a text from Topaz.

You still alive out there in the desert of dreams? Again, beware of fake figures who are in abundance! Know you've got the big guy with you, but you're still naïve as hell, Cannon. I may be a proud East Coast elite, but almost everyone in Tinsel Town is a mirage, darling; when they go to hug you, resist! Because you'll fall right through their arms and land face down on the Walk of Fame. Call me when the occasion presents itself, show stealer.

Ben-David opened the driver's side door, and she closed the text message from Topaz.

He passed the coffees to her while he got in and shut the door. "Any luck?" he asked.

She told him what she had found out about Kurt and Kitty, then said, "I think I know what our move should be after dinner."

He took a sip of coffee. "What's that?"

"Kurt Andreas has a penthouse in New York City and a beach house in Paradise Cove Bluffs, outside of Los Angeles. He also owns a private island named Santa Andreas Island in the Channel Islands off the coast of Santa Barbara. We need to start with the beach house tonight and see if we can talk to Kitty. If they're not there, we try to find out where they are. If it's the island, then we go there. If it is the New York City penthouse, we go there. If it is someplace else, then we travel there."

She picked up her coffee and drank.

"As always, I like your tenacity and optimism," he said. "Now, I'm going to try and balance those with reality." Ben-David leaned back against the leather seat. "Our best bet is the penthouse in New York City, but it's also the farthest away. How do you plan to get us into Paradise Cove Bluffs? This guy is a billionaire, many times over. He makes Artie and Misty Jensen and Saul and Pamela Knight look like paupers. I looked online while waiting for our order— go figure, it wasn't ready yet—and saw that Mister Andreas has friends in high places, including the President of the United States. His beach house looks like it's on a private drive, so not even being a Professional Investigator will get us past the gate." He paused. "The island will be even more difficult." Then, he grinned. "But, I've learned not to underestimate you. And, well, you've been a coder for twenty years. Do you have any contacts in the computer world out here who could help us access the private drive?"

She, of course, did not have any Silicon Valley contacts because she was not a computer coder. What she did have was Topaz Kennedy, who lived in New York City and could have someone check out the penthouse for them. She also had contacts in the entertainment world and, at present, enemies in the Silicon Valley universe because of the threat that A.I. posed to the publishing industry. *"I'm going to blow up the ChatGPT starship, missy; just you wait and see."*

Rachel could certainly text Topaz back and forth over the two-and-a-half-hour drive to L.A., but she had been thinking about something else ever since Tony Mallory had said the name Andre Kurt Andreas.

Life is short. Maybe it's time for me to tell Obadiah who I am. Then, I can talk to Topaz without having to hide anything. She can handle the penthouse, and she'll know someone who can get us through the gate at Paradise Cove Bluffs so that we can access the beach mansion.

In addition to being pals with the leader of the free world, Rachel had learned that Kurt Andreas also maneuvered seamlessly in and out of Hollywood's A-List circles. Most notably, there had been pictures of him walking the red carpet with actors Zachariah Lafontaine, Jessamine Jean Baptiste, and Sir Gentry Hill at various premieres. There had also been a photo of Kurt along with then-Senator Susan Kantor and, at that time, the heir apparent to Scorsese, director Massimo Bergman, who was now the most sought-after director in Hollywood. After her conversation with Topaz a few days ago, she had gone online and read that, according to unnamed Hollywood sources, Bergman was livid when Henri Pascal had come out of retirement to direct Jessamine Jean Baptiste's newest film, *The Baroness of Monterrey*. Shortly after principal photography started, rumors began to circulate that Bergman was trying to submarine the picture from the inside by using his old friend, Sir Gentry Hill. Naturally, when the rumors started, Massimo Bergman issued the statement, *"I have absolutely nothing to do with the rumored difficulties that the film is experiencing because I have no interest in it. I would never direct that type of film."*

Also, there was another item on her mind. Her award-winning audiobook narrator, Suzanne Elise Freeman, lived in Los Angeles. *Sunrise Kama Sutra* would be their final book together after a twenty-year partnership . . . and they had never met. In Rachel's eyes, Freeman had brought Adrienne and her world alive in a way that she had not thought possible, and other than telling Ben-David who she really was, Rachel wanted to meet her legendary narrator and say thank you. She knew from Freeman's interviews and social media profile that she was also a *Star Wars* fan, and so she had always thought that their meeting would be akin to Luke helping Darth Vader take off his mask at the end of *Return of the Jedi*, which was originally titled *Revenge of the Jedi*, but that was another discussion for another time. Anyway, Vader says, *"Luke, help me take this mask off,"* and Luke replies, *"But you'll die."* Vader says, *"Nothing can stop that now. Just for once, let me look on you with my own eyes."*

In a way, Riley Cannon was dying, and Rachel wanted to remove her mask for only a few critical people and look on them as Rachel Roberts, the girl whose mother had abandoned her at two years old and not only survived but became one of the bestselling authors of all time. And, now, as Rachel contemplated her answer to Ben-David's question, she realized that it had been a blessing not to find and confront her mother yet. In the everyday rhythms of life, an argument could be made that in the past three years, no one other than Topaz was closer to her than Ben-David. He didn't even know it yet, but when she had approached him to work on the first case, the murder of Kaj Reynard, he had witnessed her at her most vulnerable. Was she closer physically and emotionally to her husband Stan? Yes. But, spiritually, in the ways that only those who have been knocked down by life and stood back up to face the future would know, Ben-David had a kinship with her that she had with no one else.

Regarding her professional career, she knew there was a special bond between author and narrator that no other creative medium could rival. Even though she had never met Suzanne Elise Freeman, they were tethered by an unbreakable bond that only happens when two artists share the power of words: for Rachel, writing them; for Suzanne, saying them. Had Topaz and J. Rudolph Hightower seen the sentences, paragraphs, dialogue, and chapters in their infancy? Yes. But Freeman, and only Freeman, had seen the five full canvases before anyone else and been a partner and participant in the creative task of making that canvas come to life in the ears and minds of Riley Cannon's readers—and that was something no other artistic duo possessed. Yes, a film had a director who brought a screenplay to life, but he or she had collaborators—they didn't do it alone. For Riley Cannon's fans, there was only Riley and Suzanne. Ms. Cannon wrote the books alone, and Ms. Freeman narrated them in the solitude of her booth. There were no intermediates, no framing of what the reader or listener should experience. There was just the experience.

For two decades, Rachel had opened five emails—one for each novel—from Topaz, saying, "The email stork has just delivered the baby to her second mother." And each time she had received that email, Rachel had teared up, knowing that her friend would now bring the novel to life in her own sublime way but also that the two of them would never meet, would never get to ask each other questions, would never get to stand before each other and say thank you, and, for Rachel, she would never get to tell Suzanne that hearing her performance of that first novel had given her the courage to write the second.

I want to tell Ben-David who I am; he'll keep it to himself, but at least he'll know the real me and the whole truth about why I need to find my mother.

I want to meet Suzanne before the last book comes out. I'll probably never be in L.A. again; this is my chance.

She set her coffee cup down. "I have an idea of how we can visit the beach house in Paradise Cove Bluffs." She paused, butterflies flying in her stomach. "But, for me to tell you my idea, there is something you need to know."

He took a long pull on his coffee, seeming to weigh her words.

How is he going to take this?

Ben-David pulled the coffee cup away from his mouth and swallowed. "Okay. Lay it on me."

"Hold my hand," she said, taking his and placing it between both of hers. The proportion of their hands made it look like a baby was holding an oven mitt.

"Okay."

She met his eyes. *I owe him this.* "Obadiah, I am not now and never have been a computer coder or software engineer. I am a bestselling novelist under the pen name Riley Cannon. *I* mailed you *Dark After Midnight*, and I stood hidden in the woods and watched you open the package at your mailbox that day." She paused. "I have been working on cases with you to get ideas for my novels."

For an entire minute, he just stared at her, not moving a muscle, and she searched his eyes and face, looking for any emotion—anger, surprise, disappointment, joy, anything.

Finally, she broke the silence and said, "Please, say something."

At first, his nostrils flared, and she feared the worst, feeling that she deserved his wrath for lying to him for three years. But, just as she steeled herself, she was surprised to see his mouth break into a wide grin that even exposed his teeth, which she had only seen a few times before.

"What?" she said, smiling back.

He took out his phone, opened the web browser, and then scrolled down the different open pages until he found what he wanted and clicked on it. He showed her.

It was her picture from the back cover of *3 A.M. Phone Call.*

"I know," he said.

129

15

"How long have you known?" Rachel Roberts asked Obadiah Ben-David.

"The night you called me, remember when I said I would call you the next morning?"

"Yes, but that was about the cancer."

"It was, but I was also going to see if you wanted to meet at Darwinger's or The Peninsula Club and catch up. I was even going to bring up my relationship with Tilly on the phone to throw you off. When we met, I was going to tell you about the cancer and then hit you with the theory that Tilly and I had come up with regarding you."

"Why didn't you bring it up before right now?"

"I thought it could wait. Finding your mother was the priority, and Tilly thought you might volunteer some information on our trip, so I just sat back and observed. I'll have to call her tonight and tell her she was right. It was fun sharpening my P.I. sense while seeing if you would give anything away. I also trust you and care for you. I figured that since you hadn't brought it up, there must be a reason you didn't want to talk about it."

"Did I give anything away?" she asked.

"Surprisingly, no. I was even starting to doubt our theory."

"To the 1989 Detroit Pistons," he said. "I almost approached you about it then, but when every P.I. in Michigan had received a copy of the book . . . well, that was a nice touch to make me think twice. Then, at the retirement ceremony at the gas station, your spitfire of an aunt wearing the Detroit Tigers baseball cap . . . Aunt Jackie, was it?"

She nodded, enjoying his presentation of the evidence.

"Yes, well, I got to talking to Tilly about it, and she knows everything about the book world, and she showed me a picture of Topaz Kennedy and then played me a YouTube clip of her at a book launch party. My eyes lit up because I could never forget her eyes and her voice." He paused. "She's your agent, right?"

Again, Rachel nodded. "No one in the world like her."

"Now. Here's my question for you: Did you ever ghostwrite—"

She playfully raised an eyebrow.

"Yeah, I'm gettin' the lingo down." They shared a laugh. "Did you ever ghostwrite any of Judge Macy Ashberry's books? Remember when Tilly and I thought the Judge's style in her later books was similar to Riley Cannon's?" And now he raised both of his eyebrows. "Well, Miss Cannon?"

Of course, I did. But I cannot speak about it because of the arrangement. "Now, that is a most interesting theory," she said and then winked. "Keep digging."

Ben-David started the vehicle, and they were soon on CA-111N headed to Los Angeles. They talked for an hour about the writing life, publishing, and how Rachel had kept her identity secret. Ben-David had asked her about how she had met Ryan, and she had told him it was during the decade when she had disappeared. He had asked her if Christine Harper knew who she was, and Rachel had told him no; Christine still thought Rachel was a boring computer coder. She had then asked him if Christine had ever asked him or Tilly about Rachel, and he had said no.

She had told him about why she had re-emerged to write *Dark After Midnight* after disappearing for ten years and that, yes, working the two cases with Ben-David had helped her finish the past two books—*"What if you would have died?"* he had yelled—and, yes, she needed to meet and confront her mother before she could finish the last book in the series and say goodbye to Adrienne Astra forever. Ben-David had said, *"You know that Tilly is going to try and talk you out of it. Adrienne is her all-time favorite character. Truth be told, she's one of mine too."* That comment had put a smile on her face but had also led to her explanation that as difficult as it would be, the time was right to bid farewell to the character who had kept her alive for the past twenty years. *"You're not going to kill her, are you?"* Ben-David had asked. She had only shrugged and heard him say, *"Hey, you can't use my shrug technique against me for such a pivotal piece of information."*

Now, after introducing Topaz to Obadiah—*"Good evening, ma'am."*—and Obadiah to Topaz—*"About time I met the big guy for real! Maybe you can talk some sense into this woman about not retiring . . . You don't want to see the series end, too? See, Cannon? You can't do it! Thanks for looking after this special scribe for me, Mister Stane. Hmph!"*—Rachel was still on the phone going over the plan for the evening with her high-strung agent.

"Yes, darling, know all about Kurt. Did you know that his mega-yacht is named *Blue Kurty*? Well, it is, Cannon. But, you see, 'blue' also means 'dirty.' So, *Dirty Kurty* is what he's really going for on that one, and I must say, it fits him to a T—slime ball. Sorry, dearie, I know he may be your stepfather, but I've never been a fan of "The Outlaw of Silicon Valley." Ridiculous. Of course, with the way A.I. is seeping into the publishing fabric, I might need an outlaw right now as an ally. So, stand by, I guess. I may love Dirty Kurty by the morning hours."

"Topaz, can someone check out his penthouse for us?"

"Of course, darling. I'll have one of my pigeons fly over as soon as we're off the phone. Shouldn't take more than fifteen minutes to have an answer for you. I'm already having him run an errand for me concerning my rival Ms. Aya Gunner

. . . No, no, can't tell you about it. This is war, Cannon. I haven't given up on trying to lure you back with another three-book deal for Adrienne. If *Star Wars* can go from six to nine films, so can your series! I know you're a big fan, so I'm hitting you where it hurts, quill warrior. But—" Rachel heard ice cubes clinking in a glass, followed by a liquid being poured. "—I'm getting off track . . . or maybe I wasn't—isn't Freeman a big *Star Wars* fangirl too? Anyway, you really want to meet her tonight, huh?"

"I do."

"Can't say that I blame you, miss. Okay, I'll set it up. You'll be dining at Musso and Frank, my favorite restaurant in Hollywood. In 1927, John Mosso and his partner bought the place from Joseph Musso and Frank Toulet. Musso and Frank, get it, love? Anyhow, I've been friends with John Mosso's three granddaughters—Anne, Cathy, and Kristen—for years. Cathy's son, Mark, whom I'm particularly fond of, is the general manager. Ha! He's been asking me who Riley Cannon is for twenty years. If he's there tonight, don't dare tell him who you are, darling! I'll call Suzanne and tell her she'll be dining with someone special this evening. I'll make a reservation for four—you, Oba-wonderful, Suzanne, and her husband Scott . . . Ooo! I hope he shows up! Why? Because he knows Shawn Fabulous Frost, and he may have some fresh gossip about *The Baroness of Monterrey* for us. Have your giant P.I. probe him for the goods—he's got to know something! This is going to be perfect. Are you sure you can't postpone a few hours so I can join?"

"Topaz—"

"Right, the whole 'mom' thing. I get it, love. And I am sorry that you haven't had more success, but if Kitty Andreas ends up being your mother, I may give up scotch." Rachel heard her take a drink. *She sounds a little more upbeat since last I spoke with her. No tears yet. I wonder how she's doing, though.* "Ahhh. Just pulling your leg, of course. I could never part with my nightly victory lap. Oh, speaking of drinks, since you have made Adrienne such an expert on the subject over the years, make sure to get a martini from the bar tonight. You'll thank me later. Okay, I'll call you when I hear back about the penthouse. If they are not there, I have someone in mind who can help us access Paradise Cove Bluffs. Talk soon, and tell that large hunk of granite driving the bus, 'Welcome to the family.'"

She hung up, and Ben-David and Rachel resumed their discussion about Rachel's life since 2005 when her first novel had come out.

Twenty-five minutes later, Topaz called back.

"Penthouse is darker than Gotham at night, child. No one there except for the security guard. So, we move on to the beach estate and then, if need be, the island, correct?"

"Yes, Topaz."

"Okay, then I guessed right. First, the dinner reservation at Musso and Frank has been made for seven p.m. tonight. Freeman has no idea who she's meeting, and it sounds like she'll be bringing Sir Scott with her, so get your P.I. warmed up to ask him some questions. Second, I was a few minutes late getting back to you because I've already found a way for you to access the beach house. I called my old friend, David Killian, and he has arranged for his private limo to pick you and Obadiah up at your hotel at 9 p.m. He said it takes about an hour to get from the hotel to Paradise Cove Bluffs, and 10 p.m. in L.A. is still early, according to Killy. He said, 'No time is too late for David Killian's limousine.' What a character!"

"Will he be riding with us?"

"He didn't say."

"Well, please thank him for us, and it will be nice to meet him if he is in the limo."

"He's a charmer, that one; I almost dated him twenty years ago. Anyway, hush-hush, but he's also helping me with my Aya Gunner situation. The man has pull, and the man gets things done. What can I say? To you, Killy." Rachel heard liquid slosh and ice cubes clink against Topaz's glass. "Oh, almost forgot, retiring writer—if the beach house is a bust tonight, then Killy's tech friend, Abraham Raines, has his own mega-yacht that can take you over to Santa Andreas Island. What a prick that Kurt is, naming the island after himself. Well, anyway, if Kurt Andreas is the outlaw of Silicon Valley, then Abraham Raines is the sheriff. You've heard of him, of course?"

"Yes. Top dog in the tech sector right now."

"Naturally, darling. I'd only get you the best. Well, he's Killy's friend, and I gave him hell about it since Raines is on record for saying that his upcoming generative A.I. program could revolutionize the publishing world. Revolutionize? More like demolish! But, he has a yacht, and there you have it, lass. Oh, his yacht's name is just as preposterous as Kurt's. She's named *Abe Eye*. Get the play on words, Cannon? Ugh. Men and their bloody toys. Oh, and he also claims to be an environmentalist! Does he not think people know about his yacht?"

"Thank you, Topaz. Hopefully, I'll get my answers at the beach house tonight."

"I hope you do. Seriously, my child, I want you to find her and take care of whatever you need to take care of."

"I know you do, and it means a lot."

"Of course it does; it's coming from *me*. Now, there's one more piece of business to attend to, and I just thought of it." Topaz cleared her throat, and Rachel heard the ice cubes and liquid swish together again. "Since you've let your hubby, your P.I. friend, and are going to let Freeman know who you are, why not let the whole world know when the next book comes out? You notice I said *next* and not *last*."

"That's a definite no."

"Please, dear, hear me out."

Like I had a choice, Rachel thought while smiling. "I'm turning on the speakerphone for this part."

"Wonderful! The big fellow will be in love with my plan—er, *idea*."

Ben-David tapped his fingers on the steering wheel and said, "Let's hear it."

"It's a firecracker of an idea. Here's why. The media will eat it up—all the usual heavies—but especially your beloved *Detroit Free Press* and *Detroit News*. I'll have you on every single talk show, morning show, late-night program, major podcast, etc. We'll book you for a talk at every major bookstore worldwide— you'll single-handedly save the brick-and-mortar empire. Your image will never be tarnished once you have them in your debt. They'll love you forever, and sales will be beyond anything we ever imagined."

"And you would retain all of your clients."

"They'd be stupid not to stay with me! Anyway, hush-hush, ma'am. You've made your point, and, yes, I am thinking about how nicely it would set me up, but if my plan with Killy works, then I won't need to count on you going public with who you are, which I know you are leaning toward not doing.

"Of course, once you go public with who you are, the actors and directors attached to the films made of your novels will all want to vacation with you— Affleck, Clooney, Vergara, Egojo, Kasdan . . . everybody. Of course, you'll invite me too—package deal, miss."

"Topaz—"

"Don't you *Topaz* me right now, sweet Cannon; I'm on a roll."

Ben-David opened his eyes wide.

Rachel mouthed to him, *"Right?"*

"Here comes the kicker. We sell you and your life story to Hollywood. I've got it all worked out. Bogdanovich—God rest his sweet, talented soul—and I spoke about this very thing years ago when he was directing *Enemies in the Evening*. The stuff of your life is too good of a yarn to pass up! And I have insider information from Killy. Apparently, Emma Clarke said she would be interested in playing Riley Cannon if a film was ever made. Obadiah Jeff Bridges as your partner in crime when we get to that part of the film, right? And playing me? Get a load of this. Cate Blanchett. Naturally, I told Killy that no one could play me but *me*. But did you see Ms. Blanchett play Katherine Hepburn in *The Aviator*? She *is* me, darling!" She paused.

Rachel couldn't deny that the Hollywood angle intrigued her, but what she was thinking about right now was what would happen in Hampstead once it was known who she really was. She could see Baby Lloyd Darwinger showing up at her front door, offering security assistance. Then, there would be either Kevin Shelby or Corey Ritter, or both men, claiming, *"I've known it for years,"* to the local and national press members who would, no doubt, descend upon Hampstead.

Topaz jumped back into her plan, interrupting Rachel's thoughts. "Now, the drawbacks—one, your alma mater, Bryn Mawr, *Lord alive!* will that university's administration come a-callin' for big bucks from you; two . . . well, you already know about troublesome number two, don't you? Loss of privacy that you'll never get back in exchange for actual celebrity status and more bread than you or dear Stan can spend in your lifetimes or the lifetimes of your children. A Faustian bargain, if ever there was, Cannon. And Obadiah agrees with everything I just said!"

Ben-David went to answer but then stopped.

"As Sir John Falstaff once said, 'And so ends my catechism.' Now, think about what I have said, and give that audiobook goddess a hug for me, and see what you can find out about that film! I need details. Oba-marvelous, thank you for your support."

The phone call ended.

Rachel stared out the front window, thoughts marching across her mind as soldiers headed into battle.

"Wow. She is a force of nature. You okay?" Ben-David asked.

Topaz had forced her to consider what would happen if Rachel opened Pandora's box. *What if everyone knew who I was?* She thought of her mother. It could be true that she did not want anyone to know who she really was. *Am I like her in that way? Or am I a coward for hiding? Should I not be afraid to embrace who I am? But, this is my last book . . . or is it?*

She glanced at Ben-David. "I'm hanging in there. She just cannot accept the fact that I'm retiring."

"Don't be mad at me, but I'm not too keen on the idea either."

"I know. What did you think about what she said about me going public?"

Ben-David ran his hand over his smooth head. "Some decent arguments for doing it, I'll give her that. But, Rachel—and I know you know this—once you go public, there is no going back. You'll lose your privacy forever."

"I don't know if I'll ever be ready to give that up—not only for me but for Stan and our future children." She bit her lower lip. "She didn't even bring up estate writing."

"What's that?"

"In short, it's a way to protect and continue an author's legacy after he or she dies. For example, I could establish an estate for Riley Cannon before I die. I'd put Stan in charge of it, and he would work with an agent—Topaz if she were still alive—and they could decide to hire a writer to continue my Adrienne Astra series."

"So, your character would live on, and your family would get a cut of the new book's sales?"

Rachel rolled her eyes. "Exactly."

"Pretty good deal for your family and your fans, but it sounds like you're not in favor of it."

"I was fine with what Topaz did for *The Blue Hour Sanction*, but I don't want the character of Adrienne Astra to be written by anyone else after I'm gone."

"You don't think that author would be interested?"

"No. He likes writing stand-alone novels."

Ben-David nodded.

"Plus, I planned for Adrienne to have a specific character arc when I planned the six-book series. Any books with her in them after that will diminish her and dilute the series. No violation of art is greater than a series that has overstayed its welcome."

"All about money, isn't it?"

"That and holding on to the past, pretending it still exists."

"There's an argument to be made for wanting more of what you like."

"And there's the suspension of disbelief."

"Most people, maybe even me, can't handle pondering the realities of life. Fiction is like macaroni and cheese; we prefer it over reality after a long day of work, and you can never have enough macaroni and cheese."

"I don't think we'll run out of fiction."

"But we'll soon run out of Adrienne Astra stories, won't we?"

"Every story has an ending, or else it's not a real story."

"Kind of like life."

"That's why we're out here, right?"

Ben-David nodded. "Did you ever think about what would have happened if Adrienne's story had ended before you came back to write the final three books?"

"When I wrote *Dark After Midnight*, I rediscovered an old friend. I never knew how much I needed her, and I felt guilty for abandoning her for those ten years. I even wondered what those years would have been like if I had stuck with her." Her eyes became glassy. "Adrienne Astra was the only person who never left me. Even after I ignored her for a decade, she welcomed me back with open arms and was ready to go for books four, five, and six."

Ben-David reached over and gave her hand a quick squeeze. "I'm going to ask you something, okay?" He grinned. "But, remember, I'm an insider now."

She wiped her eyes and grinned back at him. "I'm ready."

"Let's say that you're going to hang everything up after this book. No future estate writers, etc."

She nodded in agreement.

"Are you going to kill Adrienne? That would be one way to ensure that no one ever writes her character again, even though you and I both know that writers have brought their characters back from some pretty amazing circumstances." He paused. "Or, are you going to go for the ride-off-into-the-sunset ending?"

"A lot depends on how the search for my mother goes. However, whether Adrienne dies in the book or not, neither I nor anyone else will ever write her character again. Because of that, there is a part of me that will die with her, but that will be a celebration."

"A celebration?"

"Yes. I'll be fine going on without her. And I think fans will, too. There will be other Adrienne Astras. In fact, we all already have our 'Adrienne Astras' that help us get through life—playing sports, playing video games, going to the movies, reading books, having season tickets to our favorite sports teams or performing arts . . . anything that we can count on to help us escape." She looked out at the marvelous desert landscape. "With the number of books and streaming shows coming out now, instantly available at the touch of a button, there will be plenty of Adrienne Astras."

Ben-David held the steering wheel between his knees and gave her a few polite claps before returning his hands to the wheel. "Bravo, maestro. Whatever happens in the end, it will be one hell of a ride. But, let me give you one last thing to chew on."

"I'm listening."

He became solemn, almost wistful. "If this old battered heart of mine and the twisted path that my life has taken to get me where I am today has taught me anything, it is that if you say never, make sure you mean *never*. If there is even a fraction of a doubt, then don't say it."

I will miss her, yet I'm not sure she'll ever be completely gone. As usual, he's right. Never, like forever, is for a very, very long time. "Thanks," she said. "I am certain that the next few days will bring everything into focus."

"I'll be right here with you."

"I know."

He tapped his fingers on the steering wheel again. "Speaking of never, do you think Topaz will ever retire?"

"I don't see it happening. She's the kind of person whose work *is* her life."

"Do you think she's happy?"

"I don't know. I hope so, but I've never seen her quite like this. She feels threatened."

Ben-David gave a quick grin. Rachel thought that it was one of experience and acceptance. "I think everyone over fifty feels that," he said.

"Do you miss your job?"

He smiled. "What do you mean? I'm working right now. Every time I think I'm retired, we get a new case together."

"You know what I'm saying."

He met eyes with her. "I do," he said. "And the answer is, yes, I miss it. It gave me purpose, kept me focused, and distracted me from thinking too much about how sad life can be and how little of it we actually control. To your point, I think work can be an 'Adrienne Astra' for many people. That's why so many of us struggle in retirement. If I had to guess, I'd bet that behind the evening scotch on the rocks and the adrenaline she feels from inserting herself into the middle of the latest publishing battle, Topaz is scared, just like the rest of us. And, as I learned before meeting you and finding companionship with Tilly, you miss things when work becomes too big a part of your life—important things."

"I don't want to miss those things."

"You won't." There was silence for a few minutes. "So, where to?" he asked.

"The hotel first," she said and then filled him in on the rest of the plan.

141

"Are you sure you want me at the fancy restaurant tonight? I know your agent wants me to see what I can find out about the film that is supposedly in trouble, but I want to make sure you have your protected time with your narrator."

And that is why you are going with me tonight, she thought. He was always considerate of her feelings and never assumed anything, even when it might be convenient. She thought of his cancer and hoped that nothing more would come of it. He deserved a happy life with Tilly.

Then, she thought of her father. He deserved a happy life with my mom, and she took it away.

She gave Ben-David's arm a quick pat. "You're coming with me tonight. And, now, since you know my financial situation, we will get ourselves appropriate outfits for Musso and Frank. I know you're not big on charity, but this is non-negotiable. My treat. Besides," she said, grinning, "I know that I did not pack anything dressy, and I'm assuming you didn't either."

Keeping his left hand on the steering wheel, he rubbed his beard with his right hand. "Pretty safe assumption."

"Good. It's settled. Now, give me your sizes, and I'll have the clothes delivered to the hotel. One way or another, it will be an interesting evening."

16

Musso & Frank Grill, Los Angeles

The inside of the Musso & Frank Grill throbbed with old-world charm and Hollywood lore. Red leather booths, glowing white table cloths, polished silverware, crisp, folded napkins, understated lighting from sophisticated brass wall fixtures, custom-crafted oak paneling, and lush, wine-red carpet. Yes, Romanoff's, owned and operated by his royal highness Michael Romanoff, had been king from 1941 to 1962, but the restaurant that Rachel Roberts now found herself in had stood the test of time. From the moment that she followed Obadiah Ben-David through the front door, she felt transported back in time: a time when men wore tailored suits and Fedoras, and star actresses—some with smooth, ebony skin and others with golden tans—were all covered with exquisite dresses and had glamorous jewelry on their fingers and around their necks and wrists, showcasing hairdos that looked like the ladies had just left the salon; a time of cigarette cases and lighters made of silver and of orange glows, lighting the white sticks and beautiful smoke rising to the ceiling, shrouding their owners in mystique, class, and gravitas; a time of simplicity, inside and out—a flow of warmth and friendship and rivalry inside and a temperate, street-lit atmosphere of possibility on the outside, rimmed in natural Californian beauty. Every breakfast, luncheon, and dinner was a spectacular gathering of wealth, talent, and immense power and influence—denizens of high society and the sometimes superficial world they orbited. The building was a beacon of spotlight and glamor, marking the dwelling where Tinseltown royalty had gathered in all of its lavish splendor for over a hundred years. Musso and Frank Grill had not changed, but it had welcomed change as Hollywood slowly evolved into a more open, welcoming, and diverse institution.

As soon as she entered the vibrant establishment, she heard the murmur of voices, the clinking of glasses in the bar, and the sizzle of whatever was being grilled. The smell alone made Rachel's mouth water and her stomach rumble. She both yearned for a rich steak and thirsted for a glass of red wine, but that would be after a cocktail.

As her eyes drifted to the bar, she saw the unmistakable tall and lithe form of Suzanne Elise Freeman walking toward her, wearing tan-colored heels and a short, red summer dress. Her famous audiobook narrator's eyes said, *"It's you. I cannot believe that you're here."* Rachel hoped that her own eyes said, *"It's you. Twenty years. I cannot believe that I'm here."* She smiled and stepped forward to embrace her.

Rachel wore straw sandals with a sky-blue cocktail dress, and behind her, Ben-David wore polished brown oxfords, tan pants, a white collared shirt, and a navy blazer. She had never seen him dressed up before, and she thought he cleaned up nicely. When their clothes had arrived at the hotel, Ben-David had called her from his room and said, *"Do you know how much this all costs?"* She had replied, *"Yes. You're worth it. Now get dressed. We're going to have a wonderful dinner."*

Her eyes were glassy as her arms went around Suzanne's slim and athletic form.

Twenty years . . . why didn't we do this sooner?

Suzanne whispered in her ear, "I can't believe this is happening."

She whispered back, "Right? How did you know to look for me?"

"Topaz called two minutes ago and told me who I was meeting here tonight; she said there'd be a guy with you. When you walked through the door, I knew it was you." She pulled her head back and stared down at Rachel's face. "Pretty damned close to the dust jacket pictures."

They parted, both now with glassy eyes, and Rachel introduced Suzanne to Obadiah.

After their warm handshake, Suzanne moved in close to Rachel and said, "Bodyguard?" and Rachel responded, "No, he's a P.I. Long story."

Suzanne nodded, and then Rachel observed her shift her gaze to two men speaking at the end of the legendary bar in the new room. Knowing that Suzanne's husband, Scott Brick, would accompany her, Rachel surmised he was one of the men. She would have recognized his face with his signature eyewear, goatee, and welcoming smile, but the men were facing away from her. While her romance with Ryan in Key West had been in full bloom, she had thought of writing an adventure novel set there with a Bogart-like hero and believed Brick would be the perfect choice to narrate it. Then, things had ended with Ryan, and she hadn't thought of that novel until right now.

"Is . . . that . . . Scott?" Rachel asked.

Suzanne met eyes with Rachel for a second, and then Rachel followed Suzanne's eyes as they tiptoed back across the room to the bar where the two men were now leaning over the gleaming oak top, the light reflecting off the honeycombed glass cabinet door.

Suzanne gave a polite smile. "Yes, the taller one is indeed my husband."

Rachel watched as her famous audiobook narrator studied the two men with discerning eyes.

"Who is he with?"

Suzanne pursed her lips and then gave a playful eye roll. "Shawn Frost."

Topaz would flip!

At the sound of his name, she was immediately transported back to her conversation with Topaz earlier in the day—*"Now, give that audiobook goddess a hug for me, and see what you can find out about that film! I need details."*—and then she remembered when her agent had called her in a panic years ago and said, *"Well, thespian, Killy, Freeman, and I just incinerated the video game deal . . . No, no, we did everything we could to see it through. It's the god-awful video game company! Leeches! Don't worry, though; we'll have them* crawling *back to us. Patience is power in* this *game . . . Of course, darling, Frost and Freeman are still onboard."*

"You're kidding me," Rachel said, studying the men.

Just as Shawn had turned enough for Rachel to recognize his face, he bolted upright from his slouch and started gesturing wildly—hands as stabbing weapons, crisscrossing in mid-air, then karate chops on an invisible enemy—before putting a conspiratorial arm around Scott and saying something directly into his ear. Now, Rachel had a straight-on side view of the men.

Scott took a drink from his martini glass and shrugged. Shawn registered the gesture and moved away again, shaking his head back and forth. Then, leaning forward, he clasped his hands in the classic "begging" posture. Rachel thought she could make out Scott's reply, "I don't know."

"Have you ever met Shawn?" Suzanne asked.

"Um, no," Rachel said. "Since the video game deal fell through, I haven't heard anything about him other than the new film he's staring in with Jessamine Jean Baptiste. My agent is still enamored with him, though." She smiled. "Almost as much as she is with you. Part of the hug I just gave you was from her."

146

"I *love* her," Suzanne said, giving her arm a friendly pat and squeeze. "Shawn and I are ready when the time comes. Let's go to our booth and order drinks. I'm sure Scott will be over shortly."

Ben-David said, "I'll join you both soon. I'm going to use the restroom and then say hi to the guys."

"Take your time, Obadiah," said Suzanne, "this lady and I have some catching up to do." She winked. "But don't let Shawn drag Scott out of here, okay?"

He grinned, said, "I'll see what I can do," and stepped off toward the back of the restaurant.

The hostess, waiting patiently next to Rachel and Suzanne, seemed to register the shift in attention and motioned the women toward the old room, where everything had been preserved since its construction in 1934.

"Topaz reserved us the famed Charlie Chaplin booth," Suzanne said as they followed the hostess.

Rachel's eyes sparkled at the information. In her hotel room, she had researched the renowned restaurant and wondered why she had never had Adrienne Astra meet someone there. *Perhaps that will change when I get back home and write the end of the book,* she thought.

The famous Charlie Chaplin booth was the most requested in the fabled restaurant. The booth was where Chaplin had consumed lunch daily and the only booth in the restaurant with a window. Apparently, Chaplin would horse race people, usually Rudolph Valentino, every day down the dirt road from his studio to Musso & Frank, and the loser would have to buy lunch. He and his lunch companion would sit in the window booth so that they could see their horses.

As they continued across the old room, every fixture and every piece of décor seemed to ooze with Hollywood tradition and echo of celebrity moments. As the manager had once said of the faded wallpaper that bordered the ceiling and the paneling above the booths and had never been changed, *"It's got Humphrey Bogart's cigar smoke up there."*

Just before the bar had disappeared from her sight, Rachel had taken in one last view of the men. Shawn was using his left index finger to tick off fingers on his right hand; Scott was nodding, raising his own glass to take a drink. Rachel said, "What do you think Scott and Shawn were talking about?"

Suzanne turned her head around and raised her eyebrows. "God only knows."

* * *

"And then, Brickie," Shawn Frost said, ticking off the middle finger of his right hand, "she disappears. Poof! Gone."

"Where did she go?" Scott Brick replied.

"That's the thing! She hasn't returned," Frost said. He exhaled while closing his eyes. "I might be next." He reached for Brick's martini.

"No," Brick said, sliding the glass away from him. The veteran audiobook narrator surveyed the bar and restaurant. "Where in the hell is Jo?"

"In New York for the weekend."

"Then I'm calling Killy."

"No, no, no. He'll blow his top."

"You're not even supposed to be *in a bar.*"

"I'm fallin' apart, man." He inched closer to Brick. "Somebody on that set wants me dead. I know it. Could be Pascal, could be Sir Gentry Hill, could be Zachariah Lafontaine, and it could be Massimo Bergman. I know he made his public statement and all, but the truth is *he's pissed* that he didn't get offered a chance to direct the film."

"Shawn. This. Is. Nuts. No one kidnapped Jessamine Jean Baptiste. She's the biggest draw in Hollywood."

"They did. I bet she's dead. And now they're after me. They're after *everybody*."

Brick took a drink and placed it on the bar, perhaps a bit too hard, as the bartender gave the men an apprehensive glance. "Who in the fuck are *they*, Shawn?"

A glass fell behind the bar and shattered on the floor. Seconds later, Shawn Frost was in Brick's lap, saying, "They're coming in through the windows!"

Brick gently sat Frost back down on his bar stool, Frost's eyes wide with fear. "There's no one after you, okay?"

Then, as soon as Brick had returned to his own stool, Frost leaned over, hugged him, and whispered, "Sorry, Brickie. You're the only one I could trust. I need to leave. Can't bring you into this."

"Shawn, wait a minute," Brick said.

Then, he observed Frost's face turn ghost-white, and Brick turned around. At the far end of the bar was a giant, bald man with an enormous gray beard wearing a white shirt and blazer walking toward them.

Brick twisted his head back at Frost, who said, "My. God. They've sent Obadiah Stane to eliminate me. Look! He's staring straight at me! Can you take him?"

"What?"

"Can we both take him?"

"You're out of your mind, man. We're not touching that guy!"

"He's gonna . . . Take. Me. Out. I know it." Frost swiveled his head back and forth—looking at the giant, looking at the exit, looking at the giant, looking at the exit—"I've gotta get out of here . . . good luck, dear brother."

And with that, playwright-turned-audiobook-narrator-turned-film-actor Shawn Frost dashed out of Musso and Frank Grill.

149

Brick took a sip of his martini and let it meander in his mouth for a few seconds. He swallowed, then reached into his jacket pocket and pulled out his cell phone.

Just as he was about to dial David Killian, he heard, "Scott?"

Brick looked up from his phone. It was the giant. *Hell, maybe Shawn was—*

"My name is Obadiah—"

SHIT!

"—Ben-David, and I just met Suzanne a few minutes ago. I'm here with her friend, and they're in the old room waiting for us." He sat down on the stool that Shawn Frost had vacated. "But, I thought we'd have a drink before joining them." He reached out his hand, and Brick shook it. "What are you having? I'm a scotch man, myself. This round is on me."

"Thank you, sir." Brick tipped back his glass and finished his drink. "In every other gin joint in the world, I have bourbon, but in here, it's a Ketel One martini up." He pointed to a carafe in a container filled with shaved ice on the bar next to his martini glass. "Keeps my dividend ice cold." Brick picked up the carafe and refilled his glass.

"Gin joint, huh? *Casablanca* fan?"

Brick grinned. "The greatest film ever made."

"We could use a few more Ricks in this world."

Brick toasted him and drank.

Ben-David waved the bartender over and ordered the drinks. Then, he looked into Brick's eyes, gave him a mischievous grin, and asked, "Where was Shawn Frost headed in such a hurry?"

Brick raised his eyebrows and gave a few quick shakes of his head. "I don't know where in the fuck he was going."

* * *

The old room had a more intimate and romantic vibe. The booths were fixed in size, so you could only fit three or four people in them—very conducive to conversation and privacy. The row of chairs that lined the counter—where, in the center, the grill chef cooked gigantic pieces of meat on a charcoal grill—gave that section an elevated diner feel, one of common touch, patrons taking a break for a meal and then going back to work on the current picture or project. A few booths down from them was the Marilyn Monroe booth, and at the far end of the row of booths was a telephone booth paneled in oak that had housed the first public telephone in Hollywood—there had been people actually married in that booth. Farther back, there were two more phone booths; one, in particular, had been made famous as Johnny Depp had taken a call from his agent in it and been notified of his first acting job.

"I cannot believe I am finally meeting you after all of these years," Suzanne said, taking a sip of her sazerac. She had explained to Rachel that it was the drink she had ordered on her first date with Brick at Musso and Frank and that ever since that first date, she had continued the tradition, always making it the first drink of the evening.

Rachel took a sip of her martini and then said, "I can't believe we're meeting either." Then, pointing to the far room beyond the booths, she said, "Who knows what kind of books I could have given you to perform if I had spent some time back there, soaking in the inspiration."

The back room, or the writer's room that housed the original bar from 1934 until 1955, was where the likes of Hemingway, Fitzgerald, Hammett, Welles, and Chandler sat at the bar and enjoyed, perhaps, a few too many libations. And Rachel knew that one of the many appealing things about Musso & Frank Grill was that it was still a writer's bar, where screenwriters, novelists, and playwrights would sit at the bar and write, proofread, exchange ideas, or even bounce ideas off the bartender. The irony was not lost on her that this was her *first* time entering the bar, and she was in the process of writing her *final* novel. If she lived in L.A., would she come in here for inspiration? One look at the ornate chandeliers, wood, and red-leather booths told her she would be here often.

Suzanne toasted her and said, "Those novels were just fine the way they were."

"Thanks," she replied and then sipped her martini. The rumors were confirmed: This was the best martini she had ever tasted.

They had postponed ordering until the men arrived, so Rachel and Suzanne were alone in the red leather-lined booth. "There are about a million things I want to talk with you about, but I know that this evening is going to be over like that," Rachel said, snapping her fingers.

"Me too," said Suzanne. "I usually don't get to meet the authors I work with, but over the years, I've texted, called, emailed, and sometimes even Zoomed with them. However, I have always wanted to meet you." She smiled and lowered her voice to a whisper. "And look at us, here you are, Riley Cannon. It's not your real name, is it?"

Rachel took another sip. The drink was warming up her insides, and she was feeling relaxed. "Maybe. Maybe not. What do you think?"

"I'm thinking no."

Rachel gave her a thumbs up.

"I *knew* it," Suzanne said.

"I don't want this to come across as weird, but after I listened to your performance of my first book, I felt that I had gained a friend."

"Okay, that's not weird; that's sweet."

Rachel grinned and shook her head. "I'm sorry, this is crazy meeting like this, right?"

"Better now than never. Why did you put it off for so long? Privacy?" Suzanne took a drink. "And you have no worries. I won't tell a soul. Neither will Scott. I told the hostess that you were another audiobook narrator. You're safe. Sure, some spies watched my every move when it was announced that *Dark*

After Midnight was coming out. I guess people thought that after your ten-year disappearance, we might finally meet to discuss the book. Scott and I usually have dinner here at eight, and there would be customers at the bar who would see who we had dinner with. It was nuts for a while there."

Rachel sat back and relaxed. "Mostly, it was because of privacy. I'm not a very public person."

"But you're so personable, and, just saying, you're gorgeous too."

Rachel blushed. "Well, that's very kind of you to say, but yes, I wasn't in a rush to let people know who I really was. Maybe someday I'll tell you why when we have more time."

"You better. Because you are not getting rid of me that easily." Suzanne did a quick survey of the room and lowered her voice. "What are you doing in L.A.?"

"Research."

"This *can't* be the only time we ever meet."

"I know you're right. I would love to see you again. There's so much I want to discuss."

"Well, hell, let's talk. I'll start. So, I'm dying to see how everything comes together in book six. I mean, we've got a lot to wrap up, wouldn't you say? Gideon is gone, but Control and her bodyguard are still alive, and I have to know if Adrienne and Worth will end up together. You've been teasing it for six books, and, well, I'm dying over here, ma'am."

"I'm working on it . . . don't have the ending nailed down yet, but I will."

"You've thrown me for a loop before. I always read the book ahead of time, but do you know how many times I sat on my couch, reading the book and doing my prep, and said to myself, 'Oh, she wouldn't do *that*; she'll do *this*,' and then later shouted, 'Oh my God, she's doing *that*!' In *Late-Afternoon Associates*, I totally thought that Mercedes DiMera would get away and take Byron Worth with her. That was a great seduction scene, by the way, and I knew it would take a few

153

books before Adrienne would let him back into her bedroom again." She smirked. "And I was right!"

"They've been through a lot together."

"Okay, they have to end up together, Riley, don't you think? I mean, they could both say to each other, 'Hey, I've been with other people, and so have you, but what matters is what we have together.'"

"I might hire you to write some lines! Seriously, though, it *could* happen."

"It *has to* happen. The title is *Sunrise Kama Sutra*, for crying out loud."

Rachel had no idea whether Worth and Adrienne would end up together. Did she want them to? Yes. But sometimes, her characters did not always do what Rachel wanted them to do. She was shocked when Kristy Cummings started taking drugs, and no matter how many times she had rewritten the scene, Kristy always went for the white powder. When Rachel realized that it was inevitable, she took her hands off the keyboard and screamed, *"Fine, Kristy, you want to die? Be my guest."* But Byron Worth and Adrienne Astra were different. They had a history, and it was complicated.

Suzanne gave a playful smile. "But, it's your story. Your *narrator* wants them to end up together, but I know you've got to do what you've got to do." There was silence for a beat. "But, hey, let's get one thing straight: Adrienne is going to defeat Control, right?"

"I don't think my readers would let me have it any other way, do you?"

"No way. She and her bodyguard have to go down in this one. When Adrienne took out Gideon and saved Worth in *3 a.m. Phone Call*, I cheered and then nodded through the entire epilogue. And after reading the last paragraph, where Adrienne discovers a clue to Control's whereabouts, I shut the book and said, 'Yes! It's on, bitch.'"

They both laughed and sipped from their drinks.

"It's nice to be able to share a laugh with you," said Suzanne. "There were so many times over the years that your books would make me laugh, and I never got to share that with you. With some of the other authors I work with, I can shoot them a quick text or call them, and it's fun. But, with you, I always found myself placing a thumb in the book at those moments and looking at the ceiling or out the window and saying, 'I'll never get to meet her.' I cannot count the times I said, 'Who are you, Riley Cannon? *Where* are you?'"

"I'm sorry," Rachel said. "I wanted to reach out. After the first book, you were forever on my mind whenever I wrote. I would finish a scene and think, 'I wonder what Suzanne will do with this?' It's like we've been pen pals, communicating back and forth through our respective arts."

Suzanne leaned her head to one side. "Okay, so there are two things I'm dying to know. One, why did you disappear for over ten years?" She finished her sazerac. "For the second question, I need to give some background. In *The Blue Hour Sanction*, it moved me when we found out that Adrienne had lost her brother and mother at the same time during childbirth—it explained so much to me about why Adrienne is the way she is both in her relationships and when she sets her mind to do her work. Then, in *3 a.m. Phone Call*, the whole thread about Adrienne having a lover and seemingly catching him in an affair years ago and then showing up to the houseboat where he lived and confronting him, only to find out that she had misread what she had witnessed back then and that the guy was innocent and loved her. It tore my fucking heart out, ma'am, and set things up perfectly for Adrienne and Worth to reconnect. What inspired you to write that? Where does all that stuff come from?"

What inspired me to write those things? My own life. I had something taken away from me when I was two—it's the reason I'm right here now with you, Suzanne—and it changed the course of my life and my father's life. And the thread about Adrienne being wrong about a past lover, well, that was based on my own experience with Ryan. I've never had pages come to me as easy as when I returned from Key West. Then, I had to convince Topaz and Hightower to add them before the book went off to the printers because they thought we had gone final on the manuscript.

155

After reading the revised final draft of *3 a.m. Phone Call*, Topaz had said, *"Smashing! Out-of-this-world fantastic, darling. Some of your absolute best writing. Even Hightower had nothing but good things to say . . . and if he had critiqued you, I would have let him have it! But, my dear, don't give us a heart attack like this again by dropping new pages on us in the eleventh hour!"*

Rachel looked up from her glass at her narrator and now friend.

But, Suzanne, I cannot tell you any of this—at least not right now. Not until I find my mother and . . . well, I don't know what is going to happen.

"Oh, a little bit of this, a little bit of that, I suppose. I've always thought a novel is like a mathematical function, like $f(x) = x + 2$. A function is like a machine; you put a number into the machine, and unless the function is $f(x) = x$, a new number comes out. Using $f(x) = x + 2$, you put two into the machine, and the machine spits out four. So, in a writer's case, what goes into the machine are my life experiences—including everything I've read, written, watched, and learned—the life experiences of others that I have studied, all of my ideas for the book, my agent's feedback, and my editor's feedback. The finished novel is what comes out of the machine."

"I've never heard anyone explain their writing process that way. See? That's why we have to stay in contact!" A glass of red wine arrived for Suzanne. "I get wine with dinner because I always have steak and start with steak tartar, which I recommend."

"I'm sold. Steak it is."

The waitress disappeared. "I'm already dreading saying goodbye to you," Rachel said, tearing up.

What is going on here?

"I know what you mean. You're leaving after dinner. And when the book comes out, it's *all* going away—you, Adrienne, everything. And, being here with you now, I feel . . . young, like I'm in my early thirties, and I'm just getting the phone call from Topaz about narrating your first novel. I feel like it's all just begun . . . I feel like *we've* just begun."

"I feel the same way. I promise the novel will be a hell of a bow for Adrienne."

Suzanne frowned. "And for you. Sure you don't have any more tales to tell?"

"God, you sound just like Topaz."

Suzanne gave a short laugh. "Guilty. When she called me right before you showed up, she told me to try and convince you to keep writing. 'Keep the Astra train moving, voice goddess. Bully her, blackmail her, *guilt* her into writing more. She needs Adrienne. She needs *you*. Let's go round the clock again—six new books, Freeman of Dune. Ha! That one's for your hubby.'"

They both broke into laughter at Suzanne's impersonation.

Finally, Rachel got her breathing under control and said, "She's vicious, that one. I should have known she would put you up to it."

"I can't blame her. As a fan, I know what it's like to go ten years without a book from you. I don't even want to think about *never* having another book written by you." Suzanne paused. "I don't want this to come out wrong, but has there been any pressure to have someone else write the series?"

"There has," Rachel said.

"I have an idea. What about the author who wrote *The Blue Hour Sanction*? He was fun to work with."

"I loved what he did, but it was a one-time thing. Plus, he's not a series writer—prefers writing stand-alone novels."

"There has to be another author out there who could carry on for you. Readers and listeners *adore* Adrienne. Just look at Jack Reacher. Lee Child knew he was done writing the series, but he also knew how much his fans enjoyed the character. So, he hired his brother to keep it going, which is also good for my hubby because he *loves* narrating those books. And now there's the Amazon

Prime series, and, well, that's about as perfect as television gets. You've seen it, right?"

Rachel eyeballed her. "You do not mess with the special investigators."

"Ha!" Suzanne said, giving Rachel a playful pat on her shoulder. "Seriously, would you ever consider turning the series over to anyone else?"

There was a pause.

"I'm not interested," Rachel said. "Adrienne is *my* character."

After a few seconds, Suzanne gave her a nod of approval. "And what will happen to the world when there is no Adrienne Astra to save it?"

All Rachel could do was reach out and squeeze Suzanne's hand. A tear slipped down her cheek. "The world will be fine, my friend."

"You know, in like five minutes after you're gone, I'm going to think of the right way to say goodbye."

Rachel saw Obadiah and Scott enter the old room and walk toward the booth. "Let's not think about that now," she said, wiping her eyes. "Here come the guys."

She saw Suzanne look up from her drink, and soon, the men had slid into the booth. Obadiah gave Scott a pat on the shoulder.

"Looks like you two have gotten acquainted," Rachel said.

Obadiah and Scott exchanged a grin.

"What?" Suzanne asked.

Scott laughed while looking down at his martini and shaking his head. "Shawn Frost."

Suzanne closed her eyes. "Oh, God. Now what?"

17

Santa Andreas Island – Thursday, July 3, 2025

9:00 p.m.

Kitty Andreas sat in her indigo-colored Carlisle English Arm Upholstered Chaise Lounge chair, reading Ivan Bacca's latest thriller, *After Key Largo*. An overhead fan blew cool air on the delicate skin of her right arm as she reached for her nightly smoothie—kale, chia seeds, flax seeds, blueberries, half a banana, a small scoop of peanut butter, organic cacao powder, MCT oil, and a cup of almond milk all blended. Before she had showered and put on her Victoria's Secret satin short pink iconic stripe pajama set, she had done her hour on the elliptical, followed by twenty minutes of yoga and then a half-hour-long massage.

She was seventy, but a month ago, her doctor had told her that she had the body and health of a forty-five-year-old woman. She frowned, replied, *"Only forty-five? I paid for better than that,"* and then walked out. "Paid" was a pejorative term to her when she used it after receiving disappointing news. Kitty believed that

159

she had *worked* to achieve her level of fitness and health and maintain her beauty and did not like to link her success to the money that had been hemorrhaged to physical trainers, dieticians, spiritual coaches, masseuses, physicians, counselors, and even practical worker bees like maids, contractors, secretaries, drivers, pool maintenance personnel, and hired handymen who maintained equipment like bicycles, Nautilus machines, and her custom made BowFlex exercise machine. When she hit her target, it was because of her hard work, discipline, and meticulous routine; when she did not, it was because she had not received the promised services she had paid for.

And yet, she could not make a public fuss because long ago, she and her husband had come up with her public take on money, which she delivered to perfection the few times she had been interviewed early in the marriage. The interviews ceased after a columnist for a small but popular newspaper wrote:

According to Kitty Andreas, money doesn't matter. Sunbathing on the top deck of her husband's yacht, Andreas told this reporter, "I've never been driven by money; it's never been a priority. It doesn't matter. It certainly doesn't guarantee happiness." This, of course, is easy to claim when you and your husband are worth $9 billion. When you are that wealthy, money *doesn't* matter. When this point was raised, the woman who has been called the "Second Lady of Silicon Valley" said, "There are things that are out of my control. All I can say is that money has never factored into my decisions. It doesn't motivate me the way innovation does, the way collaboration does, the way planning does, the way *philanthropy* does." As drinks arrived—a screwdriver for Ms. Andreas and a coffee with cream and sugar for this reporter—she was asked, "But is that not a rather easy statement to make?" The sunglasses lowered, and clarification was . . . demanded. It was then brought to her attention that when one has millions of dollars, let alone *billions*, it is opportune to say that money doesn't affect choices. There was no reply, but there was when Ms. Andreas was asked, "Do you and your husband consider yourself rich?" After a sip of her screwdriver—we were told the orange juice is freshly squeezed each morning—she stated, "Rich is a relative term—except for Bill Gates. Now, *he's* rich." Again, pushback was offered, namely that all rich people describe rich as someone richer than they are. This was met with a scowl and a wave to the butler waiting in the wings. The raising of *The New York Times* in front of her signaled that the interview was over, but a final question was posed: When *would* money matter? From behind the paper, she laughed and said, "Well, if one day I am only living on Social Security, come back and interview me then."

After the article appeared, Kurt Andreas, through an intermediary, bought the newspaper and fired the entire staff—to this day, no one ever knew it was Kurt—but it wasn't enough for Kitty. She wanted to explain herself, feeling that she had been misquoted. However, Kurt's publicist intervened, and she agreed to let it die. Then, in a private meeting with Kurt and Kitty, the publicist said, *"Neither of you are ever doing an interview about your personal wealth again. In fact, no wealthy person ever should. No matter what you say, it will not come across well. When you have more money than you know what to do with, you look horrible when you say stupid shit like, 'Money has never been important to me' because that is a fucking lie, or, even worse, give off the vibe that striving to be wealthy is just not your thing. Capeesh? We need to have you both embody the term 'quiet luxury.' It would be best if you seemed humble.* Underplay *your wealth and keep it out of view. Every time you flaunt it, it draws attention. You need to appear like you are just like everyone else. So, unless it's a major function, you are going undercover— a wolf in sheep's discount clothing."* And so, since then, Kitty had avoided discussing and complaining about money.

She turned the page in her book—she still preferred physical copies—and finished the final paragraph of the chapter.

She put in her bookmark—a dollar bill—and closed the book. So far, she had been impressed by *After Key Largo*. Kitty's favorite author, Jacqueline Donahue, had said on the front cover, "Ivan Bacca sits atop the thriller mountain and peers down at all of us climbers stranded at base camp." Saw Walden, the king of the military thriller, a genre in which she had no interest—fuck war porn—had said, "Every Bacca book is a heat-seeking missile that never misses its target, but *After Key Largo* should have been titled *Afterburner*. Wow! Unbelievably intense!" And though cover blurbs never sold her on a book—well, Jackie Donahue's did—these endorsements had been reasonably accurate. The novel was intense, but putting Bacca on top of the thriller mountain, well, Jackie D., that was a little much, or at least it wasn't the whole picture because the whole picture would either have Riley Cannon floating in the air above Bacca at a level he couldn't reach, even if he jumped, or there would be another, higher peak where Riley sat on the summit, looking far down at the peak that Bacca had climbed.

Cannon wasn't her favorite author, but she was queen, and there was no arguing about it. *Poor Jackie is a tad bit jealous*, Kitty thought. It had been a few years since Jackie had come to the island for a visit, and with a new book due out this October, as was her tradition, Kitty planned on reaching out and seeing if she'd like to come out for a week over Christmas. Maybe Bacca could come too.

In the first chapter, Kitty had fallen for Bacca's main character, bachelor billionaire adventurer John Hogan, when the yacht Hogan is on explodes just off Key Largo at midnight. Hogan's crew dies, and he swims through shark-infested waters to reach shore. Wearing his soaked shorts and polo shirt, he flags down a cobalt blue Ferrari 296 GTS driven by the beautiful and mysterious Lady Aston, who gives him a ride to his beach house and stays, drinking brandy by the fire while they try to figure out who would have wanted to kill him.

Kitty yawned and stared at the book while taking a final sip of her smoothie. Bacca's chapters almost always ended with zingers that made her want to turn the page and keep going, but at the end of the chapter she had just finished, Hogan and Lady Aston had just made love on his private jet as they sped back to Key Largo after receiving a tip from an informant in an abandoned beach house in Maine. She had no doubts that the next chapter would be full of suspense and tension as the two landed and followed the new lead. But, for tonight, she was at a good place to stop—she grinned and ran her hand over her large right breast as the chapter's final words ran through her mind . . . "Hogan and Lady Aston *exploded* simultaneously like the fireball that had risen into the night sky when Hogan's yacht had been blown up."

She gave her nipple a pinch and then pulled the crimson-colored fleece blanket over her chest and closed her eyes. There would be no sex with Kurt tonight. He had been distant for the past few days, meeting often with Ivan, and he would not tell her why. She knew he was stressed because he only drank vodka when something was bothering him, and she had seen him with a tumbler filled and refilled numerous times since Governor Sal Reiner had paid him a visit.

At least Reiner had left. She hated that lying little fuck and his greased-back hair and his air-headed mistress. Kitty liked Reiner's wife and told Kurt she never got to see her anymore because the island visits had become just a romp holiday for the governor and his mistress. The only reasons Kitty tolerated him were because of his political connections, his friendship with Kurt, and the fact that he went out of the way to kiss her ass during each visit, which she let him, not paying him any compliments back.

Kitty's eyes opened, and she looked over at their double king bed, which had been custom-made, and she thought back to the last time they had made love. A month ago? Two months ago? She couldn't remember the date, but she did remember that he had been more enthusiastic in bed than he had been in some time. If he did show up and showed interest, she would reciprocate.

There were other options, of course, just as he had other options. She had been with Zachariah Lafontaine a dozen or so times before, and he was mechanically sound, if not inspired, when they had sex. If he was vulnerable, which was rare, it was a different story. And then, there was her one regrettable night with his agent, Jolly Otto, that made her not want to be in his presence ever again. But he was Kurt's friend, and she did her best to appear satisfied to be in his company while also trying to avoid him as much as possible whenever he came to stay at the island or the Pacific Cove Bluffs house. And the third option was her personal bodyguard, Aymen, who was thirty-five, cut, and just outside the bedroom door right now.

Will Kurt even sleep in here tonight? She wondered. He did last night, but his mistress had arrived this afternoon and would be staying in her usual luxurious suite, two floors below the fourth-floor master bedroom. The jealousy had at least dissipated, if not disappeared entirely, when they had agreed to see other people early in their marriage, soon after she had changed her name. Kurt had been obsessed with Greek first names, so when he told her that he found her beauty and intellect beyond the basic name of Tina Haines, she had agreed to change her name to Kethryn, which meant "pure" in Greek. He had hinted at plastic surgery, but it was she who had taken the lead, and since money was not an issue, she had done precisely what she had wanted to do to herself. Later, when she started to see other men, she adopted her own nickname, Kitty, which he had fought her about at first but then relented. He said she was still the best company he had ever had but that he needed more, and so should she. *"Why limit ourselves to each other when we can have anyone we want?"* he had said. She had joked and replied, *"I agree. Kethryn means pure, but Kitty means purr, Kurt."* As always, he had found her openness and sense of humor refreshing, and they had built a life together for the past thirty years. Sometimes, while bedding a young buck like Aymen, she would smirk thinking of the men she had left behind—Guy Cole and Clark Roberts. Men who could not match her ambition.

However, Kurt having a full-time mistress was something new, and some of the long-dormant feelings of jealousy had returned. Like Kitty, she had been encouraged to change her name. When she met him, her name was Samantha Black—again, according to Kurt, basic. So, he had devised the idea of whittling it down to just one name. Samantha had been game. Now, she was only known as Andromeda—twenty-three years of age, shoulder-length golden hair, nearly six feet tall, green eyes, and a perfect smile.

Ivan, Kitty's trusted spy over the years, told her that Andromeda was a high school dropout he had found at a strip club deep in the bible belt while he was in town on business for Kurt. Estranged from her Baptist parents, she had jumped at the chance to visit L.A. and see a man interested in meeting her. The man, of course, was Kurt Andreas. After a weekend in the sack together, Kurt had determined that she should become his full-time mistress and live with him and his wife. Ivan had told Kitty that he was nervous about the arrangement. *"Kitty, watch that one. She's got an independent streak that could upset the balance if she gets her hooks into Kurt. He hasn't had a full-time mistress since Sherry-Ann."*

Kitty had heard it before, and other women had come and gone from her husband's life. She, along with Ivan, had even engineered some of their departures when they had gotten too close to Kurt, including Sherry-Ann, a professor from Berkeley with ties to the communist party who wanted Kurt to divorce Kitty, marry her, and then fund her run for the U.S. Senate. Kitty had met with Susan Kantor, and a week later, Sherry-Ann was gone. There had been a feeble attempt at retribution, but the good professor did not know that Kurt and Kitty were friends with the president of Berkeley, and the next semester, after a series of serious allegations were levied against Sherry-Ann, she resigned her position. Last Kitty had heard, she was an activist, living in Van Nuys and struggling to make ends meet through GoFundMe.

Now that Andromeda had been in their lives for a year, Kitty was already tired of her. After starting as friends—more of a mother-daughter mentorship—and having lunch together on Fridays, they rarely spoke.

The last time they had chatted was three months ago, when Andromeda had found out about the two pillars and was upset, thinking that she and Kurt were exclusive. In an attempt to get rid of her, Kitty consoled her and then suggested that she go on a shopping spree. *"No, no, dear, not clothes or jewelry. How about a few houses?"* And so Andromeda had bought a 2.1-million-dollar apartment in Greenwich Village . . . and a 26-million-dollar home in Aspen, which she had needed Kitty's help in acquiring. Both purchases had raised more than an eyebrow from Kurt. *"Why do you need a home in Aspen when I own one of the lodges? And what the fuck is up with the place in Greenwich Village? You* hated *New York City when I took you there."*

Andromeda had then dropped the bombshell that she knew about the two pillars, and Kurt promised to be more discrete, saying that she was his one and only true mistress, that he loved her, and that he planned for them to have a wonderful life together. His answer had satisfied her, and she had reported back to Kitty about what had happened and what had been said. It was then that Kitty had told her that she had known about the two long-legged ladies from Modesto for the past six months, and Andromeda had stormed off. Then, Kitty returned to her room, picked up one of her crystal bathroom glasses, and threw it against the mirror, knowing that her plot to get rid of Andromeda had failed. A quick call to Ivan had brought a contractor and a maid to the room, and she had been escorted to a guest suite for the night. In the morning, her bathroom had a new mirror and crystal glass on the counter.

Kurt sold the house in Aspen for thirty million a week later and the apartment in Greenwich Village for 2.8 million.

Now, she's going to be here over the 4th of July, and I have to play hostess, Kitty thought. *Maybe I can take a cruise on* Blue Kurty *tomorrow and avoid the festivities. I could ask*

Zachariah if he wants to go. She gave a wry smile. *We could leave Jolly Otto here to play with himself.*

The yacht was one of her favorite places to get away, mainly because it brought back memories of where she had first met Andre Kurt Andreas: Dana Point. Living with Guy Cole had been okay in Palm Springs, but, as a Michigander, she had missed the water. So, one day, when Guy was at work, she rented a car and drove it to Dana Point, arriving just before noon, where she parked and walked down the docks, admiring the yachts. About to turn around near the end of one dock to get lunch at one of the harbor's restaurants, she spotted a handsome young man having a drink on a cushioned bench in the stern. The man's name was Andre Kurt Andreas.

After she changed her name to Kethryn Pappas, they married in 1989. Kurt had a larger yacht built, and they left the beauty and serenity of Dana Point Harbor for the glamorous Marina del Rey. Sometimes, she wished they still had a boat at Dana Point. The harbor had been constructed in the 1960s and officially dedicated on July 31, 1971. It was only sixteen years old when she had met Kurt there, but time had taken its toll, and boaters had relocated to Marina del Rey. However, there was a major reconstruction revitalization project for Dana Point going on right now, and she had convinced Kurt to donate a large sum of money. It had been a whirlwind of a romance almost forty years ago. She still remembered Kurt arranging for the U-Haul so that she could gather her things at Guy's and take them to his vacation home in Malibu. His primary residence at that time was north in Silicon Valley.

In any event, the yacht, *Startup*, that they kept in Marina del Rey was the one where she had given her famous interview, but *Blue Kurty* was over twice the size of *Startup* and had to be either anchored offshore of their home in Paradise Cove Bluffs or berthed at the multi-million-dollar pier Kurt had constructed on Santa Andreas Island. Whenever the interview popped into her mind, as it had a few minutes earlier, she always took comfort in the fact that when their yacht *Outlaw*

167

had launched, Kurt had agreed to take *Startup* offshore and have it sunk. There were days when she still missed *Outlaw* and its grand staircase that had been modeled after the one on *Titanic*. She and Kurt had some of the best times in their marriage cruising the world on the yacht, but his tech-world competitors started to construct yachts that were larger than *Outlaw*, and so Kurt had *Blue Kurty* designed, which, when finished, would be the largest private yacht in the world. She still remembered when it had arrived and anchored offshore their Paradise Cove Bluffs home. There had been a cocktail party of over a hundred of their friends on the terrace overlooking the Pacific, and when the yacht had come into view, the champagne had flowed.

Thinking about *Blue Kurty* always put her in a better mood because no other women were allowed to accompany Kurt when she traveled on the mega yacht. It was a rule they had established, and Kurt had honored it. She had promised not to have any of her men travel with her when she and Kurt were aboard. Now, when one of them wasn't . . . then they were free to have anyone onboard that they liked. Hence, she was thinking of phoning Kurt, who was in his office right now, and seeing about taking a trip on the yacht with Lafontaine tomorrow. She knew the actor was embarrassed about the Senate hearing, and she would prey on his insecurities, which had always resulted in great sex.

It had been four or five years since she had attended the Oscars, but Lafontaine's performance in the drama *The Couple on the Beach*, released in May, was so powerful that she didn't think that even the botched Senate hearing would sink his nomination, and if he was nominated, then she wanted to attend the ceremony. He was actually *at* the hearing to bolster his profile for awards season, which was months away. Jolly Otto wanted to keep him in the headlines and keep the memory of his performance fresh in the Academy members' minds. It had backfired, but with talent like Fontaine's and his ability to talk his way into or out of anything, a comeback was all but assured. He would continue to hide away this week and then probably make a sizable donation followed by a short public acknowledgment—not an apology—that he continued to learn and grow as a person, imperfect as he was. Otto would have him in a light blue shirt behind the microphone. Once the acknowledgment had been delivered along with a reminder of his tithing, the focus would shift back to *The Couple on the Beach* and the quest for his second golden statue, then his next project, which was rumored to be directed by Mossimo Bergman.

At least, that is what she would do if *she* were in charge of rebuilding his public image.

Regardless, a little covert steam on *Blue Kurty* for a day or two would ease his troubled mind. And best of all, Kitty would not have to see Andromeda.

She picked up her cell phone and then put it back down. *He's been unusually distant the past few days, especially after his quick business trip. Where had he gone?* Kitty knew that Susan Kantor was in California for the 4th of July, and she remained close to Kurt, which Kitty liked even less than his relationship with Andromeda.

Kitty could never entirely forget that Kurt had almost ended their marriage to be with "Cunt-er," which was Kitty's nickname for her. And, a part of Kitty had never forgiven Kurt for what he had put her through for ten years early in their marriage. *She* was the one to walk away from men who, in her opinion, couldn't keep up. Men *did not* walk away from *her.*

After dinner, she had cornered Ivan in the dining room and asked where her husband had gone for his business meeting and why he was so distant, but her loyal insider had always been tight-lipped about particular wings of Kurt's business, and this had been one of those times. *"I cannot discuss that right now, Ms. Andreas,"* he had said when they were alone in the dining room. *"After the fourth, I think things will be better."*

"He's drinking more vodka than you drink!" she had said.

He had nodded and then hugged her. She could never stay mad at him, no matter how much she wanted to.

Kitty glanced at her cell phone again. *Things will be better after the fourth . . . all the more reason to leave the island tomorrow—give him some space.*

Is he having an issue with me? she thought. It would not be a physical issue, of course, but there had been a handful of times in their marriage when she had made an inadvisable move while running her non-profit sectors of A. Andreas Enterprises. And those times were memorable because they were the only instances when he had physically pushed her around a bit.

She did a quick inventory, scanning for missteps:

Humanitarian—she had received confirmation last week that the pallets of food and medical supplies had been offloaded at Durban, Mombasa, Djibouti, Casablanca, and Abidjan. There had been no delays.

Philanthropy—the two company planes had touched down in Haiti three days ago and delivered their bi-annual shipment of books. Like the shipments to Africa, there had been no delays, and the foreman from one of the planes responsible for the offload had sent a picture of excited children on the tarmac watching the pallets of books come off the plane.

Okay, his problem cannot be with my business responsibilities.

She tapped her fingers on the soft armrest. Was there something wrong with a man named Louis? She had heard his name come up when she entered the library without knocking on the door and found her husband talking to Ivan by the shelf with the top 100 books about Hollywood that the *Hollywood Reporter* had named a few years back. As soon as she entered, the men stopped talking, but she had heard the name Louis, and in all of her years of knowing her husband, she had never heard the name Louis before.

Then, she thought about the island's far side and what was stored there. She bit her lower lip. If something were wrong in that regard, it would be a good reason to meet with Cunt-er . . .

Then again, perhaps she was overthinking things, which she was prone to do when Andromeda was around, the skinny little bitch.

Stop it, she told herself. *You're getting triggered by past wounds. There's probably nothing wrong.* She leaned her head back against the chair's fluffy back cushion. *But if there is, what is it that's got him so spooked?*

18

Paradise Cove Bluffs – Thursday, July 3, 2025

9:45 p.m.

Rachel Roberts watched as the shiny, black limousine pulled off the Pacific Coast Highway, turned onto Sea Lane Drive, and then rolled to a stop in front of the gate that guarded the private drive to Kurt Andreas's mansion. There was a lone light on in the guard shack, and soon, a heavyset security guard, holding a flashlight and drinking from a Starbucks cup, approached the driver's side window. The privacy glass that separated the front seat from the back was raised so she could not hear what David Killian's driver, Johnny Ringo, said to the guard. Obadiah Ben-David sat across from her, scribbling in his notebook.

It had been a quiet ride since they had been picked up outside the hotel.

Rachel was sipping on a coffee; her slight buzz from the martini and red wine at Musso & Frank Grill had worn off, but the marvelous dinner had almost put her to sleep for the first fifteen minutes of the ride. "Time to find out," she said.

Ben-David looked up. "He'll let us through. Killian's powerful."

Thirty seconds later, the guard returned to the shack and opened the gate.

Ben-David winked and then went back to his notebook.

The limo started to roll, and Rachel watched as the guard pulled out his cell phone and started scrolling. *Some security.*

The vehicle passed through the gate, and the light from the guard post and gate faded as the road straightened and a mix of hedges and structures started to pass down both sides. Soon, Rachel could see the dark outlines of massive homes begin to appear ahead.

Ben-David tapped his notebook with his pencil and then put them both away. She watched him as his eyes studied the sharp angles that poked into the starlit sky from the foliage and hedges surrounding the structures. "We're in another universe now, Rachel."

The first homes in the Malibu neighborhood were built in 1936, and, from the road, most of them looked to be one story, but it was a deception. From her earlier study of the area online, she had learned many homes were built into the hillside and seemed to plummet down the bluff forever, some having separate houses built close to the beach. Some of the homes had not even been visible from Sea Lane Drive.

There were twenty-five properties in the beachfront neighborhood, with homes ranging in size from two thousand to fourteen thousand square feet; the average house was around five thousand square feet with five bedrooms and five bathrooms. The architectural styles were a spread of Modern, Mediterranean, Traditional, Cape Cod, and Ranch, and views ranged from the city lights to the ocean to the Santa Monica mountains. Kurt and Kitty Andreas's house was a sprawling, eighteen thousand square foot Mediterranean-styled main house with a similarly-styled six thousand square foot guest house. On the property was a tennis court, a full basketball court, a pool with a Jacuzzi, and then a Cape-Cod-styled, two-thousand-square-foot bungalow down on the beach with its own pool, hot tub, fire pit, and outdoor kitchen.

Ben-David had looked further into Kurt and Kitty's real estate portfolio and found out that beyond the island estate, Paradise Cove Bluffs mansion, and New York City residences, they had an apartment in Paris, a home next to Clooney in Italy, an entire lodge in Aspen, a ranch in Texas, and a house north of San Francisco on Stinson Beach. *"Let's hope they're at the Paradise Cove Bluffs beach house or on the island, but if we have to, I'm game for checking out the other places,"* he had said.

She appreciated his offer and was committed as well, but she had discovered, reading an article from 2018, that Kurt and Kitty usually spent the 4th of July holiday at the Paradise Cove Bluffs compound or on the island. There was also the possibility that they would be on their mega-yacht *Blue Kurty*, and she thought about what it would look like for her and Obadiah to steam ahead at full throttle on *Abe Eye*, tracking them down somewhere in the Pacific.

The limo slowed, and Ringo lowered the privacy glass. "We're approaching the gate," he said. "I'll call on the intercom."

Rachel thanked him, and he raised the glass.

Her phone call earlier with Stan had gone well. He had been loving and supportive, and she had detailed the dinner with Obadiah, Suzanne, and Scott. Stan had been jealous as Scott was his favorite narrator.

"Look, Suzanne is a queen, but do you know how many late-night patrols that man got me through? I mean, The Passage Trilogy? While listening to each book in the pitch black of night, I swore that my work radio would crackle to life at any moment, and the dispatcher would tell me to investigate random places in town where people were turning into virals . . . vampires."

Rachel had laughed and replied, *"I've read and listened to them too. Suzanne would like to get together again, and so would I. So, there's a chance I'll be able to introduce you to Scott."*

That had ended the call on a high note, and she promised to let him know if anything new happened tonight. In a way, she wished she was driving up to their own beach house in Lakeview right now so that she could jump out, run to the front door, and embrace him. Being away and dealing with the emotions of trying to find her mother had been difficult.

She glanced over at Ben-David.

Thank God, I've got him here.

The range of emotions she felt at this moment took her creative instincts in an unsettling direction. *What if Stan and I have a daughter, and one day* she *is being driven in a limousine to a beach house to confront* me?

She gasped.

"You okay?" Ben-David asked.

She told him what she had just thought about.

"Won't happen," he said. "If you and Stan have a daughter, then I'll be in the running for godfather, right?"

She gave him a knowing grin and nodded.

He gave her a laugh. "That's what I thought. You've got no worries, then."

She appreciated the light moment, and it had distracted her enough not to notice that the limousine had just come to a complete stop.

"Nothing like announcing whose property it is," Ben-David stated, pointing at the eight-foot-high solid gate in front of the limo.

Centered and engraved on the left panel was the letter "K" with a circle around it, and on the right panel was the letter "A" with a circle around it.

Bordering the gate that prevented access to the estate's drive were ten-foot-high hedges, no doubt covering a fence that ran the length of the property in either direction. She could only see a dark roofline in the distance beyond the gate.

"No lights," she said.

Ben-David continued to scan the property through the limousine's windows. "No lights," he replied.

* * *

In the darkened Mercedes-Benz S-Class S 500 sedan, parked twenty yards down the drive toward the ocean, Hans Millard sat in the back seat with an armed bodyguard next to him. In the front was his driver and head of security, Armand Cuvier, who was also armed. The man next to Millard had been hidden in the trunk when they passed through the gate, and the guard had bought Armand's story that the man relaxing in the backseat with a glass of champagne was paying a surprise visit to his friend, Rory Wagner, a media mogul, who lived at the end of the private drive. Millard knew that Wagner was not liked by his neighbors and that he was rude, so he had Armand hand the guard a fresh coffee from Starbucks and a hundred-dollar tip, which Millard knew was up from the standard fifty-dollar tip that visitors paid as they were allowed past the gate.

The pudgy guard had pushed the magic button for the gate to open, and Millard, in his disguise of a black wig, black mustache, and black-rimmed glasses, had turned around and watched as the guard paid no more attention to the luxury vehicle as it drove away. When the gate had closed, Armand had turned the sedan around and stopped behind a large SUV parked along the drive across from Kurt Andreas's property. Then, the bodyguard quietly slid out of the trunk, performed a quick reconnaissance of the estate, and then joined his boss in the back seat.

They had been watching the house for fifteen minutes.

"He's not in the limousine, is he?" Armand said.

Millard popped a piece of gum into his mouth to try and stave off his desire for a cigarette . . . hell, ten cigarettes. "No, the driver is talking into the intercom right now. If it were Andreas, the gate would be open by now."

"Who is it, then?"

176

Millard leaned forward. "I do not care." He started to chew his gum. "Perhaps this is a bit of luck."

Armand turned around and looked into the eyes of the man seated to Millard's right. "You're certain that the entire place was dark?"

The man nodded.

Since Millard trusted no one, they were there for two reasons. One, he wanted to see if his new arms dealing partner, the President of the United States, Susan Kantor, was setting him up. She had told him that Andreas would be staying on his island estate over the 4th of July. For his plan to succeed tomorrow, Millard wanted to verify that Andreas was not staying in his Paradise Cove Bluffs home. The last place anyone expected Millard to be was here, staking it out, and so that is where he decided to go.

The second reason they were there was also to confirm the information his source inside Andreas's security force had provided, which matched Kantor's intel that Andreas was not in Malibu but rather on his island. In his long history of arms dealing, Millard had been double-crossed before and nearly lost his life on one occasion. He needed to be able to trust his new partner, and he needed to be able to trust his source. Part II of the surprise operation set for tomorrow had been in the works for over a month, ever since Armand had discovered that Louis was the traitor. Part I would be conducted in a few hours under the cover of night. Millard's elite force of twenty mercenaries had gathered in Banff three weeks ago, and Millard had secretly joined them last week. He knew from his source that Andreas had received the package of Louis's head a few days ago, which had prompted Andreas to get into contact with Kantor . . . just as Millard and Kantor had planned. Right now, Andreas considered himself safe for the time being because he believed that Millard was in Paris and that Millard would not make a move over an American holiday.

How wrong he is, thought Millard. Tonight, Millard's twenty commandos would swim ashore from a luxury yacht named *Destination* and rig explosives near the system of underground storage bunkers on the island's western side and set them to detonate tomorrow at noon. They would not do much damage, and they were not supposed to. They were supposed to create chaos. It was also a simple means to create a diversion, sending some of Kurt Andreas's security force to the storage site. From the last report, Andreas had upped his security force at the main compound from five to ten. So, even if the explosives could only draw a few of them off, then it would create a more decisive advantage for the twenty commandos assaulting the estate.

Less than a minute after the detonation, offshore, *Destination*'s sister ship named *Jubilee*, which had been secretly armed with surface-to-surface missiles six months ago, would deliver its payload and destroy the entire arms depot complex. With the help from his contacts in the French Navy, Millard had orchestrated the modifications to the yacht, which had taken place in a remote harbor on an island in the Tuamotu Archipelago in French Polynesia, but nothing could be traced back to him. The falsified paperwork pointed to Kurt Andreas.

Right before getting into the sedan, Millard had received the report that *Jubilee* was thirty nautical miles southwest of Santa Andreas Island. Tomorrow morning, the yacht would move into position fifteen nautical miles offshore, make sure it was not in visual range of any other ships, and fire all of its missiles just after noon. Then, the captain would take the ship two nautical miles away, and she and her crew would transfer over to *Destination* and quietly scuttle *Jubilee* with precision charges wired to the ship's hull to send it into the deep quickly and quietly.

After the mercenaries planted the charges tonight, they would move east and take station, spreading out and hiding in the lush vegetation and cypress groves in the sloping hills surrounding the main Andreas compound. When the explosives detonated at noon, Millard's inside source would get the first opportunity to kill Andreas and his wife, if possible. However, the team in the hills would storm the compound at that time as well, killing anyone who got in their way and eliminating Andreas and his wife if the source had been unable to. Hopefully, the diversion drew some of the security forces away from the estate so they would have fewer obstacles to deal with. Millard and Kantor had decided that the cleanest way to transfer power to Millard was to eliminate Andreas and destroy the stockpiles on his island, thus making Millard's stockpiles that much more valuable. Scarcity would cause the price to go up: a win for Millard.

There would be inquiries and media coverage afterward, of course, as Kurt Andreas was one of the wealthiest men in the world. However, there would be no official footage of the horrors on the island. One of the informant's jobs was to disable the security camera system fifteen minutes before the explosives went off. There was always the possibility of cell phone recordings, but Millard and his team reasoned that when you are running for your life, you don't stop to take videos, and if you are hiding, then the only video you'll be able to take is of the closet you're hiding in. Hence, the press would immediately be at a disadvantage with no footage to use. Still, when the word started to leak about Kurt Andreas's arms dealing business, Susan Kantor told Millard that she would seize the moment, condemning Andreas and all illegal arms dealing throughout the world. Then, she would pivot and focus her rhetoric on arms dealing in the United States, both legal and illegal. *"I'll tour the country,"* she said, *"and make my last stop California, where Governor Reiner and I will make a joint statement. Then, I'll host a summit with Andreas's rivals in Silicon Valley and cozy up to all of them."* Millard had expressed concern that there would be a scandal because she would not be able to separate herself from her history and friendship with Andreas. She had reassured him, saying, *"Rich guy, and donor, owns an island that I visited a few times. So what? When I get through destroying Kurt Andreas's reputation, it will seem like I barely knew him and was deceived just like everyone else. We'll smear Kitty and his other mistresses, and then I'll have the justice department go after his assets in the name of national security. Believe me, you have nothing to be worried about."*

"What about the actor and his agent?"

"If they are smart, they'll hide when the bullets start flying. I'll arrange for someone to pick them up from the island before the authorities arrive, and because I kept them out of the spotlight, I'll own them even more. But . . . if they happen to perish on the island, it won't be hard to find another actor and agent willing to carry the environmental awareness torch. Then, I'll pile on along with Senator Tera Nailima from Hawaii about how, given the recent Senate hearing, it doesn't surprise us that Lafontaine and his agent were connected to Kurt Andreas. I'll have the Senator announce an investigation into the actor's travels and have my contacts in the press run with the story, suggesting that Lafontaine was a part of Andreas's arms dealing machine."

Millard had marveled at what a political animal she was, and he believed her. But still, sitting here in the dark and staring at a limousine that had just shown up at the Andreas property, he wondered why it was there. If whoever was in the vehicle was a friend of Andreas's, wouldn't he or she know he wasn't at the estate?

What if he is there?

If that were the case, then his source on the island would be dead soon . . . and so might President Susan Kantor.

He looked at the limousine again. *What if Kitty is in the vehicle?* He'd been infatuated with her for years and did not want to kill her tomorrow. *"It must be done,"* Armand had said, *"to keep things clean."*

He motioned to the man sitting beside him and then tapped the man's suppressed handgun. "Take only this, but slip outside and take up a position there," he said, pointing at a section of the Andreas property line toward the ocean. "If the limousine gains access, then go over the wall where there is no camera coverage, according to our source." He drilled his eyes into the man's. "If you see Kurt Andreas leave the house for any reason—to welcome the guest or guests in the limo, to get into the limo, etc.—I want you to take the shot."

The man gave one quick nod. "What about the limo driver and the passengers?"

Millard didn't hesitate. "Kill them and then take their valuables. It will look like a robbery. Just make sure to put on your balaclava before approaching the vehicle because you will be recorded on their security cameras."

Again, the man gave one nod. "And if the limo doesn't gain access?"

"Stay in your position until it leaves. When it exits through the gate, come back to the car."

The man left his rifle and eased out of the car, shutting the door with an almost inaudible *click*.

"Are you sure about this move, boss?" Armand said. "Won't killing him now throw off our movements for tomorrow?"

"We cannot miss the opportunity to kill him here if we have been betrayed. And if we do kill him, then it might make tomorrow easier. They'll send some people over here immediately, which will be fewer people our men and women have to deal with tomorrow. We'll also move our timeline up."

"I still thi—"

"I know what you are thinking, and I appreciate it. However, my answer is still no. If our inside source kills Andreas tonight on the island, then it will only jeopardize the missile launch tomorrow. If no one has lied to us, which it looks like we're about to find out, then waiting until tomorrow to execute the plan is worth it. Taking out Andreas, his wife, security, and stockpile in one massive sweep was always the dream, remember? Tomorrow is as much about making a statement to his allies around the world as it is about wiping out him and his island stockpile. Never forget that what we really want are his other stockpiles, and this strike will make it possible."

Armand frowned. "Okay. I just don't want anything to go wrong."

Millard took a sip of champagne with his right hand and placed his left hand on Armand's shoulder. "Everything will be all right."

And Millard believed that. After tomorrow, he and Armand would fly back to Paris and meet with his negotiating teams, which, along with sizable security forces, would then travel to each of Andreas's stockpiles and diplomatically force a turnover of the weapons and ammo caches to Millard.

* * *

Rachel watched as the two sections of the large gate parted, allowing the limousine to enter the property.

The privacy glass lowered, and Killy's driver, Johnny Ringo, said, "I just spoke to the butler. We're old friends from when I have driven Mr. Killian here for meetings. He says that Mr. Andreas won't return for a few days. I asked him where Mr. Killian might be able to reach him, and he told me the island. I know you're wondering why I didn't call ahead of time and save us the trip. Well, the butler is kind of quirky. Sometimes, Mr. Andreas instructs him to tell callers that he's not here even though he is. I remember once, he pissed Mr. Killian off so much that Mr. Killian called in a favor from one of his buddies in Pacific Palisades. Ten minutes after he placed the call, a helicopter landed on Mr. Killian's lawn and picked us up. He had me go with him because he trusted me— been his driver for over a decade now. Minutes later, we flew over to this place and saw Mr. Andreas in his pool with two women, neither of whom was his wife. Ever since then, Mr. Killian won't call ahead. We get in the limo and show up." Ringo shrugged. "Sometimes Mr. Andreas is here, sometimes he isn't."

She could see Ben-David's puzzled expression that, to her, said, *Why did you tell us all of that?*

Then, she thought, *Why didn't I ask him any of this when he had picked us up? Oh, right, I was still tipsy, and, well, there was no reason to ask him.* Killy had granted the favor to Topaz and had arranged for the yacht tomorrow, so she and Ben-David had not even thought to question the driver. She was glad they hadn't because they had enjoyed the ride over. "How about Andreas's wife?"

Ringo hooted. "Ha! Which one?"

"Well . . . Kit—"

"I'm just kidding. Sort of. Yes, his wife, Kitty, is with him, says the butler. But so is his mistress, Andromeda. How do you like that? One name. Hmph! Well, when you're that beautiful, I guess you can choose to go by one name."

"His mistress is on the island, too?" Ben-David asked.

"Yeah, that's what I said. Butler claims they're all there. One big happy, wealthy, fucked-up family. But you didn't hear me say that. I just drive the limo, friends."

Rachel crossed her legs. "Have you ever met Kitty?"

"Seen her once or twice, but she's pretty private. Seems okay."

"What does that mean?" Ben-David poked.

"I've never seen her be rude, and when you drive to as many millionaire and billionaire estates as I do, you see plenty of it, and you hear stuff."

"And you've never heard anything bad about Kitty?"

"I'm not sayin' a word, man."

Rachel slid in. "She sounds nice, but I agree with you: she's mysterious, you know?"

"Oh, yeah," Ringo said. He rubbed his neck. "Okay, you didn't hear this from me, but word is she and the actor Zachariah Lafontaine may have gotten friendly on a few occasions."

Ben-David and Rachel exchanged a glance. *Okay, all he has is gossip.* She was hoping for something substantial to head into tomorrow with.

"Do you trust the butler's word?" Rachel asked.

"About what?"

"About them all being on the island for the fourth."

"For sure," said Ringo. "It's a holiday, and only he and the housekeeper are here watching over the place. There's no reason for him to lie. Now," he said, turning around and giving them a wink, "did I volunteer that someone might be traveling out to visit the island tomorrow because of this information? No."

"Why are we heading inside the gate then?" asked Ben-David.

Ringo was looking forward again but jerked his thumb toward the back area. "I like this guy—straight to the point. He's letting us in to turn the limo around and drive out. It's much easier than turning around on the narrow drive or backing the entire way to the main gate."

Ringo brought the vehicle to a stop and said to Ben-David, "Hey, anybody ever tell you that you look just like Obadiah Stane from *Ironman*?"

"No," Ben-David said with a straight face.

"Really?" Ringo asked. "I'm surprised, boss. I must admit I kept looking back at you in my rearview mirror, thinking I had the man in the back seat. Between the three of us, I think Obadiah should have been given control of Stark Industries. Tony wasn't ready."

Rachel played along and said, "Right?"

Ben-David did not and stared out the window at the side of the main house that seemed to go on forever.

Ringo laughed. "I'm so rude. Mr. Killian only told me that I would be picking up a woman named Rachel and her friend. I never thought to ask you what your name was, sir."

Rachel bit her tongue.

"No problem. My name is . . . Ben."

"Pleased to meet you, Ben." He paused, shifting the gear into reverse. "Okay, enjoy the ride back to the hotel. There are snacks in the pull-out pantry to your right and drinks in the mini-fridge to your left."

"One last question," Ben-David said.

Ringo laughed. "Let 'er rip, sir."

"Will the butler phone the island and tell Mr. Andreas that Killian's limo stopped by?"

"No, he won't bother doing that. It's a holiday . . . might mention it after the week is over, but I doubt it. He thinks that Killian was stopping by, making a

184

social call. He's probably already forgotten it. Old veterans like him only make calls when there's an emergency."

Ben-David said thanks, and Ringo raised the privacy glass once more.

As the limousine turned around, Rachel thought she saw something outside her window—a dark shape by the shrub-lined outer wall.

"See something?" Ben-David asked.

Her eyes searched the darkness for a few more seconds, and then she looked at her partner. "I thought I did . . . over there, by the wall," she said, pointing, "but maybe not."

The limousine left the Andreas estate, turned right, and headed toward the guard shack.

* * *

Thirty seconds after the limousine passed by the guard shack, the back door to the sedan opened, and Millard's bodyguard got in the car and shut the door.

"Nothing," said the bodyguard. "The lights stayed off, and no one came out to greet them. Whoever is in the house must have let them in so they could turn around more easily."

Millard leaned forward and stared at the closed gate. "He's not there." *Looks like both sources told me the truth. One last check.* He leaned back. "Text our source on the island and verify that Andreas is there and will be tomorrow."

Armand pulled out his phone and began typing.

Two minutes after hitting send, he received a reply and showed it to Millard.

Fireworks are here. Ready for a great show tomorrow night.

Millard tapped him on the arm, and Armand put the phone away.

"Let's watch the house for ten more minutes."

185

The bodyguard left silently once again to take up his station in the spot where the security camera did not cover.

After ten minutes of silence and no movement anywhere, the bodyguard returned.

Armand lowered the back window closest to the Andreas property, and the man whispered, "Nothing."

Millard said, "Good," and the bodyguard moved to the rear and climbed quietly into the trunk.

Armand raised the window and said, "To the safe house?"

"Yes," said Millard. "The men and women will be leaving for the island soon."

Armand started the engine, and in a minute, they rolled past the guard shack, waving to the sentry, and soon were on the Pacific Coast Highway heading south toward San Clemente.

PART III

Sunrise

19

Onboard *Abe Eye*, offshore Santa Andreas Island – Friday, July 4, 2025

Rachel Roberts could see the beautiful and mountainous Santa Andreas Island off the bow of *Abe Eye* from the starboard bridge wing. It was 11 a.m., and the morning fog had lifted like a veil earlier, revealing Santa Rosa, then San Miguel, and finally Kurt Andreas's private paradise.

The wind blew her hair back, and she smelled the sweet-scented air. With each breath, she became more and more awake, alive. She felt like Adrienne Astra on a secret mission for a moment, and that feeling began to spark ideas in her mind for *Sunrise Kama Sutra*'s climax.

A high-tech yacht.

An island.

Control versus Adrienne Astra.

Hmmm.

She turned around and saw Obadiah Ben-David standing behind her with his eyes closed, the wind blowing through his enormous beard. She wondered if his mind ever returned to his night on *The Big House* and his long swim to Beacon Island. *Probably every time he's on the water*, she thought.

The voyage to the island had been pleasant, and one of the young stewards onboard—he was *maybe* old enough to drink—had told them about the famous Channel Islands. There were nine islands in total. Five came under the jurisdiction of Santa Barbara County, including Santa Andreas; two were under the jurisdiction of Ventura County; two were under the jurisdiction of Los Angeles County. Santa Andreas was ten square miles and the westernmost of the northern Channel Islands. Five of the islands formed the Channel Islands National Park, which was established in 1980. The steward had told them that the park offered beautiful hiking trails—he'd hiked all of them—and that there were picturesque places to camp. *"You can also snorkel, whale watch, and kayak,"* he had said. *"Are there a lot of people who visit?"* Rachel had asked. The steward seemed annoyed with her question. *"Of course!"* he had exclaimed. *"We're talking close to one hundred thousand tourists a year, most venturing out during the summer. It really is the place to be."* He had paused. *"Now, if you're into luxury,"* he said, rolling his eyes. *"Then, you probably won't travel farther than Santa Catalina Island. Most people visit Avalon, the resort city on Catalina, and never go anywhere else. The hell with it. Start north and then work your way down to Cost-a-lina."* He snickered. *"I didn't misspeak. Bring your credit cards, folks. You're gonna need 'em. Everything costs more in California, and I don't like it one bit. But . . . Hey! You're on this yacht, so what do I know? You've probably got enough cash to buy Cost-a-lina! No offense."* They had tears in their eyes because they were laughing so hard. *"I like this guy,"* Ben-David said, putting a hand on his shoulder. *"Me too,"* added Rachel. *"Well, there's your tour. Back to my work,"* he had said and then disappeared.

The Captain, a fortyish-year-old, tall man with thick blonde hair and a deep tan, wearing sunglasses, joined Rachel and Ben-David on the bridge wing. "We'll anchor in another ten minutes and get you both into the launch. Should take only ten minutes to get to the dock, so," he said, looking at his watch, "you'll be at the estate by quarter to noon. I know you wanted to be there earlier, but I didn't want to chance anything with the fog."

She raised her hands. "No complaints from the peanut gallery here, Captain. Everything will be fine."

Ben-David said, "Thanks, Cap. It was a smooth ride."

The Captain motioned for them to follow him back inside the bridge, and after they had all entered, he said, "When we anchor, I'll radio the dock. We've brought Mr. Raines out here to visit Mr. Andreas before, so you'll have no problem, but, as I told you earlier, they will ask for your names." He picked up a clipboard and pen. "What should I tell them?"

Rachel didn't hesitate. "Ed Crandall and Tina Haines."

He gave a wry grin, knowing their real names, and wrote the fake names down. "Don't blame you. The dock has a security shack on it, and inside, they have someone look up the names and do a quick background workup. Now, with a party arriving from a ship they don't know, I can see why they'd do that for security reasons. But to check someone out who is aboard *Abe Eye*? Ridiculous. I'll tell them that you are both old friends of Mr. Raines on a holiday cruise that he'll be joining later this evening. I'll add that while the yacht was abeam of Santa Andreas Island on its way out to the deep blue, you both wanted to drop by and pay your respects to Kurt and Kitty." He chuckled. "They love hearing stuff like that on this island, so you won't have any trouble at the dock. In fact, I bet they will hurry to take you to the house to meet Kurt and Kitty."

"Why?" Rachel asked.

"Because they will see it as an opportunity to host friends of a competitor and see what gossip they can charm out of them. It's happened before—happens all the time in rich circles." He peered out the front windows for a second. "Anyway, it will be fun to see what the security team comes up with in the dock

191

building after I give them your names." His eyes moved to the digital navigation monitor, a sixty-inch screen mounted above the chart table, and then he smiled back at them. "Okay, we're almost to the anchorage. Head on down."

Rachel had discussed the names they would provide after the Captain had first told them about it shortly after they had left port in the morning. She had picked "Ed Crandall" for Ben-David because Crandall was Adrienne Astra's father, and the veteran P.I. had been like a father to Rachel just as Topaz Kennedy had been a mother figure in her life. What she hoped would happen when the dock reported to the main estate that "Tina Haines" was also here to visit Kurt and Kitty was clear: If Kitty Andreas was Rachel's mother, then hearing her former name would entice her to meet Rachel face-to-face—that is if her glamorous mother would not be embarrassed by her daughter's appearance.

Rachel had worn casual attire for the other possible meetings in Michigan and Palm Springs and decided not to break with her style for the island meeting. She wore khaki shorts, a plain white T-shirt, socks, and navy-colored Nike running shoes with a white swoosh. Her hair was pulled back into a ponytail, and the only jewelry she had on were her earrings, wedding ring, and smartwatch. Ben-David wore black Brooks running shoes, jeans, and a black t-shirt with a front pocket over the left breast. He had on his smartwatch, which he hated. They were hardly the glamorous guests of Abraham Raines, but then again, Rachel had seen plenty of wealthy folks who did not flaunt their status with the clothes they wore. She was one of them.

She gazed up into Ben-David's eyes; her own eyes were glassy.

"You're ready," he said.

She smiled and wiped her eyes. "I am."

They headed down the ladder toward the aft deck.

Fifteen nautical miles southwest of Santa Andreas Island, the Commanding Officer of *Jubilee*, Marty Foster, sat in the specially designed Weapons Control Center, a deck below the bridge. He sipped his coffee and looked at the two giant screens before him.

On the right-hand display was a satellite image of Santa Andreas Island with neon-colored range rings extending to fifty nautical miles from the center. *Jubilee* was a tiny orange triangle between the ten and fifteen-mile rings. They were now in position and awaiting the final orders to execute their mission. The only other orange triangle on the water was of the ship *Abe Eye* that had just anchored to the north. Foster had called Millard and asked if it was a problem. Millard had said no. Foster had requested to use one of the missiles currently scheduled to blow up the island's arms depot to destroy the yacht, but Millard had denied the request. *"C'mon, you won't let me destroy* Blue Kurty. *At least let me sink* Abe Eye. *It'd be fun—like that video game you and I were playing in Paris,"* Foster had said. *Global Invasion. What a game changer it had been when the designers allowed for two-person teams to use a missile if they collected enough kills,* Foster thought. There had been silence at that point in the conversation, and he felt he had pulled the correct string as Millard loved violent video games. And Global Invasion? Millard was a certified addict. However, the answer from his boss had still been no. Innocent lives and all that shit. *Fuck Abraham Raines,* Foster said to himself. *He's just as guilty as Kurt Andreas for turning the world upside down with the proliferation of A.I.*

Foster sat back and then chastised himself. *You dumbass. Without computers and computing power, you wouldn't be playing Global Invasion.* He shook his head. *Life is one big sandstorm nowadays—not one goddamned thing clear about it anymore.*

But, hey! What if someone on Abe Eye *starts recording everything?* He frowned. *Naw, they'll weigh anchor and speed away. Cowards. Every single one of them. Even if they get some footage, it will be at a distance, and the main playpen for our commandos will be* inside *the mansion.* He sneered and flipped off the screen with both of his middle fingers.

193

He zoomed in on the island using the joystick on the control console before him. Next to the pier was Andreas's mega-yacht, *Blue Kurty*.

These motherfuckers and their toys.

He zoomed back out until the two yachts were small, orange triangles again. A smirk came across his face, and he took a drink of coffee. *Shit, maybe I'm just jealous that my two yachts are half their size. And later today, I've gotta sink the one I'm on. What a fuckin' waste, man.*

On the left-hand display was the view of the Andreas estate on the island from the commando team leader, who was a few hundred yards up the slope of the mountain that rose behind the southern side of the mansion.

Foster checked his watch.

It was 11:20 a.m.

20

Santa Andreas Island – Friday, July 4, 2025

Rachel Roberts had never seen a sitting room like this before.

It must be a thousand square feet in here, she thought.

The space's overall shape was rectangular, with French doors marking the entrance. Two large couches with floral patterns and glass-topped end tables faced each other, with a glass-topped coffee table in between. There was a fireplace on the far end with two chairs with ottomans facing it. Behind one of the couches was a writing desk and chair, and behind the other couch was a nook with large windows and an aquamarine-colored cushioned bench that had a white fleece blanket folded on top. There was an ornate chandelier high above the coffee table, and two white-bladed ceiling fans hung from the ceiling on either side, equidistantly spaced between the chandelier and the far wall with the fireplace on one side and between the chandelier and French doors on the other.

The space's flooring was wood with two lush navy rugs—one that covered the entire seating area dominated by the couches and one that cushioned the two chairs by the fireplace.

A butler, old and wise, with thick white hair parted and combed to perfection, wearing a tuxedo with a white jacket, led her and Obadiah Ben-David to the couches. A pitcher of ice water, a pitcher of coffee, and a tea kettle rested on a silver tray. A smaller pitcher of cream and an assortment of sugar packets and tea bags were placed next to the large pitchers. There were four delicate porcelain cups with thin aquamarine stripes near the brims that rested on saucers with aquamarine circles just inside the circumferences on another silver tray, along with tiny silver spoons that rested on folded white napkins with thin aquamarine stripes. Next to that tray was a smaller tray with four water goblets.

The butler had not provided them with his name, and there was no nametag on his white tuxedo jacket, so Rachel did what she usually did when she was not given a person's name: she made one up. In *The Blue Hour Sanction*, a similarly dressed character named Mr. Lobby had been a flight attendant for Worth-Gideon, Inc. and had served the Director, Kerrie Raven, cold glasses of Kors vodka on the flight from Oregon to Michigan. Hence, Rachel would now refer to the butler as Mr. Lobby in her head. *Writers and our imaginations*, she said to herself.

With a smile that said, *"Your mere presence enchants me,"* he welcomed them to sit on one of the couches.

Why, thank you, Mr. Lobby.

A young female server dressed in a black suit and white shirt entered the room, her black heels clicking on the wooden floor as she approached the coffee table. She filled all four water goblets and then stood next to the butler. With the practiced movements of centuries in the profession, the old boy slid to the side and reviewed the drink options before adding with a self-deprecatory grin,

"Or, we always have something stronger to propel you into the far reaches of the sunny afternoon."

Both Rachel and Ben-David opted for tea, and the server placed a bag in each of their China cups and then poured hot water from the tea kettle over the bags. After setting the kettle down, she punched buttons on her phone and poured coffee into the other porcelain cups. Finished, she stood to the side of the couch. "A 3-minute steep, and then tea will be served, ma'am, sir."

Ben-David pulled his hand back that had been reaching for the cup.

What should I call her? Rachel thought, studying the young woman. She was tall and thin with auburn hair that fell just above her shoulders. Her tan was deep, and her fingernails were painted red and manicured to perfection. Emerald eyes stared out behind her black-rimmed designer glasses.

It was not a perfect match, but she reminded Rachel of Flo. There were times in the past twenty years when she wondered what Adrienne's career would have been like if Flo had not been killed. There were even years when she considered crafting an entire story to account for the fact that Flo was not dead but being held as a prisoner in a dungeon by Control. Hell, a similar story thread had worked on *Days of our Lives*. But, ultimately, Topaz and Hightower had won out. Flo needed to die for Adrienne to reach her essence. *"She's gone, darling, and there's never bringing any of us back again,"* Topaz had said.

Rachel gave the server a quick grin as if in defiance of Topaz's long-ago statement. *Flo it is.*

Then, the words *there's never bringing any of us back again* took Rachel out of her creative game that was distracting her from facing her situation. *I might be seconds away from meeting my mother.*

She checked her watch.

11:51

"Mr. and Mrs. Andreas will be here shortly," the butler said. "They are both looking forward to meeting you, Mr. Crandall and Ms. Haines."

"It was nice of them to make some time for us, especially on short notice and because it's a holiday. I hope we didn't interrupt anything," Rachel said.

"Not at all," said *Mr. Lobby*. "They both like to keep things lowkey during the day, but we have a spectacular fireworks show planned for this evening."

She gave him a warm grin. "And, we apologize for our attire. On vacation, you know?"

He waved a friendly hand. "Don't think twice about it. Everyone is on vacation here."

What a kind gentleman you are, Mr. Lobby.

They talked about the weather for another minute, and *Flo*'s phone started vibrating.

She tapped the screen and said, "Tea is served."

"We won't be disturbing lunch, will we?" Rachel said to *Mr. Lobby*, reaching for her cup of tea.

"Absolutely not," he said. "Lunch is served promptly at 1:30."

Ben-David took a sip of his tea and said, "Thank you."

Rachel took a sip and felt her nerves calm as the warm liquid slid down her throat and into her stomach.

"Well, any friends of Abraham Raines are friends of mine," said a man's voice from the direction of the French doors.

Rachel turned and saw a short but trim man approaching the couch wearing red flip-flops, white linen pants, and an untucked blue Hawaiian shirt with white palm fronds. He matched the description of Kurt Andreas, and so did his watch. A stainless steel Doxa Sub 300 Professional with the classic orange dial. She had read that he was a fan of Clive Cussler's Dirk Pitt series, and Pitt wore a Doxa. However, she knew the watch because she had chosen it for a villain to wear in one of the series she had ghostwritten for. To her, the characters who made the most interesting antagonists always believed in what they were doing—they didn't think they were doing anything wrong and felt completely justified in their actions.

Was Kurt Andreas a villain?

To some people, probably. Topaz had delivered the sermon on money and enemies—the number of enemies you had was directly proportional to the amount of money you had . . . unless you had a pen name. Then, your pen name had the enemies and not you.

There was no one behind him.

She and Ben-David stood up and shook hands with the man; the P.I. towered over him, his hand almost swallowing the shorter man's.

"Kurt Andreas," he said, making eye contact with both of them. He neither smiled nor frowned, and his shake was firm. "Happy fourth. Kitty will be right along."

"Your coffee, sir," Mr. Lobby said, motioning Kurt to the opposite couch.

"Ah, many thanks, Benson."

Benson! Knowing the real name always ruined the game. Where was his wife?

Kurt sat down and took a sip of his coffee. "Still the best on the planet, Norrie," he said, winking to *Flo*.

Damn, now the game is officially over. *Okay, Benson and Norrie, it is.*

Kurt looked at their cups. "How's the tea?" he asked as if he were a salesperson for the tea company.

"Tasty," Rachel replied.

She waited for Ben-David to say something, but he stayed quiet for a moment, alternating his eyes between Kurt and Norrie a few times. Then, he stared straight into Kurt's eyes, gave a slight smirk, and finally said, "Good."

Rachel's eyes scanned over to Norrie. *Is she blushing?* Then, Rachel's brain processed what Ben-David had noticed, and she thought, *of course, she is blushing. They've been together.*

Evidently, Benson noticed it as well and said, "I'll handle the refills."

Norrie turned and left.

The situation reminded her of their dinner conversation last night. When Scott Brick and Ben-David had joined her and Suzanne Elise Freeman in the Charlie Chaplain booth, Scott had told them that when Shawn Frost had shown up unexpectedly at Musso & Frank Grill and was out of his mind, Shawn had said, *"It's the goddamned picture, Brickie,* The Baroness of Monterrey! *Everybody is sleeping with everybody, and they're all on coke! I'm in deep shit, and that's not all, man."*

She sipped while watching Kurt's eyes follow Norrie out of the room. *Everybody is sleeping with everybody.*

Yes. They. Are.

Kurt set down his cup with a clink. He crossed his legs and focused his attention on Rachel. "So, how is Abraha—"

"Hell-oh, everyone!" said a woman's voice entering the room, cutting Kurt off.

All three rose, and a woman wearing leather sandals, white stretch pants, and a red-and-blue-striped linen shirt with her sleeves rolled up approached the couches. Her hair was pulled back in a bun, and her makeup was immaculate— the red lipstick glowed.

Rachel saw it first. Kitty's eyes—their shape and perfectly proportioned separation from each other—were the same as Rachel's, as was the shape of their heads and hairline.

No doubt she and her husband had undergone rounds of plastic surgery— people that old should have more wrinkles—but Rachel thought that other than Kitty's much larger bust, her build was similar to Rachel's . . . too similar. As she reached the couch, Rachel saw that her height was around five-foot-six, which matched her mother's height. Kitty had kept herself in incredible shape, and seeing it up close was impressive.

She glanced at Rachel and took her position next to Kurt, whom Rachel was now watching.

He could not hide his surprise as his eyes darted between Rachel and Kitty. Rachel swiveled her head toward Ben-David, and his intense look into her eyes told her that he knew it, too.

Kitty Andreas was Rachel's mother.

Benson closed the French doors and took the lead, making introductions as hands crisscrossed and smiles were delivered. When Rachel felt Kitty's firm grip, she heard her say, "Nice to meet you, Tina."

All she could get out in return was, "You too."

Her insides were churning as they sat down. *I feel it all now—abandonment, fear, sadness, joy, empowerment, loss, disillusionment, confusion, helplessness, power, disappointment, betrayal . . . and* rage.

For a moment, her body felt transported to the Kalamazoo Meijer store, and Harold was sitting across the picnic table from her, saying, *"Yeah, the divorce . . . I'm sorry for what I'm about to say. Your mom didn't want you."*

Like other writers, sometimes she struggled with speaking in certain situations. Immediate replies were not Rachel's strong suit, especially when her emotions were ruling her as they were now. Topaz had summarized it as, *"As novelists, you all can write anything, darling, and can usually think well on your feet, but very few of you can speak well while you are in the moment. You freeze into bloody statues, which is okay because I don't."* However, whenever Rachel had worked with Ben-David, she had surprised herself with her wit and ability to ask well-placed questions and provide helpful on-the-spot commentary. Now, staring at her mother, all of her confidence had evaporated along with her words. *I should have just written her a letter—I would have nailed it.*

She could see the lined paper in front of her now, her thoughts appearing on it as they came to her mind . . .

Why did you leave Dad and me?

Why didn't you want me in your life?

Do you know how hard it was for him to raise me by himself?

Do you know what he gave up to devote all his time and energy to me?

You bitch.

You selfish, horrible bitch.

I dreamed of the day you would come back into our lives.

I used to stay up after I was supposed to go to bed and look out at the dark street through the blinds covering my window.

I would wake up and run for the front door.

I deserved a mother.

You quit.

You are weak. I am stronger than you are.

I remember feeling love for you when I was tiny.

I remember crying after you left.

I remember crying in school and college and after getting a coffee and not knowing why.

Why did you never come back?

You never wrote. You never called. You never showed up.

Dad was a good man.

He's gone now, and you're the one who should be.

I was a good kid.

Hug me. Apologize. Say you made a mistake.

We can talk.

You ruined it all.

No, you didn't. We made it. I made it.

I'm right in front of you now, and I earned my money. You didn't.

I hate you.

I love you.

I want to know you.

I want nothing to do with you.

You took everything away.

I beat you.

I just want to say . . .

Kurt's arm went around Kitty, and he cocked his head away from his wife's, donning his Kurt-for-mayor smile. "Well, what's new in the world of Abraham Raines?"

Rachel ignored him, not breaking eye contact with Kitty.

There was silence for a few beats, and then, out of her peripheral vision, she saw Kurt look down at Kitty's shaking right leg.

Rachel drew in a breath, her eyes glassy but firm. She said, almost in a growl, "You know why I am here."

Ben-David put his hand on Rachel's knee.

Kurt Andreas squinted and tilted his head as if someone had asked, *"Why are you sitting there naked, Kurt?"* After several starts and stops, he at last got out, "Kitty . . ."

Kitty Andreas reached up and dotted the corner of her eye with the tip of her index finger. She swallowed and said, "I know why you are here."

A tall man wearing jeans, a black Polo shirt, and a utility belt with a gun in a holster opened the French doors and entered.

"What is it, Jake?" asked Kurt, his tone a mix of seriousness and annoyance.

Jake continued to walk toward the couch. Rachel saw that the utility belt also held a knife, a flashlight, handcuffs, and extra clips of ammunition.

Benson moved to intercept him. "Is there something I can assist you with?" he asked Jake.

Then, Rachel heard a series of loud bangs, all coming from outside . . . in the direction of the wall with the fireplace.

Kurt shot up from his seat and said, "What—"

He stopped talking as Rachel watched Jake pull out his gun and raise it toward Kurt.

21

J ust as Rachel Roberts's eyes opened in disbelief, she saw another figure—a man wearing jeans, a red Polo shirt, and a similar utility belt—emerge behind Jake. Not waiting to reach the room, he pulled his gun out of its holster and fired at Jake.

The bullets entered Jake's back, and he lurched forward, his arm holding the gun lowering in response to the force of the rounds. He squeezed the trigger, and a round went into the floor, splintering the wood.

"Ivan, get him!" Kurt shouted.

The man in the red shirt continued to fire, and Rachel watched as Jake's body twisted with each impact until he fell over and crashed to the floor.

Automatic weapons fire broke out from what seemed like every direction. The windows to the sitting room shattered, and Ben-David pulled Rachel to the ground, which pushed the glass-covered coffee table toward Kurt and Kitty.

They were now flat against the wood floor between the couches, and Rachel looked up and saw Jake's lifeless eyes staring at her, a pool of blood forming on the floor underneath him.

Ivan dropped down and felt Jake's neck; then Rachel watched him crawl over to Kurt and Kitty. "The security system is down."

"How long for?" asked Kurt, his voice panicked.

"I don't know. We've got to get you both to the panic room."

"What is going on?" Kitty asked.

"Follow me. Low to the ground," Ivan commanded.

They took off for the French doors—Kitty looked back at Rachel for a second and then continued crawling behind Kurt and Ivan.

Rachel thought about what to say, but the trio reached the doors and took a right into the hallway outside the sitting room. A second later, she heard Kitty scream, "Oh, Norrie. No!" Then, there was silence. A few seconds after that, she heard Kurt yell, "Andromeda! God, nooooooo!"

Then, there was the sound of a string of tremendous explosions in the distance, and they put their heads down for a moment.

When the sounds ceased, Ben-David asked, "You okay?"

She looked at him. "Yes. You?"

"I'm good. Sounds like Norrie and Andromeda aren't, and what we just heard can't be good." He glanced at the open French doors. "Be right back."

She observed him crawl over to Jake's body. In less than thirty seconds, he had returned with Jake's gun and utility belt in hand. "Here," he said, motioning for her to lift her hips. She arched up, and he slid the belt underneath her and then adjusted it to fit her waist, always keeping an eye on the shattered windows and the French doors.

He took the knife off the belt and put it in her hand. Then, he slid the two extra magazines out of their sleeves on the belt and put them in his jeans' back pocket. "Okay, you've got a flashlight and handcuffs on the belt." He held the gun in front of her. "This is a Beretta M9 handgun. Jake got off 1 round, so we've got fourteen left." He patted his back pocket. "Each magazine has fifteen rounds, so we're looking at forty-four total." He paused, pursing his lips. "This looks like an inside job to get Kurt gone semi-wrong. Unfortunately, we won't be able to trust any of Kurt's security team members if we see them. It doesn't mean they were all in on it, but if something looks wrong, we shoot first and talk after." He frowned. "Rachel. If I go down, take the gun and the magazines. You can slide them back into the sleeves on your belt."

"Obadiah—"

"It's okay. We're getting you off this island. You've got a whole life ahead of you with Stan."

But I don't want to lose you! Again, the words were clear in her mind, but she could not speak them.

They heard more gunfire outside, followed by shouting and then screaming. For now, the inside of the house was quiet.

He hugged her and said, "Our best bet is to get to a place where we can see if making a run for the dock is possible. My bet is whoever is out there was working with Jake and is after Kurt, and if we can make it to the dock and jump in the water, they'll leave us alone. We can swim toward the yacht. I'm sure someone from *Abe Eye* will send a boat to get us if they can, but we may have to swim the entire way. Do you see any other options?"

She thought about finding where Kurt, Kitty, and Ivan had gone, but that was out of the question. The inside of the mansion would be a maze. "No," she said. "Your plan sounds good."

He looked at her hand that was holding the knife. It was shaking. "That's a—"

"Fixed-blade knife," she said, cutting him off.

"You know?"

"Adrienne Astra does."

"So you know how to stab with it, right?"

She did. The research that she had done over the years was suddenly front and center in her mind. "If I have to."

"You might," he said. "Okay, I'm going to crawl over and try to look out the shattered windows. Get behind the end of the couch and watch the opening into the hallway." He locked eyes. "We're going to be fine."

They moved, and in seconds, she was behind the couch, and Ben-David had made his way to the wall next to the blasted-out windows. She focused her attention on the hallway outside of the French doors.

Suddenly, a woman wearing camouflage fatigues with a red bandana tied around her blonde hair, holding an assault rifle, ran across the opening. Rachel heard her footsteps echo down the hallway.

Ben-David was soon beside her. "Okay, I don't see anyone out front. If we can get to the front door and take an immediate right, there is cover at the end of the porch—red, white, and blue bunting everywhere—and we need to stay low. We can work our way through the shrubs that line that side of the yard, which will get us near the dock. If the stupid fences weren't on either side of it, we could jump right in the water, but climbing a fence that high would expose us for too long."

"Did you see the woman wearing camouflage fatigues run by the doorway?"

"No. Was she armed?"

"Assault rifle. Looked like an AK-47."

"Okay. Let's wait a few more seconds to see if she returns or if others follow her."

They crouched down and waited.

* * *

Zachariah Lafontaine hid in the pool house with Jolly Otto.

"What in the fuck is happening?" he whispered to Jolly.

"They're starting the fireworks early, asshole. Now, here, put this on before we go back out," Jolly said, throwing him a terrycloth robe.

Lafontaine peered out at the pool deck through the open plantation shutters for a few seconds and then put on the robe. *Am I overreacting again?*

The *moment* the explosions had started, he had fallen off his lounger into the deep end of the massive pool with only a towel around his waist. And because his streak of bad luck—disastrous senate hearing, losing out on a major film role, etc.—had continued, the towel had come off while he was under choking on the water he had sucked in when he fell overboard. Jolly had been at the swim-up bar with two female "lifeguards" who were topless and had mere pieces of butt floss on for their bottoms. Lafontaine admitted to himself that he was waiting for everyone to get nice and soused before he moved in for the kill. As usual, when there were two wet beauties drinking with his agent, Jolly had a habit of overindulging and getting whiskey-dick—as Shakespeare once said about drink, *"It provokes the desire, but it takes away the performance . . . makes him stand to and not stand to."* However, when that happened, Saint Otto would admit the error of his ways, feeling the sin in his belly shrink the snake in his pants, and graciously remove himself from the battlefield before embarrassment followed hard upon the dropping of his drawers. Lafontaine was sure that was the case today, and when it happened, Lafontaine, who had pretended to be going drink for drink with them but was, in reality, having just tonic water and lime while he floated around the pool, planned to give the two goddesses . . . well, he planned to give them an afternoon with Zachariah *Lafontaine*. And it had appeared that it would be the case today as Jolly had pounded rum and cokes, and the ladies had made two pitchers of margaritas vanish in the late-morning hours. Then, the distant thunder of what he thought were actual explosions, followed by the popping noises and *rat-a-tat-tat* sounds, had surprised the hell out of him and sent his flailing body into the deep. When he emerged from the pool naked, the ladies and bartender were sprinting toward the guest lodge at full speed, and Jolly had tripped over a lounger and was sprawled out on the pool deck, a shattered glass of rum and coke on the concrete next to him.

So, Lafontaine had offered Jolly a hand up, and his agent had shouted, *"Where's everyone going?"*

"Those were assault rifles going off, Jolly, I swear. And that massive thunder from the other end of the island . . . Something horrible is happening."

"No, those were fireworks."

Jolly was lit, but maybe he was right. So, Lafontaine had turned toward the main house at that point, naked, and shouted. *"But, hey, how about a little warning!"*

Then, they had heard the *rat-a-tat-tat* again, and he had pulled Jolly into the pool house where they now stood.

"This is ridiculous," Jolly said. "We're going back out there. Did you *see* those women at the bar?"

"Just hold on," he replied, grabbing his agent's arm.

Watching the classic movie, *The Baron of Arizona*—Kitty's suggestion—had put him in a foul mood that had continued this morning. Somehow, he, *Zachariah Lafontaine*, had lost out on the male lead in *The Baroness of Monterrey* to Shawn Frost, of all people. *It's all because of that film he starred in for Spielberg,* Lafontaine had thought. Although he knew his annoyance was fueled by jealousy—Frost had been perfect in the lead role, and the picture had dominated the box office— Lafontaine had thought, *Well, good for him. He's acting again but belongs in New York City on the stage or in his booth. Leave the big screen to the big actors, Frost.* Lafontaine was so sure he would be chosen as *The Baroness of Monterrey*'s male lead that he had a basket of grapes, wine, cheese, crackers, champagne, and chocolate delivered to the actress he had wanted to work with forever: the legendary Jessamine Jean Baptiste. She had sent him a kind note in return, and he had told Jolly Otto, "She knows what we can make this film." Then, the call had come from Director Henri Pascal—*Why in the fuck didn't he stay retired! Massimo Bergman would have chosen me!*—who told Lafontaine that he was all wrong for the role and that it would go to Shawn Frost. *"It's because he's hot right now, isn't it?"* he yelled into his phone. There had been a pause, and Pascal had answered, *"It's a small film, Zachariah, and the attention will be on Jessamine. There will be better fits for you and her to work together later."* The call had ended, and Lafontaine had broken two antique chairs in his den and then wept.

When the casting was announced, it had set off a gigantic war between Jolly Otto and David Killian. Jolly had lost. Then, all the bullshit about traveling using fossil fuels had come up at the senate hearing, and, well, he was here to forget all of that. *I should have never watched that movie last night! Kitty tricked me. I can't say no to her!* After the film ended, Kitty suggested they go off on *Blue Kurty* together the next afternoon, and his spirits lifted. However, the morning's promise had only turned into more suffering as Kitty informed him that she had changed her mind. He was furious, and his desire for her had turned to spite, and he had planned to flaunt his disappointment by having a long roll in the hay with the two women at the swim-up bar. *I'll have them bouncing up and down on me all afternoon, a bounce for every word I have ever uttered in a film! Shit, that's a lot of bouncing,* he had thought. *The hell with it. If Kitty's sweet, seventy-year-old bronze body—that I can't get enough of when I'm down—doesn't want me, I'll move on to other divinities.*

Movement on the pool deck pulled him from his mind's cycling disdain for Lady Andreas. One of Kurt's security guards was sprinting across the pool deck with a gun in his hand. Suddenly, there was a string of loud *pops*, and blood burst from the guard's chest as he fell to the ground next to a human-sized cardboard statue of Uncle Sam. Behind the fallen security guard was a man wearing camouflage fatigues holding a rifle and continuing to pour lead into the guard as he advanced toward the bloody man on the deck.

"Holy fuck!" Lafontaine shouted.

Jolly Otto pulled him down and said, "Okay, so you're right. Now, there's a bunch of tubes and other blow-ups in the back room. Let's go."

Seconds later, they were hidden behind the floaties in the darkened room. Zachariah Lafontaine had a snorkel in his hand to use as a billy club, and Major

Otto had a squirt gun that looked like a rifle that Lafontaine had used in the science fiction movie *Bug Hunt* that he had starred in early in his career.

They waited, and the only thing that Lafontaine smelled beyond his fear was the alcohol on Jolly's breath.

"I've got an idea," his agent said, flicking on the light.

The next thing Lafontaine knew, Jolly had pulled down his swim trunks, popped off the cap on the water rifle, and began peeing into the gun's water reservoir. "Anybody comes at us, and they're getting a face-full of Jolly's special cocktail."

"You brilliant warhorse," Lafontaine said.

Main-vein Otto finished and turned off the lights. "Come and get it," he said.

* * *

Kurt Andreas held hands with his wife as they ran down the hallway, following Ivan. The second set of explosions had sickened him. *They almost certainly just took out my supply depots,* he thought. *Millard is making his move. But that is impossible . . . No. Jake just tried to assassinate you.* Nothing *is impossible.*

How did this happen? *Security was tight, and I just met with Susan Kantor, the President of the—*

In an instant, everything became clear to him. *It was her. She thinks Millard is stronger.* He gritted his teeth. *Our relationship . . . thirty-plus years! That backstabbing witch! They killed Andromeda . . . in my house! When I get out of here, I'm going to—*

Ivan stopped at the intersection of a long hallway. Kurt and Kitty stopped, and Ivan quickly looked behind them and saw no one coming. "Keep your eyes on our rear," he told Kitty. "If you see anything move, tell us."

Kurt watched his wife nod. Her chin was vibrating, and she gripped his arm tightly. Around the corner to the right and five doors down on the left was the

211

entrance to a walk-in linen closet; the space's back wall was the secret entrance into the panic room. They were almost there.

Ivan poked his head out, looking right and left down the long corridor. Immediately, he pulled his head back. "Empty in both directions," he said, turning toward them. "Let's hurry."

All three of them entered the hallway, and Kurt felt his lungs burn as he sprinted behind Ivan, pulling Kitty along. They passed one door.

Two doors.

He was breathing hard. Ivan's red shirt was like a bullseye he was trying to hit.

Three doors.

A door on the right side of the hallway opened perhaps ten yards away, and a man wearing camouflage fatigues turned toward them. There was something in his hand . . .

Ivan shot off five or six rounds, hitting the man in the chest, but it was not enough to stop the man's throwing motion with his right hand.

A green object the size of a baseball left the man's hand as he shouted out in pain and started to fall to the floor.

"Grenade!" Ivan yelled.

Kurt stopped and held back Kitty as the grenade hit the floor a few feet in front of them and a few feet behind Ivan.

He went to jump the other way but saw Ivan turn and jump on the grenade at the last second.

In a grotesque explosion, Ivan's body blew apart, scattering body parts, blood, bone, and gristle all over the hallway, walls, and Kurt and Kitty.

Shaken by the explosion and the blood that had splattered his back and the back of his head, Kurt tried to get to his feet. Then, he felt an awful pain tear through his right arm, and it was then that he heard the familiar sound of an AK-47 being fired.

His arm disintegrated in a shower of blood, and then the pain moved over to his chest, where wet, red holes started appearing.

He dropped to one knee and saw Kitty's body writhing on the ground, and bullets poured into her small frame. He took one look up and saw a female mercenary approaching them, continuing to shoot.

Kurt fell next to Kitty, and for a moment, the bullets stopped.

Blood was leaking out of Kitty's mouth, but she was able to say, "That woman . . . in . . . the . . . sit-ting room. She . . . w-ah-s, my d—"

Her eyes froze, and her head slumped, and Kurt knew that Kitty was gone.

Two mercenaries were now standing over him—one male, one female—and the last thing that Kurt Andreas ever saw was the end of the barrel of the flagship weapon on which he had built a secret empire, the gun that Mikhail Kalashnikov had invented out of his own horrifying experience in World War II when he had witnessed the Germans invading the motherland, his country, with automatic rifles . . . the AK-47.

* * *

Rachel stopped just behind Ben-David, holding the knife in her sweating hand. They were now just to the left of the shot-out windows in the room next to the estate's grand front doorway.

"What do you see?" she asked.

"Nothing . . . and that's what scares me. No one in the front yard, and no movement on the pier. I still can't see if there is a boat we can use, so we should still plan on swimming if we can get to the water."

They had encountered no one in their journey from the sitting room down the expansive hallway and along the narrow corridor leading to their current position. It had been a few minutes since they had heard any gunfire.

"There could be a smaller boat," she said.

"Maybe," said Ben-David. "Depends on who controls the pier. Either way, we can't wait here forever. This might be our best chance."

From somewhere in the house behind them, they heard an explosion followed by automatic rifle fire.

"It's definitely from the interior," Rachel said, her heart thumping.

"Okay, let's make our break for the far property line. Stay behind me and keep an eye on our rear."

She nodded.

"I love you, kid," he said.

"I love you too," she replied.

They exited through the front door, checked all directions, and sprinted for the hedges.

22

achel Roberts was surprised at Obadiah Ben-David's speed as they bounded across the thick front lawn of the Andreas estate. Every few bounds, she would turn her head and look behind her. She saw no one so far.

Her primary thoughts leaned toward survival, but there were also thoughts of Stan and their life together and their *future* together, along with the sinking feeling that her mother had not made it to safety and the realization that she would never be able to speak with her again. If given a second chance, would she have said all of her thoughts to her aloud? She wanted to believe she would have, but something inside her said, *No, it was never your responsibility to say those things to her.*

And Ben-David. He had told her that he loved her, and she had told him she felt the same way. It was not a romantic love, but this unexpected, life-and-death scenario had brought their unspoken sentiments to the forefront. She was happy that they had expressed what their relationship meant to each other. Unlike her encounter with Kitty Andreas, it was genuine, uncomplicated; it was real.

They were twenty yards from the hedges.

Fifteen yards.

Ten.

A shot rang out, and Ben-David's right leg bent inward. He started to fall to the ground.

Rachel did a quick survey of the area. There was a woman soldier who had just come around the side of the house and was running toward them with a pistol raised.

Ben-David landed on the ground and rolled just as another round hit where he had fallen. Blood from his thigh was now staining the lush green grass. Rachel dove to his side and watched as he raised the gun and aimed it at the mercenary. He pulled the trigger.

He pulled it again.

And again.

At least one shot had hit its mark as the woman dropped her weapon and felt her upper chest. But she kept on running toward them.

Then, gunfire came at them from across the lawn by the entrance to the pier. There was a man with an AK-47 shooting at them.

Ben-David returned fire, and the man dove for cover.

Rachel held her knife the way Adrienne had been instructed by Flo, which Rachel had written. *"Remember, Adrienne, slip it into the flesh between the bones."*

"She's still coming," Rachel shouted to Ben-David over the gunfire. "I'll take her. You focus on the asshole on the pier!"

Gunfire strafed the hedges behind them, but the rounds went high as Ben-David engaged.

The mercenary was a few yards away from Rachel. Blood was soaking the upper chest and right shoulder area of her fatigues as if a small jar of Ragu had been poured on it. Seeing the knife in Rachel's hand, she went for her own knife.

As Ben-David peppered the pier with bullets behind her, Rachel sprung at the oncoming woman.

Her force knocked the soldier to the ground, and Rachel seized the momentum, getting on top of her. The woman slashed with her knife and barely missed Rachel's midsection, and Rachel used her left hand to block a second attempt. Everything was happening fast, and she did not have time to make a calculated stab, so, without hesitation, she drove the knife into the woman's stomach.

The mercenary screamed in pain, and Rachel smelled her foul and hot breath. The woman was much larger and stronger than her, and Rachel did not know if she could parry another blow. *Create distance!*

She pushed her knife in deeper, let go of it, and rolled off the soldier just in time as the woman's blade sliced through the air where Rachel's neck had been.

Rachel continued to roll away.

I've lost my weapon, but I'm still alive.

She heard a gunshot.

Her roll stopped, and she turned to face her opponent.

But there was no opponent.

Ben-David had shot her in the head, and the lawn around what was left of the woman's skull was a mess of goo.

"You okay?" he asked, ejecting the magazine from his Beretta, keeping an eye on the pier.

She low crawled over to him. "Yeah. How's the leg?"

He removed a fresh magazine from his back pocket and slammed it into the Beretta. Just as the man with the AK-47 appeared on the pier again, Ben-David unloaded on him, and Rachel watched as the man flailed and then fell off the dock into the water.

Ben-David swept his gun across the pier, the yard, the house, and then behind them. There were no more visible threats.

He reached into his back pocket and withdrew the final magazine. Then, holding both in his large hand, he extended his arm toward her. "Here, take these," he said, wincing in pain. "I'll only slow you down. Get to the pier and get to the yacht. You know I can't swim like this."

She took the gun and magazine. *He's right. There is no way he can swim.* Her eyes continued to scan for threats as she evaluated the situation. She could only see Andreas's monster yacht, *Blue Kurty,* dominating the pier. Was there a smaller speed boat tied up farther down? From her angle, she couldn't tell. She decided it was worth a shot. She was not leaving Ben-David here.

"C'mon," she said, bending down. "I'm going to help you to the pier. There might be a boat."

"Rachel—"

"I'm not leaving you here, and that is final," she said, cutting him off. Her words were delivered with a tone of uncompromising determination.

What I say goes right now, she thought.

"Okay, I'm not talking you out of it," he replied.

He held on to her arm and rose from the ground . . . and then the five-foot two-inch Rachel Roberts helped the six-foot eight-inch Obadiah Ben-David start limping toward the pier.

* * *

Jolly Otto . . .

Aimed his squirt gun at the mercenary who had entered the back room of the pool house. Without hesitation, he squeezed the trigger, and a stream of yellow urine shot into the soldier's eyes and mouth. As the man dropped his AK-47, Zachariah Lafontaine, in his hooded, terrycloth robe, an actor-monk-enforcer, seventeen feet tall, *The Baron of the Pool House,* burst out from behind the stacked floaties and swung the snorkel in his hand like a policeman slicing the air with a baton.

Look at that actor go—right in the middle of it! Jolly thought. *Get him.*

The snorkel found its mark against the startled man's nose . . . and did nothing. Thankfully, Jolly had also emerged from behind the blow-up cover and picked up the man's weapon. *I didn't watch all of those Schwarzenegger, Stallone, and Willis films in the 1980s for nothing,* the agent thought as he raised the AK-47 and unloaded a handful of rounds into the man's chest.

If they got out of this, they'd be heroes. *He'd* be a hero. The man who saved the world's best and most bankable actor. The agent *The Hollywood Reporter* had nicknamed "The Man Who Would Be William Morris."

Jolly. Otto.

The Lion in Summer.

The soldier of fortune fell as his blood dripped onto a giant-sized floatie of Mr. Spock, who was raising an eyebrow with a phaser in his hand. "You sonofabitch," Jolly snarled at the man who was spitting up blood . . . and reaching for his gun. "Oh, no, you don't!" Jolly yelled and emptied more bullets into the mercenary's chest. *You don't vandalize a piece of property that has the legendary Vulcan on it. No sir.*

Lafontaine dropped his snorkel, and the man lay motionless, blood oozing from his multiple wounds.

"Got you, bitch," Jolly said and then heard more dripping and looked at Lafontaine. *Oh God, tell me he isn't hit.*

The mega-agent-turned-Rambo saw no blood anywhere near his client. Then, he looked at the bottom of the robe and the floor underneath it . . . and rolled his eyes.

Lafontaine had pissed himself.

Then, the dead man's radio crackled to life. "All units, all units, objective attained. Move to rendezvous bravo, out."

✻ ✻ ✻

Rachel and Ben-David reached the pier, and as they started to move down the structure past *Blue Kurty*, she saw the body of the dead mercenary that Ben-David had killed being torn apart by sharks in the water to the right. There was blood and foam and splashing everywhere in the feeding frenzy.

She could see *Abe Eye* in the distance.

Good, the ship hasn't left yet.

She squinted. There appeared to be a smaller boat in the water. "Is that the speedboat that brought us here earlier?" she asked Ben-David.

After a few more steps, he said, "Stop for a minute." They did, and he concentrated on the water. "Yes, I think they're headed this way."

Her spirits lifted. "Thank God. Let's get to the end of the pier and make it easy for them."

Behind them, gunfire sounded, and Rachel turned around while Ben-David balanced on one leg.

She saw three mercenaries running away from the estate toward the hills beyond, and one member of Kurt Andreas's surviving security force was giving chase, shooting at them with an Uzi. She swung her weapon in a tight arc, looking for threats headed her way.

A few seconds passed, and Andreas's man and the three combatants moved out of view.

She turned around and took some of Ben-David's weight as he leaned down on her, and they continued down the pier.

A few minutes later, they reached the security shack. It was riddled with bullets, and she could see three shot-up bodies inside. Rachel handed Ben-David the Beretta and dashed inside. From one of the bodies lying on the floor, Rachel picked up the man's Beretta, took the spare clips off his utility belt, and placed them inside the sleeves of her belt. In a few seconds, she was standing next to Ben-David again.

"Good," he said, holding the gun in his free hand. Rachel checked the magazine in her weapon. It was almost empty. She ejected it and inserted one of the full ones from her belt. There was no watercraft tied up to the pier beyond *Blue Kurty*. The inbound speedboat would be their only way out of there.

They pressed on.

Ten yards from the end, they witnessed the speedboat from *Abe Eye* sharply turn toward the pier. A woman was driving the boat, and two crew members were armed with automatic rifles. One of them gave Rachel and Ben-David a wave. Rachel waved back.

In seconds, the boat was alongside the pier, and Rachel and one of the men helped get Ben-David onboard—it was a drop of a few feet from the pier's surface to the speedboat's gunwale.

Suddenly, a series of shots sounded behind Rachel, and she dropped to the deck. The speedboat lurched forward and sped away while the two armed men onboard shot their weapons in the direction of the pier.

Rachel twisted her head and saw a mercenary running toward her with an AK-47 in his hands. *Where did he come from?*

She got the answer to her question as a second mercenary jumped down to the pier from a ladder hung on Blue Kurty.

They had been onboard the boat. *Why?*

The men fired a few more rounds and then took off in the other direction.

Why are they running that way?

She looked over at *Blue Kurty* . . . and the answer entered her mind.

"Rachel, we're coming for you!" Ben-David yelled from the speedboat.

One of the men had moved forward on the speedboat and was now firing a bow-mounted machine gun at the retreating soldiers on the pier. Rachel watched the gun cut the two mercenaries to pieces, and she dropped her weapon and removed the utility belt. Then, she tried to wave the boat off. "The yacht is going to explode!" she yelled.

Ben-David gave her a thumbs up and then motioned her to *c'mon!* He relayed the message to the woman driving the craft, and she nodded.

Rachel didn't wait. She moved back perhaps fifteen yards, turned around, and sprinted for the end of the pier.

Ten yards.

Five yards.

One yard.

As her feet found purchase at the end of the pier, Rachel Roberts, pen name Riley Cannon, pushed off.

Her body floated through the air as a massive explosion—a fireball and spray of fiberglass, chrome, glass, and other material—blew Kurt's yacht to pieces.

She closed her eyes and trusted her angle into the water.

Like Adrienne jumping into the ice-cold waters of Lake Superior to save her own life the night she ran the island course, Rachel was diving into the shark-infested Pacific Blue to save her own life.

She entered the water and kicked hard for the deep.

As she pulled, she felt disturbances in the water—pieces of *Blue Kurty* falling in and sinking all around her—and she prayed that nothing would land directly on her.

She pulled and pulled.

Had the sharks finished with the man that Ben-David had shot? *Will they now come after me?* She pushed the thought away and dug deep inside herself. *You're going to make it!*

Rachel reached the bottom, and her lungs began to ache. *A few more pulls . . .*

She heard a motor ahead. *They made it,* she thought.

Her head started to pound, but she pulled twice more before pushing off the bottom with her legs, exhaling a stream of bubbles on the way up.

Rachel's right hand broke the surface first, followed by her head. She gasped for air, taking in deep breaths as she looked around. She heard Ben-David shout, "There she is! Get over there, damnit!"

There were pieces of *Blue Kurty* all around her, and she felt weak. The sound of the motor grew louder and louder.

She was starting to sink. *Adrienne's time is up . . . maybe mine is too.*

Then, two huge hands closed around her wrists, and she felt herself lifting from the warm water and into the breezy air. Her eyes opened, and she saw Ben-David pulling her up.

"I've got you," he said.

I know you do, she thought. *You never left me.*

5 Months Later . . .

Landon Beach

23

South of Hampstead, Michigan – December 2025

2 p.m.

S nug and safe in her Christmas pajamas, Rachel Roberts sat at her desk in the second-story writing room and looked over the top of her laptop's glowing screen and out the window at the snowflakes falling. She joined her hands and stretched her fingers. A minute before, her husband, Stan Atwater, had placed a fresh mug of hot chocolate, topped with whipped cream, on top of her desk next to her laptop, kissed the top of her head, and then quietly exited the room.

Rachel reached over and picked up the mug, smelling the heavenly scent as the rim of the mug touched her lips. She took a sip and then felt Hemy rub against her right leg. Before she could reach down to pet him, he had left, crossing the carpet until he was in front of the ottoman. He plopped down, purring.

She set the mug back down and watched as steam rose from its top. Feeling a shiver, she swiveled in her chair to face Hemy. "This is it, furball," she said to the cat, whose eyes started closing.

A gust of wind blew outside, making the house creak and moan, and she shivered again. *It's time.*

Rachel spun her chair back around and stared at the screen. She saw the words MEETING PLACES centered a third of the way down the page. For the final book, she broke with her tradition of using chapter numbers and gave them titles instead. She had also broken the novel into four parts: Dharma, Artha, Kama, and Moksha. Topaz Kennedy may have thought that Rachel's title, *Sunrise Kama Sutra,* was an over-the-top allusion to the tension between Adrienne Astra and Byron Worth, but Rachel had other purposes beyond that hint. She had learned that the text from India, written in Sanskrit, recognized the Hindu concept of Purusharthas, which outlined four main goals of life. Rachel had summarized them in her notes.

Dharma—the preferred moral behaviors that make life possible and fulfilling

Artha—the material means of life that one properly and ethically gathers and employs to reach his or her desired state

Kama—the experiencing of pleasures and aesthetic enjoyment of life while still acting in accordance with Dharma and Artha

Moksha—liberation through the achievement of self-actualization

So, she wrote the novel in a way that forced Adrienne to reflect on her career and interrogate her actions and experiences through the lenses of Dharma, Artha, and Kama. Now, in Part Four, *Moksha*, it was time for Adrienne—and Rachel—to achieve release and freedom. However, Moksha could also be interpreted as completing the cycle of life, which ultimately meant dying before one could be reborn. On Santa Andreas Island, Rachel and Obadiah Ben-David had nearly completed their cycles of life, and Rachel now planned to bring that experience to the page, for the final novel was about endings, not beginnings, closure to what had been, not resolutions to influence what would be.

Ben-David's leg had healed, and he was now up to walking three miles daily with Tilly. He had also taken some long hikes with Rachel, talking about what they had gone through together. For the first month, she had visited him at his house where he was recovering from what he had told everyone outside of her, Tilly, and Stan was "an attempted mugging" in L.A. They had watched the news together, thinking there would be footage released of them at some point, but there never had been. Then, they remembered hearing Ivan's report to Kurt in the sitting room that the security system had been disabled. No one except Abraham Raines, David Killian, and the crew onboard *Abe Eye* had known Rachel and Ben-David were there. After a brief chat with Raines and Killian at Raines's private hospital, where Ben-David had surgery, it was determined that it was in the best interests of all parties concerned not to disclose that the yacht had been anywhere near Santa Andreas Island. Raines had grinned and said, *"Our secret is safe. I've got an entire team that leverages A.I. to scour the internet and remove anything that puts me in a negative or questionable light. Even if anything does show up, we can always say the pictures and video must be a deep fake. Hell, it's what everybody else does."*

President Susan Kantor had given a prime-time address from the Oval Office, declaring a war on illegal arms dealing, telling the entire nation that her longtime friendship with Kurt Andreas had blinded her, but that would not deter her from disrupting and dismantling the network he had been a part of. Then, she had gone on a tour of the country—a campaign trip like no one had ever seen before—to talk about her plan for a safer world. At each stop, she would also reveal a new, devastating piece of information about the former "Outlaw of Silicon Valley" and his wicked wife, who had both been found murdered in their island estate.

At that news, Rachel had wept. Mostly, it had been in response to the finality of her search for Tina Haines, but a small part had been in response to the overwhelming loss she had felt her entire life.

Then, there had been the circus of a press conference with Zachariah Lafontaine and Jolly Otto. Both men had been surrounded by adoring fans who had already forgiven Lafontaine for his disastrous Senate hearing. The screaming fans were energized as the legendary actor and his famous agent pledged their loyalty to President Kantor's crusade to disrupt and eventually end the illegal arms trade, and the press conference had ended in a frenzy of possibility as Lafontaine signed a large check to fill Kantor's mission coffers. *"This is one war we cannot afford to lose,"* Lafontaine had said. However, days after the publicity stunt, there had been rumors that Jolly Otto had an AK-47 mounted over the basement bar in his Pacific Palisades home. And, as they had after the Senate debacle, the two went into hiding . . . somewhere. There had even been wild rumors that Lafontaine and Otto had been on the island, but Rachel and Ben-David had not seen them there.

As for her own nightmarish experience of fighting and stabbing the female soldier on the island, Rachel had told only Stan about it, and he had been comforting and understanding. She had surprised herself with how well she handled it, but her writing had been different these past months as she made her way to the ending she knew she could not avoid. She thought her action scenes had an element of realism that wasn't there before; they were shorter and more intense and did not always go according to plan. When she was on top of the mercenary on the island, she knew where to stab her knife, but in the actual moment of struggle, it was not as easy as she had written it before in other novels. Topaz and Hightower had loved the pages since she had returned from California. *"They're so lean and tight, darling! Talk about* muscular prose—*you invented the style, and this book is the closing argument in your case for mastering it. Hurry up because I've got to know how it ends!"*

Rachel tapped her desk with her fingertips and thought again about the title, *Sunrise Kama Sutra.* She also knew that the ancient text was indeed about sexual pleasure, love, positions, and rituals. In that way, the *Kama Sutra was* about meeting and joining—the art of living well and finding a life partner, like Byron Worth and Adrienne Astra—and what sustains unions. And yet, people also met to destroy—*fuck*—each other, and Rachel intended to use this interpretation to her advantage as she wrote the final chapter. For, in the end, as she had planned it years ago, the series' moral center had always been anchored to this question: *When Adrienne Astra and Control finally met, who would achieve the ultimate deliverance in eliminating the other one?*

And still, there was a final question that followed that one:

What would be the cost?

Rachel had ended the previous chapter, titled "THE RISE OF THE SUN," with a cliffhanger. Adrienne Astra had finally learned Control's name, Robi Starr, which translated to "famous star," and Adrienne, along with Byron Worth and Ulysses King, had located her. Starr was on her speedy yacht named *Voyager*—a self-aggrandizing title Control had given the vessel to suggest that her work with A.I. rivaled the two Voyager satellites launched in 1977 that had now entered interstellar space. Now, *Voyager* was steaming at full throttle toward an island in the Pacific nicknamed "The Spider's Web," which Worth, Tipler, & Associates had recently discovered housed Control's secret base. In homage to Disney's *20,000 Leagues Under The Sea*, Rachel had modeled the island off Captain Nemo's island of Vulcania, which was made of volcanic rock, and his secret nuclear base there that surrounded the hidden, interior lagoon. "The Spider's Web" had a lagoon, accessible only by an underwater passage, and vast subterranean features along with palm trees, and there was a tricky reef that surrounded three-quarters of the island. Control had used A.I. along with her contacts in the military to fabricate a whole history of the island going back to the 1950s when it was supposedly used for atomic bomb testing, and, hence, was radioactive, and hence, there were warning signs for passers-by to stay away. Until recently, Control had also been able to manipulate the satellites that passed over the island so that there was no pictorial or video evidence of what was happening there.

Now, for the first time in the entire series, Control was on the run and had been cornered. United States Warships from the Pacific Fleet were on their way to the island, and Control was desperately trying to reach the island to destroy everything like Nemo had. But there was a twist: she also planned on firing her entire nuclear arsenal of missiles at as many countries as possible. A few chapters before THE RISE OF THE SUN had been a time of great tension as Adrienne had worked with the Space Force, C.I.A., and Pentagon to disrupt Control's A.I. superiority and remove her ability to fire the missiles remotely. Now, Control had only one option: to reach her deserted base first and manually fire the weapons before blowing up the entire island.

And only Adrienne Astra could stop her.

Dark Star vs. Famous Star.

Every other plane, warship, and submarine would not make it in time. Even Byron Worth's yacht, *Net Worth*, was out of intercept range.

But there was hope for the forces of good because Adrienne, Worth, and Ulysses were already onboard Control's yacht.

The original plan had been to sabotage the engines and bring the yacht to a stop, but when Adrienne had killed two of Control's armed guards and entered the main engine room with a backpack of explosives and demolition equipment, she had seen enough wired TNT to blow up Miami. If any component were damaged, the yacht would explode. So, they altered their plan to take over the bridge and slow the ship that way while still hunting for Control.

But, right at the end of the previous chapter, Control's seemingly immortal bodyguard, Gardell Valorous, was sneaking up on Ulysses King, who was positioned below decks near the yacht's stern . . . and Adrienne and Worth were just past amidships, heading toward the bow. They would not be able to get to the Weapons Division Head if he was in trouble.

He was on his own.

Topside, it was nearing the end of the morning's blue hour, the period of time right before sunrise.

The final question came into focus and ran through Rachel's mind like a digital display, the same information scrolling across the screen repeatedly: *What would be the cost?* She felt a lump in her throat, and suddenly, she was not only a writer but one of her future readers who would be on the edge of her or his seat, wondering if one of the series' favorites, the beloved tech expert and Weapons Division Head Ulysses King, would make it.

Licking her lips and tilting her head to the right, Rachel placed her fingers on the laptop's keyboard.

She said, "I'm pulling for you, Ulysses. If anyone can make it out of this, it's you." Then she reminded herself of one of the reasons that the series was so successful: Readers knew that Adrienne would be around for six books, but what they didn't know was if Adrienne could always *save* the people she cared for or set out to save from the evil clutches of Control.

The titles scrolled through her thoughts . . . *The Blue Hour Sanction* . . . *Morning Glory Mayhem!* . . . *Late-Afternoon Associates* . . . *Enemies in the Evening* . . . *Dark After Midnight* . . . *3 a.m. Phone Call* . . . *Sunrise Kama Sutra.*

She closed her eyes and said, "I love you, Adrienne. Thank you for what you have given me."

And then, Rachel Roberts, pen name Riley Cannon, wrote the final chapter of her legendary series. There would be no epilogue . . . only *MEETING PLACES*.

The Final Chapter of *Sunrise Kama Sutra*

MEETING PLACES

Onboard *Voyager,* somewhere in the South Pacific

U lysses King crouched low in the passageway and spoke into the microphone on his headset. "Adrienne, Byron, I'm in position near the aft hatch—should be able to take care of anyone who comes this way."

"Roger that. We're still heading forward," came the voice of his long-time co-worker and friend, Adrienne Astra.

"Security system has been disabled. They have no visuals below or topside. Be ready if I have to flush some baddies your way," Ulysses said.

"Born ready," said Adrienne. "Dark Star, out."

King grinned and focused his attention on the darkened passageway ahead of him. He trained his Uzi on the center of the narrow space and swept it slowly back and forth, looking for any movement.

They were almost done with their mission—a mission that had taken over twenty years to complete. There had been triumphs, betrayals, disasters, and loss, yet he was still standing and proud to be by Adrienne's side in what should be their finest hour. On the Worth, Tipler, & Associates front, Munny, Flo, and

Raven had been dead for two decades, Gideon for over a year, and Rose Varga and Kristy Cummings for almost five years—although Munny and Flo were the only ones who had not been traitors. On the enemy front, Adrienne had defeated Victor Lars Junius, Imperia Rex, Brandon Gold, Samuel Ingraham Michaelson, Geoffrey Cashmere, Mercedes DiMera, and Aristotle Baron, sending them all to meet their maker.

As he continued to scan for threats, Ulysses knew he was a different person now than the wiry kid who had joined Worth-Gideon in his early twenties. And, at 46, Adrienne was different too, and so was the 61-year-old Worth. The three of them bore the physical and emotional scars that came with twenty years in the business, and Ulysses couldn't help but think of what he had told his husband, the still-on-the-air talk show host, Dr. Michael, right before he had left with the team: *"We'll take the kids on a trip to the beach. This is the last leg of my team's journey, Michael. The world will be a safer place when I return—and then I'll retire."*

The years spent tracking down Control had taken a toll on their relationship, and he had missed key events in his young children's lives over the past two years. *It's time to end this and get those years back,* he said to himself.

He felt a rush of air on his neck before he heard the creak behind him. Part of his brain told him that there was only a bulkhead to his rear . . . while the out-of-the-box and creative troubleshooting part of his brain that had kept him alive throughout his career signaled danger and that the bulkhead must have a hidden compartment.

Ulysses spun and ducked, hearing a round hit the opposite bulkhead. Instinctively, he thrust his left hand upward while his right still held onto the Uzi. His effort paid off as the pistol held by Gardell Valorous flew out of her right hand. Then, he felt two things at once: a searing pain in his back and the Uzi being ripped from his hands. As he finished his turn, he witnessed the immense physical presence of Gardell Valorous as she withdrew the serrated knife from his back and threw the weapon to the deck. The shorter and now wounded

238

Ulysses reached up and tried to claw at Valorous's eyes, but his movements were sluggish as hot blood poured out of his back and splashed on the passageway's gleaming, waxed floor.

"We've had enough of you," Valorous growled and then plunged her dripping knife into Ulysses' chest.

He dropped to one knee, struggling to breathe as his right lung filled with blood. A sick, gurgling sound came from his mouth as he inhaled. In a desperate attempt, he reached for the Beretta in the holster on his waist . . .

Gardell Valorous kicked his hand away. Then Ulysses felt the full force of a blow to his neck, and his vision became a field of stars until his head slammed against the deck, and everything went black.

He thought he heard the sound of a gun being cocked, and his last thought was, *I've failed you, Adrienne.*

✳ ✳ ✳

Adrienne Astra moved swiftly down the passageway, holding in front her hush puppy with a suppressor attached, sweeping it back and forth. Worth was right behind her, covering their rear with his suppressed Glock 22.

She saw a ladder twenty feet ahead. *Good. That should lead us right up to the bridge.*

She whispered into her headset's mic, "Ulysses, this is Dark Star, over?"

There was no reply.

"Ulysses, this is Dark Star, over?"

Again, radio silence.

She felt an empty, uneasy feeling in her stomach, one that she had never had before concerning Ulysses. Adrienne gave Worth the signal to halt, and they stopped, perhaps five feet from the ladder. She covered her mic and said to Worth, "Switch to backup channel."

239

They adjusted their radios, and Adrienne said, "Byron, I think he's gone."

Worth gave her a pained nod. "It's just us."

Her pain was immense. When she had started as an assassin near the turn of the century, she had been able to keep her emotions from interfering with her work. However, as the years passed and her relationships matured, she became aware of her vulnerability. Her lover Worth and her eternal teammate Ulysses were family to her, and she had wanted to take on this last mission alone. *"You've got a husband and kids. I'll take care of this,"* she had said to Ulysses. He had replied, *"Remember the vow we took on the boat after leaving Robin's Nest? Nothing on earth, including you, could stop me from helping you finish what we started."* And now he was likely gone. *I'll never forgive myself,* she thought.

She took a deep breath and accessed the remaining reservoir of determination and courage inside of herself. *I will finish this.*

"Okay, it's now or never," she told Worth. "We storm the bridge."

* * *

Gardell Valorous stood over the body of Ulysses King and took out her radio after listening to Adrienne Astra try and contact the dead Weapons Division Head. She keyed the mic and said, "Control, King is dead. Worth and Astra are still onboard."

There was a pause, and then Valorous heard Control's voice. "Find them. They're either headed for the engine room or the bridge, although I've lost comm's with the engine room guards. Hurry. We're almost to the island."

She said, "Yes, Control. If the two guards are dead, then it's just you, me, the helmsman, and the bridge guard. Stay in your safe room. Valorous, out." She entered the secret passageway and headed for the engine room.

Two minutes later, Valorous stood over the dead engine room guards. She radioed Control, "Both engine room guards are dead, but Astra and Worth now know they cannot sabotage the engines. I'm headed for the bridge."

"Copy," was all she heard from Control.

"Bridge, this Valorous, be ready for action. Astra and Worth headed your way."

There was no reply.

"Fuck!" said Valorous as she headed topside to try and enter the bridge from the top hatch.

* * *

Adrienne was inside the bridge instantly after Worth had blown the port-side bridge wing hatch and lobbed in two concussion grenades.

She saw two dazed figures lying on the deck and fired a pair of rounds into each of their skulls. Blood, hair, and bone exploded outward from their disfigured heads and coated sections of the helm and navigation consoles.

Worth entered and ran to the helm station, where he pulled back on the throttles, slowing the craft.

Adrienne could see the imposing island's reef line in the distance. She examined the rest of the bridge, including the chart room, sweeping her hush puppy from side to side, expecting an armed guard to appear.

The space was silent.

"How many do you think are left?" Worth said, watching the yacht's speed drop on the digital display above the helm console.

"At least Control and Valorous. And that's enough."

"You said this thing had a submarine onboard. Do you think they're headed down to the diving well to leave on it?"

"They might. But, it's still faster to get where they're headed on the yacht."

241

Suddenly, an overhead hatch opened, and a figure swung through the opening. Before Adrienne could bring her hush puppy up, a boot connected with her face, and she fell backward.

Stunned, she landed on her back and dropped her weapon, watching it slide across the deck. There was a sizzling heat throughout her nose, and the vision in her right eye was blurry. Through her left eye, she saw the imposing figure of Gardell Valorous land near her feet and reach for her holstered weapon.

But, just as her fingers found the grip, Adrienne watched Byron Worth slam into her side, taking her to the ground.

Adrienne watched as they rolled over and over again until Worth was on top and using his weight to keep her from flipping him. Adrienne rose to her feet and took a step, but the blow to her head had thrown off her equilibrium, and she fell to her hands and knees. She shook her head and started to crawl toward the two figures.

Then, Valorous kneed Worth in his groin, and his body leaned slightly to the left, and he lost his leverage. With one visceral exertion, she rocked her hips, and he toppled over, hitting his head on the corner of the radio console.

Adrienne watched as blood started leaking from his head onto the deck. Worth moaned and tried to raise his hands in self-defense; with both of her hands now free, Valorous reached for her gun again. "I killed your little techie," Control's bodyguard said.

"No," groaned Worth.

"Felt good to get him finally, but not as good as this will feel."

The hell it will! Adrienne pulled out her Tom Brown Tracker #1 knife and, from a crouch, sprung.

Valorous had just removed her weapon when the blade of Adrienne's knife went through her left forearm. She shrieked and released her grip on the gun.

Adrienne's view of her enemy was a mix of clear in her left eye and blurry in her right, and somehow, through all the years, Raven's words—the island looming in the darkness beyond the monstrous seas—came back to her. *"You are animals. And in our line of work, you will be going up against* animals . . . *And I need to know which of you three has the best chance to survive if things don't go our way. I need to know how much of an* animal *each of you really is."* She gritted her teeth and pressed her body down on top of Valorous. Adrienne's agility was not what it once was, but in her forties, she had gained muscle mass in her arms and shoulders, and what she had lost in her reaction time, she had gained in overall strength. Valorous was in her early fifties and past her prime, but she was still formidable. *If I don't eliminate her now, she will kill me, and then she will kill Worth.*

With one powerful and direct motion, she pulled the knife out of Valorous's arm and then slashed the bodyguard's neck. A sickening gurgling sound came out of her opponent's mouth as she brought her hands to her throat, and Adrienne witnessed them become covered in blood as Valorous gasped for air.

Adrienne leaned over her, staring into her eyes, and said, "For Ulysses and the others," and then thrust her gory knife into Valorous's chest.

Again.

Again.

And again . . .

When she pulled the knife out after her last stab, she heard, "Adrienne! Look out!"

Out of the corner of her eye, she saw a blurry figure enter the bridge, an arm raised with a pistol in it. At the last possible second, Adrienne twisted away but felt a tremendous force hit her left shoulder. She dropped her knife.

Adrienne landed face down on the deck and heard another shot. A window in the pilothouse shattered. She felt a surge forward and looked at the helm console. A tall, stocky woman wearing black combat boots, fatigue trousers, and an olive t-shirt grappled with Byron Worth. The throttles had been shoved all the way forward, and the yacht was gaining speed through the water toward the island.

Adrienne looked at her left shoulder and saw blood soaking her black t-shirt around the hole where the bullet had entered. She quickly tested her shoulder's motion by trying to raise her left arm, but the pain was excruciating. She winced, looking down at the lifeless body of Gardell Valorous, blood spreading on the deck around her head and neck and starting to slide aft with the boat's forward motion.

Her eyes rose to Worth and the brunette woman he was struggling with. *Control!* Adrienne had never seen her—no one had—and now she wanted to kill her more than ever.

She rose to her feet, using the radio mount with her right arm, but Control slammed Worth against the helm console. When he pushed off, their locked arms pulled the port throttle back, and the boat twisted hard to port. As Adrienne held onto the radio mount, she watched helplessly as Worth sailed past her and out the open port hatch. He tried to check his motion before hitting the port bridge wing, but instead, he lost his balance, and she watched in horror as he went over the side.

Control got a hold of the port throttle and slammed it forward. Then, she turned the wheel hard to starboard to correct the yacht's course. Just before the boat heeled over, Adrienne saw Worth in the ocean, swimming for shore.

The yacht's screws dug into the water, and the motion caused Adrienne to lose her grip on the radio mount. She tumbled toward the helm console.

Like a bowling ball heading down the lane, Adrienne crashed into Control, knocking her to the deck.

They were both standing in seconds, but Adrienne had gotten behind Control and wrapped her right arm around Control's neck, squeezing and pulling her adversary's head back. Choking her was Adrienne's only move until she could locate a weapon.

They were now a few feet aft of the helm console, and she looked out the bridge's large front windows. The yacht was racing straight toward the island through a gap in the reef line.

I have to stop this boat. But she knew that to do that, she would have to let go of Control. Adrienne pulled her right arm back with all of her strength. *Just a few more seconds, and she should black out. . .*

But, it was difficult as her left arm was now useless, and Control must have sensed it immediately as she used her arms to elbow Adrienne's ribs. Then, Control snapped her head back, connecting with Adrienne's broken nose.

Blood erupted from the wound, wetting Control's hair, and Adrienne felt a level of pain that was much worse than when Valorous had kicked her face. The room was spinning, but she held on, refusing to release Control's neck. They stumbled backward, now a good ten feet from the helm console.

Then, the woman who had tried to rule the world for the past two decades uttered her final and fatal words, "Fine. Together then."

Knowing what she meant, Adrienne let go of Control's neck and lunged for the throttles . . .

As Adrienne sailed through the air, she thought of . . . Ulysses, dead somewhere below decks on this machine of death . . . Byron, and the promise they had made to each other before this final mission: *"We're getting married and retiring from this business,"* . . . Grid, now Daphne Brighton, visiting a theme park with her husband and two kids, safe and enjoying life . . . Jock Gideon—the stunned look on his face as Adrienne appeared before him, and then the satisfying view of him falling before her with two bloody holes in his forehead from Adrienne's hush puppy . . . Rose Varga—the *moment* that Adrienne realized that Rose had betrayed her . . . Flo—their last meeting on Adrienne's back patio when Flo said, *"Don't let the work we do consume you—always have something meaningful to come back to until you decide it is time to walk away,"* . . . the cabin—her first kill as she aimed her weapon at the drug king pin and heard, *"Oh my God, I'm reaching you.*

You do understand me, don't you? Woman to woman," . . . the island—the screams and then the feeling of the cold ground against her feet as she sprinted toward her paddock's gate . . . the last 100 meters of her final heptathlon—feeling her energy surge as she moved into a tie for first place, then pulling back to earn a spot with the company, and, after the race, looking up at Raven and Gideon seated high up in the stands . . . the day her mother and brother died—her father, with tears in his eyes, sitting down next to her in an empty hospital room and saying, *"Mama and Tommy are going away on a long trip,"* and her asking him, *"How long?"* and her broken father wiping his eyes and replying, *"A long, long time."*

Adrienne's right hand was inches away from the throttles, a collision with the island perhaps seconds away . . .

She felt the impact as Control drove her own body into Adrienne's back . . . and her outstretched fingers missed the throttles.

✳ ✳ ✳

Byron Worth stopped his crawl stroke a few yards short of the reef and trod water, watching the yacht zoom toward shore. In the past few seconds, the boat had turned to port, away from the sandy beach, and was now headed directly for the rocky cliff face. His stomach suddenly felt empty, and his eyes opened wide, realizing Adrienne's fate if the yacht was not stopped soon. *C'mon, stop the ship or jump off,* he said to himself.

The yacht began to turn to starboard . . . but did not slow down.

No . . .

Seconds later, the sea and cliff face exploded.

Worth dove deep and clung to the side of the reef to avoid the debris flying outward in all directions. Soon, pieces of the destroyed yacht began landing on the surface far above and then began to sink toward their watery grave all around

Worth, as if a monster were taking a bite out of the sea and its teeth were closing down on him.

His lungs began to burn, and he knew that he would have to surface soon, but all he could think was, *She's gone. I've lost her forever. The world has lost her. I can't face the reality above the water.*

He shut his eyes, holding on to the sharp, bony reef and his memories of Adrienne Astra. *I can stay down here forever* . . .

He could not.

Finally, Byron Worth's body conquered his shattered mind, and he kicked for the surface.

7 Months Later . . .

EPILOGUE

South of Hampstead, Michigan – Tuesday, July 7, 2026

Rachel Roberts and Stan Atwater walked hand-in-hand on the beach leading down to the navy sheet of glass that was Lake Huron. The blue hour sky was clear, and the sand felt cool underneath her feet as they approached the water. The sun would rise in five minutes.

She wore jeans and a red fleece, and Stan was in cut-off jean shorts and a Detroit Lions hooded sweatshirt. In their free hands were stainless-steel mugs of coffee, and, so far, other than "Good morning," they had not said anything to each other, simply enjoying the quiet rhythms of their routine and the first rejuvenating sips of coffee.

"Big day," Stan finally said.

"It is," she said.

Last night, they had discussed the launch of *Sunrise Kama Sutra* the next day during their romantic dinner on the back deck—steak, crab legs, curly French fries, and Caesar salad. He drank merlot, and Rachel drank . . . sparkling water.

Because she was three months pregnant.

Tonight, Christine Harper was coming over along with Obadiah Ben-David and his new wife, Tilly Michaels. Stan's parents would be there, and Topaz Kennedy was flying in for the occasion, as was Suzanne Elise Freeman—Tilly couldn't wait to meet her. Scott Brick and David Killian had been invited, but right now, they were tied up dealing with Shawn Frost and the strange rumors circling the production of *The Baroness of Monterrey*. Topaz had tried to persuade her friend who had penned *The Blue Hour Sanction*, but he was overseas researching a new novel—Rachel was bummed but understood and said they would have to get together sometime soon.

Tonight, they all planned on celebrating four things:

First, Ben-David had received encouraging news from his doctor. There was no tumor growth; his bloodwork looked good; and his Gleason score was low. The recommendation was to continue surveillance.

Second, Topaz Kennedy had officially conquered Ana Gunner and taken all her clients. How had it happened? Rachel had written eight letters—one to each of Topaz's clients and one to each of Aya Gunner's clients. In the letter, she explained why working with Topaz was the best experience of her life, and with the uncertainty of the publishing world's future, it was more important than ever to have the right agent . . . a veteran and powerful player who would know how to navigate the upcoming wars and secure big paydays for her clients . . . and that Topaz had no knowledge of what Riley Cannon was doing. She had emailed the draft to David Killian, who had massaged some wording and then sent it back to her. She personalized and signed them, and then Killy had eight couriers visit the eight authors and hand-deliver the letters and a $100,000.00 care package from the retiring writer. Loyalty talked, but money talked louder—an old lesson from the agent she was attempting to save. The result—all four of Topaz's writers stayed with Topaz, and all four of Aya Gunner's clients fired her and broke for Topaz. And the only person that Aya Gunner could blame? Riley Cannon—a writer whom no one, minus Rachel's trusted few, knew the true identity of.

"Tonight is all about me, darling! Sorry, but it's true—and I'm hanging with Freeman all night. Won't be able to meet her better half, but all in due time, Cannon. All in due time. I sent over a bottle of my favorite scotch and a few bottles of the audiobook deity's favorite red wine. Deal with it, retired author. My present to you is that I won't talk to you about writing another Astra book for at least ten years for what you did for me, you sensational saint! And Killy, well, if he weren't so caught up in those delicious film rumors, I'd fly out to L.A. and plant a big one right on his cheek. Incredible. Both of you. Fuck Aya Gunner."

Third, they would raise a toast to Riley Cannon's final novel and celebrate her legendary career.

Lastly, Rachel and Stan would share the good news about the pregnancy, which they had told no one about, not even Stan's parents.

However, before all that, the first surprise would be for Rachel to let Christine know that she was Riley Cannon. As was tradition since *Dark After Midnight* had come out, Christine had been given an exclusive interview with Riley Cannon. However, for this book, she had been notified that it would be a telephone interview and take place on the evening of launch day. Christine had called two days ago and told Rachel that she would have to cancel because she could not miss this interview. Rachel had smiled on the other end of the phone and said, *"You're coming. Don't worry, the party starts at seven. If you get called before then, fine. If not, you can take the call here and use my office upstairs."* Christine had agreed, and while Topaz and Suzanne hid in a downstairs bedroom, Rachel would take Christine upstairs at 7:10 p.m. to "check the room over." Then, Rachel would pull out her cell phone and call Christine when they were in the room.

"How do you feel about everything?" Stan asked and took a drink from his mug.

"At peace," she said.

"I know you don't look at reviews, but since the book dropped at midnight last night, you already have more than six thousand reviews on Amazon. Can you guess which titles are ranked number one through six for book, Kindle, and audiobook?" He paused and took another drink. "The entire 'Round the Clock' series."

"Glad the audiobook is up there," she said. "Suzanne turned in a performance for the ages. I can't wait to introduce her to you tonight."

"Thank you again for allowing me to listen to the proof recording."

She kissed him on the cheek. "It was something I wanted to experience together."

"Can I say again that I am sad about not being able to meet Scott?"

"You can," she said.

"Yeah, well, I wish he was coming. What in the hell is going on with that film and with Shawn Frost, anyway?"

Rachel shook her head. "I don't know." She brought his hand up to her mouth and kissed it. "I'm not supposed to tell you this because Suzanne is going to 'surprise' us both tonight, but they invited us out to a beach house they're renting in Maui this November."

"You're kidding me," Stan said.

"No. And we're going. It will be our babymoon."

"How long have you known about this?"

"She broke down and told me last week when we were finalizing plans for tonight." She gave him a smirk. "So, don't ruin her surprise."

He stopped them both and held her, giving her a long kiss on the lips. "I will not ruin this," he said, jumping up and down.

"Hey, easy with the pregnant lady."

His face turned white. "Oh, shit. Sorry, sweetie. Just—"

"A bit happy," she said, cutting him off.

He dropped down to one knee, kissed her belly, and then lightly tapped on it with his knuckles. "Hey, sorry in there. Your dad is still a kid, and sometimes he gets excited about things."

She laughed while he stood back up. "You know, two of the many reasons I married you were that you still acted like a kid and that I knew you would always make me laugh."

"And that I love Christmas."

"If you hadn't, it would have been a deal breaker."

"I knew when you returned from that research trip in Key West that we were meant to be together." He chuckled. "Remember how you told me you were attending an A.I. retreat there? Ah well, you couldn't tell me that you were really researching for the book that comes out today." He looked into her eyes. "And I did like the opening Key West scene where Adrienne and Worth talk about their past together."

Rachel said nothing but nodded with a closed-eye smile.

"God, that was a special Christmas! But, you know what? This one is going to be even better. And don't even get me started on the one after that. Our baby's first Christmas, are you kidding me? It's going to be amazing."

I love you, Rachel thought. *I love you, I love you, I love you.*

She continued to walk with him toward the water, thinking about becoming a mother in January and wondering what it would be like. It was as if her main character had passed the baton to her and said, *"You've got this."* Adrienne had never been given the opportunity to get married or have kids, and Rachel thought it fitting for her to end the series with Adrienne unmarried and childless. There was no future for a married assassin with children, as Flo had found out. Eventually, the innocent became targets, and Rachel was not sure she wanted to explore that aspect of Adrienne. However, if there was anyone who could balance family life and still save the world, then, of course, it was Adrienne Astra.

And today marked the end of their journey. As evidenced by Stan's report, thousands of readers had already discovered how the series ended, and today, many more would too. A writer was saying goodbye to her favorite character; a parent was saying goodbye to a child.

She thought of her father.

More than anything, she had wanted to share today with him, the man who had been forced to give up any dreams he had to raise her by himself. All his life, he had told her how easy it was to start something but how difficult it was to finish it. After what she had gone through to complete this book, she now believed him more than ever. She just wished that she could have told him in person.

As for her mother, well, she had chosen her path, which led her to where she was: a graveyard. All the fame and fortune that she had craved and received had not been able to keep her alive for one more second. Rachel had always wondered: *What if she had stayed with my dad?* Now, she was no longer interested in the answer. She had risked everything to meet her, and the reward had been the peace that had filled her soul after Rachel had said goodbye to Tina Haines, not to Kitty Andreas. Stan, Obadiah, Tilly, and Topaz had been wonderful in the aftermath of the terror on the island, and, as Rachel had suspected, she had been able to finish the book after that finally.

However, there were still instances when the moment she had stared down her mother and said, *"You know why I am here,"* came back to her, and she would remember her mother dotting the corner of her eye with her index finger. *Did she have a tear? Or was she just scratching her eye?* Then, the thoughts would leave her mind, and she would return to the present moment as if nothing had happened.

She stopped, and Stan stopped along with her. She turned her head and gazed at the vacant two-story house, four down the beach from her place. After hearing that she would not be going public with who she was, Topaz had called her in May. *"Okay, missy, it looks like there is no changing your mind. The world's loss, child, because you are one of the good gals. Now, I need to let you in a bit of a secret. My sister knows who you are."*

"Your sister?"

"Yes. Five years older than me and, for sure, the more level-headed of us. Don't you ever tell her I told you that!"

"I'm probably never going to meet her."

"Oh, but you have, many times, my dear Cannon."

"What?"

"Miss Mary, four houses down the beach." She paused. "Yes, darling, she's my sister. I had her move in right after you did years ago. Wanted to keep an eye on you and make sure that nothing happened to you. And she did it. I'll never be able to repay her. Of course, now that you're officially retiring and not going to announce to the world who you are, she will probably be heading down to Florida for good. She's there right now, but you already knew that, didn't you, lady, because you've been looking after her place for her like you have the past few years when she's traveled south. Ha! Did you ever notice that she only started doing it after you and Stan became an item? I told her I thought you were in good hands with your policeman, so she spread her snowbird wings and flew south. Well, I'm sure she'll say a proper goodbye when she returns in another month, but she did enjoy bumping into you over the years at Lakeview Villages or on the beach, always thought you were a kind person, which, naturally, I told her I knew already. Well, she kept you safe for all those years. That's the point, I suppose. She almost had to blow her cover during your first case with Mister Too-Tall—some scary stuff with those rich kids and all. Bye, Miss I-didn't-know-I-had-a-guardian-angel."

With the loss of her mother for a second time in her life the past summer, Rachel had been touched to know that for the entire time that she had lived in Lakeview, Topaz had her sister watching over her. Mary had always been so welcoming, and Rachel had always walked away from their chance encounters uplifted. Now, looking back on the years, Rachel realized that Mary's gestures of kindness—a pot of chili here, a raspberry pie there, a knitted scarf one Christmas, and a candle and a knitted blanket before a big winter storm hit during another— had always come when she needed them the most, which did not take away from Mary's visits but only made Rachel appreciate Topaz more because it had been Topaz who tipped Mary off that Rachel was hurting.

257

Their goodbye last month had been emotional as Rachel thanked her for watching over her. Mary had assured her that it was a pleasure—she had lost her husband to a heart attack a year before she moved to Hampstead, and Topaz's mission for her had given her purpose and had kept her alive. She also confessed that Adrienne Astra had kept her going as well. *"I've got the hardcover and audiobook pre-ordered. The book will be delivered to my new place in Boca Raton on pub day, and the audiobook will appear on my phone. I love listening to Suzanne while following along in my hardcover."*

They had embraced in Mary's driveway, and Rachel and Stan had watched her pull away in her car.

"Hard to believe she's gone," Stan said, looking at the darkened house.

"Today is all about change," Rachel said, "but Mary moving is one change I did not want to happen. The more I think about her, the more I miss her."

"I stand by my previous prediction. Someone will buy it by the end of the summer."

"Knowing that she was there watching over me for all those years, I hope it stays vacant for a while. Do you know what Topaz told me last night over the phone? She said she visited her sister there a few times a year and had even fielded phone calls from me while she was staying in the second-story guest room." Rachel pointed to the house. "And, once, she stood behind that corner window and talked to me on the phone while watching me walk down to the beach and stand at the water's edge while listening to her."

"Why didn't you tell me that last night?"

"You were already asleep."

Rachel blew a kiss toward the house, and they continued walking until they reached the water's edge.

They stood, facing the water and drinking from their coffee mugs.

"Should be any second now," Rachel said, seeing the orange glow in the shape of a semi-circle above the sharp black line of the horizon. There were no clouds, and she knew they were about to witness a perfect Lake Huron sunrise. *Appropriate for today,* she thought. Destiny *might be the right word.*

Hampstead was still crawling with tourists visiting for the 4th of July and staying until the end of the week. Stan had been busy, but he had taken today and tomorrow off for the quiet celebration.

She was about to go through today's schedule with him again when . . . it happened.

A small flash was followed by a crescent of glowing gold that broke the horizon and grew brighter by the second.

The water was still; there was no wind; and the only sound came from a few birds singing their wonderful morning songs.

Rachel took a sip of coffee, and her eyes scanned over to Beacon Island.

She thought of Ben-David swimming ashore almost forty years ago. Without him, she might not be alive. They had joked that they were now equal; he had saved her life from the psychotic Knight twins, and she had saved him from the mercenaries on Santa Andreas Island. Whenever strangers saw them together, they gave them a puzzled glance. She admitted they were an odd couple, a friendship between people over twenty years apart. Other than Stan, no one knew her better than Ben-David, especially after what had happened on the island. After she had finished the book and after he and Tilly had been married, Rachel and Stan had gone out to Ben-David's house every Thursday night for dinner, and she had finally brought Hemy out, and he and Ben were the embodiment of Rachel and Ben-David: two beings who didn't look like they belonged together but were best friends.

Last Thursday, she had pulled him aside and said, *"The book comes out on Tuesday. I'm not ready to say* never *yet."*

And he had smiled and replied, *"Then don't. Not until you're sure."*

She sometimes wondered if her stab would have killed the mercenary she had fought with on the island. Thankfully, Ben-David had saved her from the burden that would have come with taking another person's life. However, the memory of the encounter had convinced her that she was ready to take a break from writing . . . especially from writing action novels.

Having lived it, she no longer needed to write it.

Stan let out a whistle, motioning his hand across the peaceful and glowing horizon. "You couldn't have written a better scene than this."

"Perfect, isn't it?"

"Speaking of scenes, I have to say it one last time: I still can't believe you killed Adrienne Astra."

Rachel continued to stare at Beacon Island. As the rising sun's rays illuminated the island's features, casting a butter-yellow glow across the terrain, the image morphed into "The Spider's Web," and Rachel saw *Voyager* speed the last hundred yards toward the looming rocky cliffs . . . and then blast apart.

She blinked and saw herself diving off the pier at Santa Andreas Island, *Blue Kurty* exploding behind her.

Rachel turned toward Stan, raised an eyebrow, and said, "Did I?"

They held each other's gaze for a few moments, their faces devoid of expression.

Then, as if a film director appeared a few feet away from them and said, *"Action,"* Stan and Rachel's eyes opened wide, and they shared a smile.

AUTHOR'S NOTE

Thank you for reading or listening to *Huron Sunrise*. As an independent author, my success greatly depends on reviews and referrals. If you enjoyed the book, it would help me out if you left a quick review and then passed on the recommendation. If you want more information on upcoming books and discounts, please sign up for my email list through my website (landonbeachbooks.com) or follow Landon Beach Books on Facebook, Twitter, or Instagram.

Huron Sunrise. I hope you found the final leg of Rachel and Obadiah's journey as satisfying as I did when I typed the final period, my friends. It is never easy to say goodbye to characters you have lived with for years, let alone wrap up their arcs in a meaningful and complete way. The callbacks to characters from *Narrator* were fun, and, yes, there may be another Shawn Frost novel on the horizon. It has to be right for me to do it, but the wheels started turning when he met my two favorite narrators and friends, Scott Brick and Suzanne Elise Freeman, in Musso & Frank Grill. I am especially grateful to Scott and Suzanne for being game for that particular chapter when I approached them with a draft. You could say that my entire career has been built on the philosophy of "Treat other professionals in the business with kindness and then throw out the rule book. Life is short. Let's have some fun." Will I ever bring back Rachel and Obadiah to investigate some more mysteries along the shore of my beloved Lake Huron? Well, I have also learned in this business to "never say never."

Okay, it's time to finish the Great Lakes Saga. Look for *The Bay* in the future.

Many thanks to MB, EL, DB, JB, and RR, who all provided helpful comments on early drafts of the manuscript. I would also like to thank my wife and two daughters for their love, patience, and encouragement during this particular project—I will never forget it.

Happy Beach Reading!

L.B.

If you enjoyed *Huron Sunrise*, expand your adventure with *The Wreck,* the first book in the Great Lakes Saga. Here is an excerpt to start the journey.

THE WRECK

Landon Beach

PROLOGUE

LAKE HURON, MICHIGAN
SUMMER 2007

The Hunter 49's motor cut, and the luxury yacht glided with no running lights on. Cloud cover hid the moon and stars; the water looked black. A man in a full wetsuit moved forward in the cockpit and after verifying the latitude and longitude, pushed the GPS monitor's "off" button. The LCD color display vanished.

Waves beat against the hull, heavier seas than had been predicted. He would have to be efficient or he'd need to reposition the boat over the scuttle site again. The chronometer above the navigation station read 0030. This should have been finished 30 minutes ago. Not only had the boat been in the wrong slip, forcing him to search the marina in the dark, the owner—details apparently escaped that arrogant prick—had not filled the fuel tank.

He headed below and opened the aft stateroom door. The woman's naked corpse lay strapped to the berth, the nipples of her large breasts pointing at the overhead. A careful lift of the port-side bench revealed black wiring connecting a series of three explosive charges. After similar checks of the wiring and charges in the gutted-out galley and v-berth, he smiled to himself and went topside with a pair of night vision goggles.

A scan of the horizon. Nothing.

He closed and locked the aft hatch cover. Moving swiftly—but never rushing—he donned a mask and fins, then pulled a remote detonation device from the pocket of his wetsuit. Two of the four buttons were for the explosives he had attached to the outside of the hull underwater, which would sink the boat. The bottom two were for the explosives he had just checked on the interior.

He looked back at the cockpit and for a moment rubbed his left hand on the smooth fiberglass hull. What a waste of a beautiful boat. How much had the owner paid for it? Three...Four-hundred thousand? Some people did live differently. With the night vision goggles hanging on his neck and the remote for the explosives in his right hand, he slipped into the water and began to kick.

Fifty yards away he began to tread water and looked back at the yacht. It listed to starboard, then to port, as whitecaps pushed against the hull. He pressed the top two buttons on the remote. The yacht lifted and then began to lower into the water; the heaving sea had less and less effect as more of the boat submerged. In under a minute, the yacht was gone. He held his fingers on the bottom two buttons but did not push them. The water was deep, and it would take three to four minutes for the boat to reach the lake bed.

At four minutes, he pushed the bottom two buttons, shut the remote, and zipped it back into his wetsuit pocket. He treaded water for half an hour. Nothing surfaced.

He swam for five minutes, stopped, scanned the area with his night vision goggles, and swam again.

After an hour of this, he pulled the goggles over his head and let them sink to the bottom. He continued his long swim to shore.

1

HAMPSTEAD, MICHIGAN
SUMMER 2008

The sand felt cool under Nate Martin's feet as he walked hand-in-hand with his wife down to the water. A bonfire crackled away on their beach behind them—the sun had set 30 minutes ago and an orange glow still hung on the horizon. The Martins' boat, *Speculation*, bobbed gently in her mooring about twenty yards offshore.

They parted hands and Nate stopped to pick up a piece of driftwood and toss it back toward the fire. Brooke Martin continued on and dipped her right foot into the water, the wind brushing her auburn hair against her cheek.

"Too cold for me," she said.

Nate took a gulp of beer before walking ankle deep into the water beside her.

"Not bad, but colder than when I put the boat in," Nate said.

"Glad I didn't have to help," Brooke said and then took a sip from her plastic cup of wine.

"Not up for a swim?" Nate joked.

"No way," Brooke said.

They started to walk parallel to the water, with Nate's feet still in and Brooke's squishing into the wet sand just out of reach of the lapping waves.

Four zigzagging jet skis sliced through the water off the Martins' beach. Two were driven by women in bikinis and the other two by men. They weren't wearing life jackets, which usually meant these were summer folk who spent June, July, and August in one of the beach castles smoking weed in mass quantities. These four were probably already baked.

One girl cut a turn too close and flew off.

"Crazies," Nate said.

She resurfaced and climbed back aboard. Her bikini bottom was really a thong and her butt cheeks slapped against the rubber seat as the jet ski started and took off.

"Should they be riding those things this late?" Brooke asked.

"No," said Nate, "but who is going to stop them?"

They continued to walk as the sound of the jet skis faded. A quarter mile later, they reached the stretch where the larger homes began. The floodlights on the estates' back decks illuminated the beach like a stage. The Martins turned around.

When they arrived at their beach, Nate placed a new log on the fire and sat down in his lawn chair. Brooke sat down but then rose, moving her chair a few feet further away from the heat.

"What are your plans for tomorrow?" Nate said.

"I think I'll lay out. I looked at the weather report and we're in for a few good days until rain arrives," Brooke said, "then I'll probably go to the bookstore." Her voice trailed off. She gathered her thoughts for a moment. "We need to make love the next four nights."

"Okay," Nate said.

"You could work up a little enthusiasm," Brooke said.

He had sounded matter-of-fact. "Sorry. It's just that scheduled sex sometimes takes the excitement out of it. We're on vacation. We should just let it happen."

"So, you get to have your strict workout regime everyday, but when I mention a specific time that we need to make love in order to give us the best chance at conceiving, it's suddenly 'We're on vacation'?"

She had a point. He thought about trying to angle in with a comment about her obsessive need to clean the house the moment they had arrived earlier today, but as he thought of it the vision of his freshly cut and edged grass entered his mind. If they really were on vacation, as he had put it, then the lawn being manicured wouldn't be so important to him. Damn.

"What is your plan for tomorrow?" She said.

A switch of topics, but he knew she was circling. "I'm going to get up, take my run, and then hit the hardware store for a new lock for the boat."

"What happened to the lock you keep in the garage?"

"It broke today," Nate shrugged.

"How does a lock break?"

"I put the key in, and when I turned it, it broke off in the lock."

"You mean our boat is moored out there right now without a lock?" Brooke asked, while shifting her gaze to the white hull reflecting the growing moonlight.

"Yep."

"Do you think someone would steal it?"

"Nah. The keys are in the house. If someone wanted to steal a boat worth anything, they'd go down to Shelby's Marina and try and take Shaw's *Triumph*." Leonard Shaw was a Baltimore businessman who had grown up in Michigan and now summered in the largest beach mansion in Hampstead. Once his two-hundred foot custom-built yacht was completed, he'd hired a dredging crew to carve out a separate berth in the marina to dock the boat. With the dredging crew working mostly at night, locals and vacationers complained of the noise and threatened to pull their boats out of Shelby's. Nate was glad he had avoided the hassle by keeping *Speculation* moored off of his beach.

Brooke swiveled her eyes between Nate and the boat. "Why didn't you get a new lock today?"

He moved behind her and started to kiss the back of her neck. *We're on vacation, relax, baby.* "Is that a hint? Do you want me to swim out and sleep on board tonight?"

"Of course not," Brooke whispered back, enjoying the foreplay. "Are you trying to get a head start on tomorrow night?"

"No. Just trying to enjoy *tonight*," Nate said. "Can we concentrate on that?"

She leaned her head back and he kissed her lips.

Ten minutes later, the fire started to die with two empty lawn chairs sitting in front of it.

2

Sun rays peeked around the edges of the horizontal blinds in the Martins' bedroom window. Nate opened his eyes and looked at his watch, eight o'clock. He was normally up by six. Brooke was snoring, and he eased out of bed and lifted one strip of the blinds. *Speculation* was in her mooring. He smiled and dropped the blind back into place.

After putting on a pair of shorts and a tank top, he grabbed a pair of socks and his running shoes and exited the bedroom. The hallway was dark as he made his way to the kitchen. He pressed "start" on the coffee pot, and the coffee he had prepared the night before began to brew as he put on his shoes.

The past year had been a revolving door of pain, uncertainty, and disappointment. They had been trying to conceive for six months when his father died. Only last month had it felt right to try again. He hadn't been himself in the classroom either. His ninth grade physical science lessons at W. M. Breech High School had wandered aimlessly, his tests were rote memorization, and the usual passion he brought to each day had been missing; his students let him know they knew it.

His mother had lasted in the beach house until Christmas. The original plan had been for Nate and his older sister, Marie, to share ownership when their parents were unable to handle the upkeep, but Nate had bought Marie's half and the house was now his and Brooke's. His mother had left in January to move in with his sister in St. Petersburg.

He pushed the brass button on the doorknob and closed the door behind him. After wiggling the knob to make sure it was locked, he hopped off the small porch onto the stone walkway, went past the garage, and followed the dirt driveway until he was parallel with their mailbox. After stretching, he looked at his watch and started to jog down Sandyhook Road.

Each lakeside house had some sort of identifying marker next to its mailbox. A red and white striped lighthouse carved out of wood. A miniature of the house painted on a three foot by three foot board. A post. A bench. Something with the owner's name and the year the house had been built on the marker. This five miles of beach, once sparsely populated with neighbors in similarly sized residences, was now dominated by beach mansions that looked more like hotels than houses. The lots were owned by lawyers, congressmen, real-estate tycoons, government contractors, Detroit businessmen (of the few businesses that remained), and a few others who had money. Some were migrants from the already overcrowded western shore of Michigan. White collar Chicago money had run north and was moving around the Great Lakes shoreline like a child connecting the dots to make a picture of a left-handed mitten.

The sun flickered in and out of Nate's face as he ran under the oak trees spanning the road. He thought of the advice his father had given him when he was searching for his first teaching job: "Make sure that you buy a house east of the school so that when you go into work you'll be driving west, and when you come home from work you'll be driving east. That way, you'll never be driving into the sun. Just a simple stress reliever that most people don't take into consideration—that is, until they rear-end someone for the first time." As with all of Nate's father's advice, it had sounded too simple but ended up being right.

Last June his father had been diagnosed with stomach cancer. Three months later, on an overcast September day, Nate had buried him.

Brooke heard the back door close and rose from bed. She turned off their box fan and opened the bedroom blinds. The entire beach was motionless, and their boat was still moored, surrounded by flat water. The aroma of coffee drifted into the bedroom as she put on her robe.

By the time she reached the kitchen, Nate had already filled his mug and was headed down to the water. She poured herself a cup and started a bacon and eggs breakfast.

The sand parted with each step as Nate walked toward the water. Bordering both sides of the Martins' property was a wooden fence; the spindles were flat, painted red, and held together by wire with a metal rod driven into the ground every fifteen feet or so. The fence was not only a "beachy" way to mark property lines but served its primary purpose of trapping sand. Nate took off his shoes and set his mug down by the end of the northern fence line. He began to walk south.

The water ran over his ankles and then receded. It was cool and felt good on his tired feet. The beach looked abandoned. No more than twenty yards from where he started, Nate stepped down with his right foot and felt something sharp. He stood, balancing on his left leg as he inspected the bottom of his right foot. No apparent cut. No bleeding. He rubbed in circles and the pain went away. As he stepped back down onto the wet sand, he saw something sparkle in the place he had stepped before. Glass? A toy left behind by some toddler? As Nate picked the object up, he saw that it was neither. He submerged the object, wiping the wet sand off it, and then dried it with the bottom of his tank top. He held the object a foot in front of his face and studied it. In his hand was a gold coin.

* * *

Brooke saw Nate returning from the water. Assuming that he was coming in to complete his morning routine of running three miles, taking a walk to the water with his coffee, and now eating breakfast and reading the newspaper, she rose to unlock the sliding glass door from the deck. However, he walked right by the deck and headed for the garage. She unlocked the door anyway and refilled her cup. She took a seat at the worn kitchen table, which she wanted to replace but didn't as it had been in the family since Nate was a child. She had plans to redo many parts of the house, but Nate was adamant that the table remained and that the bedroom he stayed in as a boy not be changed. When his father was alive, Nate would have coffee with him in the morning and read the paper at this table. Brooke would still be sleeping and his mother would be cooking breakfast. He had remarked to her that at times he still felt like a visitor, expecting his father to pull up a chair and start a conversation with him about the old days and family stories he'd heard over and over again.

Brooke finished the paper, breakfast, and her cup of coffee and Nate had not come in yet. What was he doing? His bacon, eggs, and toast were cold. She grabbed the coffee pot and headed to the garage.

Nate heard the garage door open as he stared at the coin through a magnifying glass, mesmerized by it.

His wooden writing desk sat in the middle of black carpeting that covered one-quarter of the garage's concrete floor. Two bookcases that he had constructed from odds-and-ends left over from the addition that his parents had done a few years ago rested against the wall behind the desk. Favorite authors had taken up permanent residence on the top two shelves of the first bookcase, and the remaining three shelves were full of paperbacks, read according to his mood at the time he had purchased them. On the top shelf of the second bookcase rested a pair of fins and a mask that he used when cleaning off the bottom of his boat. His father's dive knife was next to the mask.

The shelf below the diving gear contained books that Nate had almost worn the covers off: a Marine Biology desk reference set, half-a-dozen books by Dr. Robert D. Ballard from the Woods Hole Oceanographic Institute, a few by Jacques Cousteau, and five years' worth of magazines from his National Geographic subscription.

The bottom shelves contained books about Great Lakes ports, navigation rules and aids, and boating regulations. Next to one of the rows of books were rolled up charts and a navigation kit. Nate had taught himself how to navigate and routinely took *Speculation* out overnight.

Brooke arrived at Nate's desk and refilled his coffee mug. "Are we rich?" She asked looking at the coin.

"Very funny," Nate said, "I found this on our beach this morning."

"Is that gold?" Brooke asked, more serious now that she had a better look at the coin.

"Maybe. I don't recognize any of these marks or the language that is engraved on it." He put the coin and magnifying glass down and pointed to the bookshelf. "Hand me that book."

Brooke reached up to the top shelf and grabbed a heavy, hardcover book. She looked at the title—*The Golden Age of Piracy*—and tried to hide a grin.

Nate knew her expression meant: *only you would have a book like this, Nate.* "Thanks," he said, laughing at himself with her. "I'm glad to see that I'm still a cheap source of entertainment for you."

She giggled back, and then kissed him on the cheek.

Nate began to leaf through the book.

Brooke set the coffee pot down and picked up the coin and magnifying glass.

After checking the appropriate pages, he closed the book and looked up at Brooke. "Nothing in here that resembles the markings on this coin." He took a drink of his coffee.

Brooke passed the coin and magnifying glass back to Nate. "I can't make out anything on it either." She picked up the coffee pot. "Well, I'm going in to take a shower and then head out to do a little shopping. Your breakfast is cold, but it's on the table if you still want it," she said. "I looked down the beach this morning and I think the Gibsons are up."

Nate was once more absorbed in the mystery of the coin and only grunted in reply.

"I wonder if anyone will make us an offer on our place this summer," Brooke wondered aloud.

A few Hampstead locals had hung on to their homes, repeatedly declining offers that were made for their property. In some cases, it was enough money to bankroll them for a decade. The ink on the paperwork transferring ownership of the house from his mother to Brooke and him hadn't even dried yet when they had been approached. It was over Easter weekend, and they were at the beach house furnishing it with some of their own things. The doorbell had rung, and after five minutes of polite conversation, Nate and Brooke had said no; the prospective buyer and his trophy wife had stormed off.

Some of the mansion owners had even tried to sue the cottage owners, claiming that the cottages detracted from the beachfront's beauty. They wanted the locals out. Most of the locals wanted the castles bulldozed.

Nate set the coin and magnifying glass aside for a moment. "You think that the local kids have all the lawn jobs sewn up yet?" His father had once told him of an unofficial lottery held at the town barbershop to determine who would be allowed to apply for the summer mansion mowing jobs. It had been one of their last conversations.

"Probably," said Brooke. "I've felt stares at the dime store from Judge Hopkins and Sheriff Walker. I know they're wishing we would just sell our cottage already."

"How wrong is that?" Nate said. "The town leaders turning on the townspeople."

"What do they gain by us selling?"

"New mansions mean more opportunities for their sons or daughters to mow a summer resident's lawn," Nate said. "And if their kid does a good job, then maybe, just maybe, they'll get invited out for a summer party."

"Funny how some people get fooled into thinking they're moving up in the world," she said.

"If they only knew that they look like the person who walks behind a horse and picks up its droppings."

He couldn't help but laugh at the scene he was now picturing.

"What?" Brooke said.

He continued to laugh.

"Naaayyyyyte," she said, poking him with her finger.

He gathered himself. "I started to envision some of the people we know who want to break into that circle walking behind the Budweiser Clydesdales at the Fourth of the July parade picking up piles of shit and waving to the crowd. Agree?"

"One hundred percent. Oh, the pictures you paint, Mr. Martin," Brooke said.

"You're the only one that can see the pictures I describe, sweetie."

"When are we getting our internet connection?" Nate said.

"They can't make it out until next week."

"Damned cable company. We're supposed to have cell phone reception out here next summer too. I'll believe it when I see it."

She kissed him and then left the garage.

He picked up the coin again and then looked out the window at the spot on the beach where he had found it. Where had it come from? Were there more? He put the magnifying glass and coin in the top drawer of his desk and reshelved the book. He stood with his hand resting on the dive gear for a moment. *Let's have a look.*

He entered the house through the sliding glass door and could hear the shower running as he walked down the hallway and grabbed a towel from the linen closet. He exited the house and as he stepped off the deck, he noticed that the blinds were now open on the lakeside windows of a house two down from them. No doubt the owner had his binoculars out and was watching to see what Nate was up to. The man spent more time prying into other people's lives than living his own. The beach mansion owners had one complaint that held weight: the locals were nosey.

Nate passed by the stack of unused wood in the sand and made his way to the water. The lake was placid and the sun had risen far enough to see the sandy bottom. He positioned himself at the approximate point where he had found the coin. He looked back toward the house to make sure it had been found on his property. It had.

After strapping the knife to his right calf, he pulled the mask down past his face so that it hung by its strap around his neck and rested on his upper chest. He entered the water holding the fins above the surface and probed the bottom with his toes for more coins as he walked out up to his waist. Feeling none, he put his fins on and pulled the mask over his head. He spit into the faceplate, rubbing warm saliva all over, and then dipped the mask into the cold water. After securing it to his face, Nate verified his alignment with the spot on the beach where he'd found the coin and dove under.

The water's temperature was probably in the high fifties, and Nate kicked to warm his body, seeing nothing on the bottom at first. Then, his own anchor auger, wire, and buoy appeared. He surfaced next to *Speculation*, took a deep breath, and dove to the bottom to test the auger. Holding onto the steel pole, he pulled from side to side, then up and down. Neither motion moved the mooring. He checked the wire which ran through the auger's eye to the buoy and back to the eye: they were secure.

A few summers back, he had applied for a job as a navigator on a yacht out of Shelby's. The local paper had advertised that a crew was needed for the vessel's summer voyage up Lake Huron to Mackinac Island, down Lake Michigan to Chicago, and then back to Hampstead. Perhaps "applied" was too strong a word. Thinking that mailing an item like a resume would be too formal, he had shown up at Shelby's to inquire about the job. The marina owner, Kevin Shelby, had finally opened his office door after Nate's third stream of knocking. Shelby had a cigarette and cup of coffee in one hand and was running the other hand through his greasy hair. There had been an open bottle of Baileys on his small desk.

After hearing Nate out, Shelby had said, "Fuck if I know. I've never even heard about the cruise, you sure you've got the right marina?"

And that was the end of his career as a navigator—and possibly berthing his boat there.

Nate swam under *Speculation* and after seeing that the hull was fine, he surfaced and kicked further out until the water was approximately ten feet deep. He took a deep breath and dove.

He traced the bottom and swam in a zigzag pattern out to a depth of twenty-five feet. Odds-and-ends were scattered across the sand: rocks, a tire, a rusted can but no coins. He surfaced. The sun hid behind a cloud making the water darker as Nate treaded. A breeze had started and *Speculation* wandered around her mooring. Where did the coin come from? Nate rotated in a slow circle watching the waves and hearing the distant cry of a seagull.

The sun came out from behind the cloud and the khaki colored bottom illuminated under his black fins. He dove and kicked back toward shore while hugging the lake bed. Had he hoped to find something? Sure. Did he really think that he would? No. At least he knew the boat wasn't going anywhere.

As he dried off on the beach, Brooke emerged from the house.

ABOUT THE AUTHOR

Landon Beach was born and raised in Michigan but now lives in the Sunshine State with his wife, two children, and their golden retriever. He previously served as a Naval Officer and was an educator for fifteen years before becoming a full-time writer. Find out more at landonbeachbooks.com.